To Liz
With thank you for
your enthusiasm
Love from Charmian Stewart

HIGHLAND
ENCHANTMENT

Charmian Stewart

D1375916

Pen Press Publishers Ltd

This novel is a work of fiction.
Names and characters are the product of the author's
imagination and any resemblance to actual persons,
living or dead is purely coincidental.

First published in Great Britain by
Pen Press Publishers Ltd
25 Eastern Place
Brighton
BN2 1GJ

ISBN13: 978-1-906206-17-8

Printed and bound in the UK

A catalogue record of this book is available from
the British Library

Cover design by Jacqueline Abromeit

PROLOGUE

February 2006

They were pulling and tugging at her, trying to raise her upright, their fingers plucking at her clothes. She gave a small crushed whimper and tried to turn away. Her hands beat at them in an attempt to resist them, but weakness overcame her and she slipped back.

The voices were all around her, whispering, planning. Her eyelids parted, but the glare of the white walls wounded her eyes, and the white coats scared her. A man's red face floated into her vision. She stared, fascinated by his full, greedy lips. What did he want of her? Money? She didn't think she had any. She didn't care really. She just wanted to be left alone to sleep. She moved restlessly. Where was Peter? He shouldn't have left her so long alone.

Someone jabbed her hand. A pen was thrust into her fingers. A pillow was shoved behind her back and she was bolstered up.

'Come along, Grizelda, let's get this done.'

The group surrounded her, hemming her in, their eyes glittering avidly. She crouched lower in the bed sheets.

The large lady in the grey suit was familiar. She smiled kindly. 'Come along, Grizelda, just sign your name, and then you can go back to sleep.'

Sleep – that was what she wanted. Peace too. Peace to dream.

The figures moved and regrouped around her. The scene dissolved and blurred, but now the misty outline of a young, red-haired woman hovered behind them. She lifted her head from the pillow and stared at her. Her mouth tried to form some words, but only a string of silent bubbles slipped out.

The fat man sucked on his lips and leaned closer, his heavy kilt flattening the flowers that lay on the bed. Her head drooped and she exhaled a weary breath, allowing him to fold her fingers round the pen and move her hand. If she strained her ears, she could just make out the rhythmic tramp of feet and the skirl of the bagpipes outside the window. She felt her body being drawn by an invisible thread, her limbs stirring. Surely at last they were coming for her.

She smiled as they guided her fingers to form shaky black letters.

CHAPTER ONE

June 2006

Alyssa Mead was lost.

The road in front of her had dwindled into a narrow sheep track. Jerking to a stop, she jumped out of her car to examine the terrain. The evening air was knife-sharp on her cheek as she scrambled up the grassy bank at the side of the road. Far below she could just make out the dark glimmers of a loch and with a shiver she stepped back quickly, catching her breath. One slip of her foot and she'd plunge into its black depths.

The silence seemed to roll down from the hills around her, and the shadows crept closer as the twilight of the Scottish highlands faded into night. Alyssa banged the car door shut just to check she hadn't suddenly gone deaf and the loud clang re-echoed through the lonely landscape, startling her.

She clambered over a fallen pine tree, catching her immaculate grey trousers on a jagged branch. Why on earth hadn't she stopped at the lonely wayside petrol station sometime back to buy some food and a bottle of Coke? She was light-headed from lack of nourishment, and her imagination was much too lively. It was easy to picture a white horse or water kelpies creeping out of the loch, and what about the last wolf in Scotland? What was that shadow hovering in that clump of pine trees silhouetted against the sky? Did wolves still exist? She shivered again, and this time not with cold.

Scotland wasn't all bagpipes and kilts, that was for certain. The long drive up from Edinburgh airport in her rented car had taken its toll on her and negotiating the narrow, twisty roads for hours had left her exhausted. Sudden blind corners kept looming up so that her eyes stung with the strain of watching out for unexpected obstacles. But her determined stubbornness forced her onward on her journey to the remote Island of Mora on the west coast of Scotland, linked only by a single causeway to the mainland.

She'd driven across the causeway earlier that evening as the tide lapped at the worn asphalt of the road. Putting her foot down hard on the accelerator, she'd had to speed across the bumpy surface, splashing through the seawater before it swirled over and completely obliterated the link.

Black-winged birds whirled and swooped overhead in the waning light. Or maybe they were leather-winged bats, she wasn't sure. She got back into the car again and set it in motion. It lurched forward with a strange knocking sound, but she managed to shift gear and inch further along the track as it meandered up the hill. She was getting more uncertain by the minute that this was the right road to her great aunt's house.

Back home in London she could drive with confidence through the congested traffic, but up here she seemed to be going round in circles, the narrow roads as confusing as a small, tight maze. How could anyone have built a house in such a remote part of the island? Or had she taken the wrong fork of the road?

The car engine coughed alarmingly and then died. The needle of the petrol gauge wavered a little but there still seemed to be enough fuel. She sat back in her seat. What else could be wrong? Perhaps an overheated engine from all the steep hills she'd driven up in low gear? Lack of water? A defective fan belt?

Alyssa sat for a moment, considering her next step. Maybe she shouldn't have been so impetuous. The Scottish lawyer's letter about her inheritance of a large house on this remote island had arrived like an arrow from the blue-unknown. She'd grabbed the challenge and come rushing up from her London home to see what it was all about.

But out here alone, with the dark falling around her like muffled velvet, she began to wonder if it had been such a good idea to come to this distant island after all.

She gritted her teeth. She had to get out of here some-how. And the only way seemed to be to retrace her tracks, back down the way she'd come. She restarted the engine and forced the gear lever into reverse, 'just you dare give up on me!' she threatened the car, and turning her head, she began to negotiate the narrow track, hugging the side furthest away from the steep banks of the loch.

The road seemed entirely deserted so she rounded the bends at speed in her haste to get back to the little village she'd passed earlier. Perhaps she could get a warming supper and, with luck, a bed for the night. The car slewed too fast round a corner. Powerful headlights blinded her vision. She tried to jam on the brakes, tried in vain to spin the steering wheel to avoid the impact. But with a grinding of metal and a tinkling of broken glass the car came to a violent stop. She jerked forward against the steering wheel, and the airbag released itself with a startling whoosh.

Her face engulfed by the airbag, Alyssa shut her eyes and groaned. Suddenly out of the darkness a hand gripped her arm and a voice spoke. 'Are you hurt?' it demanded.

Alyssa raised her head and stared straight into the eyes of a tall man. 'No,' she said shortly, and sank into the embrace of the airbag again.

'You'd better get out and let me have a look at you.' The man was insistent. 'Can you move your arms and legs?'

A draught of cold air blew into the car from the open door. Alyssa gathered her scattered thoughts, and moved first her right arm, then her left. Her right leg, then her left. There didn't seem to be much wrong with her.

Leaving the protection of the airbag, she squinted against the strong yellow headlights of the other vehicle. The man held out his hand to her and she stepped out of the car. A Land Rover stood enmeshed with the flattened boot of Alyssa's small car, its engine still running. One side of the larger vehicle's bumper was twisted like the crumpled horn of an ox, but otherwise, except for the fact that one of the headlights cast its beam higher than the other, the Land Rover seemed to have survived the encounter quite well. But what about *her* car?

As she stood on the roadside, the man's arm went round her, supporting and constraining her. She felt his breath stirring her hair. Steeling herself, she pulled away from him and looked up into a pair of clear and observant eyes.

'Are you okay?' His voice was deep and pleasing with the hint of a Scottish accent, and his hand felt her arm gently and probingly.

'Yes, yes, I'm fine.' She swallowed down a slight feeling of nausea, and straightened up.

'Well, you're very lucky. You could've got yourself killed, driving backwards at such speed. If I hadn't been on the lookout for sheep on the road, and managed to slow up quite a bit, it could have been the end of you and your car.' The man's concern had suddenly turned to anger.

His harsh words struck her like a blow. 'Well, I'm really sorry, about *your* car.' she retorted, trying to shake his hand off her arm. 'I've never driven up here before. I never expected to meet another soul at this time of night and I think your roads are a disgrace!'

'Who are you anyway? What are you doing here?' he shot back, staring at her, one eyebrow lifted.

She brushed down her jeans, then faced him defiantly, her eyes hurting in the sharp beam of the headlights. She caught the clean masculine smell of him. A whiff of tangy aftershave, tinged with disinfectant. He stood tall and immovable as a rock, one hand on his hip, waiting for Alyssa's reply.

Her heart began to pound with fear and anger. 'And who do you think *you* are?' she cried. 'Lord of the Isles or some such feudal despot! I suppose that's why you were hogging the road. You must think you own it.'

All of a sudden he shook with laughter. 'And I suppose you're the fairy queen of the night? Are you lost? We always have trouble with visitors up here. They expect traffic lights and zebra crossings. Instead they get sheep in the burns and punctured tyres.'

He stretched out a hand and picked a strand of grass out of Alyssa's hair. She stepped back quickly flinching at his touch, but she held his gaze, her chin determinedly up. His hair was dark and a little overlong, curling over the collar of his open-necked shirt. He wore washed-out jeans and

5

strong rubber boots. And he had the bluest eyes she'd ever seen.

She'd have liked to sit down on the bank beside the road as her knees were shaking in the aftermath of her fright and her lack of food, but she wasn't going to admit to any weakness. Instead she asked him, 'If you're one of the locals, perhaps you can set me on the right road to Balvaig House.'

'You want to get to Balvaig House?' The man seemed genuinely surprised. 'Nobody's lived there for months and the roof leaks. Who are you anyway?' A suspicious note had entered his voice.

Alyssa wrapped her arms tightly around herself. 'None of your business,' she said. Now she regretted her impulsiveness in mentioning the house. He seemed to know a lot about it. She debated what to do next, but realised she couldn't let even this vigorous stranger leave her alone on the desolate hillside. There might not be another vehicle along the road before morning, and perhaps not even then. She took a deep breath and tilted her chin. 'Perhaps you can tell me the way to a hotel or pension for the night.' She was annoyed at the quaver in her voice.

'Hotel or pension? Or Balvaig House?' His attractive Scottish voice mimicked her precise English diction. 'You'll have to make up your mind, you know.'

Alyssa debated his words. It was probably too late to arrive at a strange house with no food or provisions, but she wasn't going to let him see that he had influenced her. Her mouth firmed. 'Hotel or pension would be best.'

'Why certainly, your highness! But you'll never be able to move that car now with the airbags floating around. And the boot of your car has taken quite a lot of damage. It'll need some serious repairs before you can drive it again. I'll give you a lift down the road and you can sort it out in the morning. There's a small hotel near the village where you can probably spend the night.'

Alyssa stepped forward trying to push past him but he stood like a solid rock of granite, barring her way and watching her intently. There was a scrabbling in the back of the Land Rover, and suddenly two black and white collies and a smaller ginger-coloured one erupted from the vehicle. The ginger collie rushed up to Alyssa and sniffed her eagerly. The other two dogs swirled round her, brushing her with their silky coats.

Alyssa put her hand out automatically to calm the dogs. More and more she felt as if she had entered a dream. She was so used to being in control. She always knew what to do; what steps to take next. She had to. No one would have employed her as a management consultant for their business if she hadn't been decisive, quick-thinking and professional. She was adept at dealing with the most belligerent customer, soothing ruffled feathers and setting people on the right track.

But here on this island she seemed to have lost all her skills. She was floundering and uncertain. The tall powerful Celt in front of her was certainly in no need of having his feathers smoothed. He stood calmly among his eager dogs, apparently awaiting Alyssa's next move.

She hesitated for a moment. She'd have to turn the car round. Could she take the risk on such a narrow road? The edges might give way, and she'd probably get entangled in the voluminous airbag, and not be able to move the car at all. Suppose she plunged it down into the black waters of the loch. That is if the car would start at all. Worst of all there was an ominous seepage of liquid onto the ground under the rear wheels.

She swallowed her pride. There was nothing else for it. Trying not to fall over the swirling dogs, she fixed her eyes on the stranger. 'Yes, thank you, I'd really appreciate a lift from you,' she said.

'And how the hell did you get up this far?' He wasn't going to let her off lightly. 'You must have driven through the gate two miles back. It's a private road or didn't you notice?'

'I was looking for Balvaig House, and I must have taken the wrong fork. I've already been down one track, which ended in a field where the cows were sunk in a bog or something. It looked very unhealthy to me.'

The man studied her inquiringly. Alyssa realised that, of course, he wouldn't expect a city person to know anything about cows.

'Can you help me or can't you?' She tried to stay calm and focused, but her fear of being abandoned out here alone kept running through her mind.

The stranger gave her a look of cool appraisal, setting off a strange tingle in the pit of her stomach. Could she trust him?

'Lucky you didn't run over a sheep! It's not often we get a visit from the fairy queen who gets stuck among us ordinary mortals.' He seemed to be enjoying her discomfiture.

The eerie highland light bathed the scene, and the man's powerful air convinced Alyssa that the Celtic myths were true. Anything could happen here. She fancied that the faerie folk were all around her with their eyes and ears open, their hands covering their mouths as they shook with mirth at her predicament.

'Okay,' he said stirring her out of her reverie. 'I'll try and move your car into the lay-by. He held open the door of the Land Rover. 'Just get in. Have you got any bags or anything else you need? And perhaps your highness would like to tell me her name?'

'It's Alyssa Mead,' she said reluctantly.

'And a very delightful name for a fairy queen,' he said coolly.

'And your name is?' she demanded, stiffening her spine.

'Rory MacDonald at your highness's service,' he replied with a mocking bow. He whistled to the dogs, who rushed to the back of the Land Rover, jostling to be first on board. The ginger collie gave Alyssa's hand a quick lick before dashing off to jump into the vehicle with the others.

The dog's affection gave her a slight sense of comfort. She looked out from her seat to watch Rory MacDonald managing to get the small car started and he reversed it into the lay-by.

Then carrying her heavy case, he returned to his own vehicle and tossed her keys into her lap. The engine started smoothly under his hands and ticked over evenly. Making a quick turn in the next lay-by he drove fast down the narrow, twisted ribbon of the road.

'You'd never have got back down the road with all that oil that's dripping out of the car,' he said.

Reaching the bottom where the road widened, he turned right and drove toward a long white building with the discreet sign, 'Inverdarroch Hotel' outside the door.

He swung into the parking lot and got out of the Land Rover. 'I'll get someone to bring your car down in the morning. Here's the hotel. Mrs Nicholson will look after you. You can start your quest for Balvaig House in the morning.' He turned his penetrating gaze on her. 'It's an awful dump, you know!' He handed her case to her and then strode swiftly away.

Alyssa was shaken by his parting words. She followed him with her eyes until he vanished from view. Now she stood alone on the gravel sweep in front of the hotel. The windows were dark as mountain pools. By the weak moonlight, she managed to read her watch and saw that it was after midnight. Of course, the witching hour. It was all of a piece up here in the lonely highlands.

There was a ramshackle sign on which she could just make out the word 'Reception' and she stumbled toward it along the narrow gravel path which led to the front door.

She scrabbled around until she found a small brass doorbell which she pushed. She waited for a few moments. Then thank goodness, there seemed to be some signs of life. She heard the lock being turned. The front door opened and light streamed out. A woman in her dressing gown and wearing large spectacles peered out at her.

'Are you Mrs Nicholson? Would you possibly have a room for the night?' Alyssa shivered again, more as a result of her ordeal than the actual cold of the night.

The woman looked at her sympathetically 'Yes, dear, I'm Mrs Nicholson and yes, I do have a room for you tonight. Have you come a long way?'

'I've driven up from Edinburgh,' said Alyssa. 'But actually I come from London. It's a long time since I've been in the Scottish highlands. I've come to visit a house left to me by my great aunt.' She stopped. Really there was no need to start on her life story, just because somebody was looking at her kindly. She'd never have done that in London. The pace of life there was much too fast.

'That'll be Lady Grizelda's place. God rest her soul,' said Mrs Nicholson. 'Come in, come in. We've got a nice room for you upstairs. Did Mr Rory bring you? I thought I saw him with you.'

'Yes, so you know him?' Alyssa dragged her heavy case inside.

'He's the son of the local minister. Well, the old man's retired now because of ill health, and Mr Rory has come back from Edinburgh to keep an eye on him. He's the local vet, you know, and very pally with Mr MacDonald's housekeeper.' Mrs Nicholson pursed her lips as if she'd said too much.

'Did you know Lady Lovat of Balvaig Farm?' Alyssa saw her chance to learn more about her unknown great aunt, who'd left her the inheritance.

'Folk called her Lady Grizelda round here. She was Miss Grizel to everyone when she was young. So she was your great aunt? I didn't know she had any relatives, except the one.' Mrs Nicholson's eyes shone with curiosity as she studied Alyssa.

'The one...? Alyssa prompted.

'Och, here I am standing gossiping with you, you must be fair exhausted after your long day.' Mrs Nicholson reached over to help Alyssa with her case and ushered her into the warm hotel.

*

Next morning, fortified by a large breakfast and carrying a map drawn by Mrs Nicholson, Alyssa set off at a brisk pace to walk across the island to inspect Lady Grizelda's house.

11

Glad that she had put on her jeans and heavy shoes, she hoped she would blend in with the local people.

The path wound uphill and she was soon short of breath. She drew some of the sweet fresh air into her lungs to revive her. She'd been sitting too much in front of her computer and she was getting unfit. She promised herself she'd get out a lot, and run up and down the hills on the island. Her footsteps were the only sound in the quiet countryside. It seemed that nature was holding her breath as Alyssa passed.

Her hand brushed against a cluster of pink foxgloves or fairy bells as the country folk called them. She couldn't resist picking a spray to make the popping sound, like bursting a tiny paper bag, as she used to do as a child.

She jumped across a burn as it trickled brown and secret between the stones. Suddenly the water was struck by the sun's rays in a bright filigree of silver bubbles. Alyssa stood mesmerised for a moment. Then she pressed on following the winding trail of the stream as it led her through the rough grass. Sunlight sieved through the leaves of the birch grove, dappling the path.

Ahead of her a ring of ancient stones stood silently, clad in their lichen robes of grey and gold. Alyssa hesitated for a moment, an unseen barrier holding her back. Then squaring her shoulders she entered the circle and bent forward, trying to decipher the runic squiggles on the first stone. A half-remembered shadow began to wake and stir just beyond her vision. Old magic reached out to touch her, and she felt the hairs rising on the nape of her neck. Her instinct told her that this was a boundary she shouldn't cross. Her heart raced erratically, and the palms of her hands felt clammy.

A frightened bird ejected itself from the grass and took flight, its ear-piercing squawks shattering the silence. Perhaps she wasn't alone after all. She looked around for a large stick as protection and found a long branch covered with moss. Not very strong, but it would have to do. Then she gave herself a mental shake. Probably the bird had been frightened by *her*. What an idiot she was! She must have been more affected than she realised by her wanderings along the loch side last night.

What an attractive man Rory MacDonald was with his laughing blue eyes. He must be descended from the ancient Celts, who had erected this ring of stones, now standing as sentinels to the past. Great power emanated from the circle, and she felt herself drawn into the centre as if called to judgement by a higher court. But resisting the magnetic pull, she backed away.

Rory MacDonald was so obviously part of the island. But he was far too sure of himself. Anyway she hadn't come all this way up to Scotland to get entangled with one of the local inhabitants. She was only here to sort out the ownership of the house, arrange for it to be put on the market and sold. Then she could return to her life in London. It wouldn't suit her at all to be buried up here on an isolated island, with no theatres, galleries or film shows, and probably not even a decent restaurant…

Alyssa pushed her heavy auburn hair back from her forehead. The truth was she'd come rushing up here to get away from London and its memories of Jeff and his treachery. She thrust the thought of him out of her mind, and determined to enjoy the charm of the island and the magic of the place. Turning resolutely, she left the standing stones and picked up speed, following the path through the resin-scented pine trees and out on to the narrow road once more. When it divided into two she checked her map, and took the left fork.

She walked swiftly along, now following the bends of the road up the hill. Rounding a corner she stopped aghast. Straight ahead of her, a forbidding black house loomed up. Surely that couldn't be it? Great Aunt Grizelda's Balvaig House? The tall gable stretching high up one side of the house ended in a broken chimney. The whole structure hung like an unsteady threat in a garden filled with rough grass and knee-high weeds.

Alyssa approached the ramshackle gate, which leaned precariously on the stone wall encircling the garden. Had she travelled all the way to Scotland just for this?

Drawing closer, she saw several of the side windows of the house had been boarded up. Now they stared at her with blank, hostile eyes. Some bricks were missing from the house walls. Disappointment flooded through Alyssa. Great Aunt Grizelda's house was almost a ruin. Perhaps uninhabitable. A sad, neglected dump.

Just as Rory MacDonald had said.

A few faded pink roses clung tenaciously to the walls of the house. Some marigolds and marguerites had managed to survive, and they vied with the grass that was doing its best to smother the whole garden.

Alyssa struggled with the heavy gate, which threatened to topple over. It slipped through her fingers and crashed down, just missing crushing her foot. She scrambled over it, catching a sharp splinter in her hand. She walked up to the front door and then tried to peer through one of the broken windows.

Wild barking broke out behind her and she whirled round. One thing was certain: there were far too many dogs on this island. From the red caravan parked in the no-man's-land round the back of the house, an old man with a stick limped speedily towards the fallen gate. He shouted something at Alyssa, but his words wafted away on the breeze. A shaggy black dog of indiscriminate breed rushed out in front of the angry looking old man. The animal growled and bared its teeth, ready to attack Alyssa if she didn't move smartly. She wasn't welcome here, that was for sure, and she decided not to hang about to hear what the man had to say.

A sharp jag of panic crossed her chest. She looked round for an escape route. The big stick she'd picked up by the standing stones lay forgotten beside the fallen gate. Although she'd dropped her weapon of defence, she could still run fast. On winged feet she tore across the garden and vaulted effortlessly over the high stone wall. Landing on the other side with a bump, she pulled herself up into a sitting position and surveyed her surroundings. A huge expanse of green grass stretched all around her. The trees stretched their gnarled and twisted branches toward her.

Where was she now?

CHAPTER TWO

The world reeled on its axis as Alyssa fought the whirling sensation that enveloped her. A sharp dragging pain in her chest almost choked her, and she gasped, trying to get air into her lungs. Grey tendrils of mist washed around her, blocking out the sun. A sharp breeze whipped her hair across her face, and slow shadows crept closer. A tall figure shimmered in front of her. A strange, red-haired woman was peering down at her. Alyssa squeezed shut her eyes, and turned away as a wave of nausea engulfed her.

Her breathing was getting easier and she tried to still her fast-beating heart. Then she opened her eyes again and blinked painfully as the sun's rays beat directly down on her. She was alone. The strange woman had gone.

Alyssa's left hand was throbbing. She looked down and winced at the large splinter of wood, which was embedded in her palm. Three drops of blood splashed onto her blue jeans while shudders of pain reverberated up her arm. The trees seemed to bend towards her like twisted serpents. Then full awareness came flooding back: the falling gate, the frightening old man, and her headlong leap over the wall to escape the dog. And who was the strange-looking woman? Alyssa rubbed her eyes. Could she have fainted for a moment?

Her vision cleared and she found herself sitting on a large, green lawn which formed the centre of a beautifully kept garden. On her right was a bed of lush pink roses. The scent of the heavy blooms was so strong it almost overwhelmed her in her dizzy state. She scrambled to her feet, and her glance caught a familiar Land Rover parked in the gravelled driveway.

Oh no! Not her mysterious saviour of last night. The shock of the discovery hit her with full force. How maddening that he had turned up just when she was in trouble again. But to her surprise, a warm feeling flowed into her jarred body, reviving her.

The front door of the grey stone house opened wide and Rory MacDonald himself came out. He looked strong and capable. In fact, very delectable.

He stared at her, complete surprise on his face. 'Good God, it's the fairy queen again,' he said, a tone of mockery in his voice. 'Did you have an accident on your broomstick?'

Alyssa straightened up, and swallowed determinedly. 'You could say that.' She took a deep breath to calm herself and gather her defences. 'Is this your garden? Because, if so, I don't think much of your neighbours. In fact they're positively unfriendly. I've been attacked by a very nasty old man who set his dog on me.' She stopped because she had run out of breath.

A frenzied barking came from the other side of the wall.

'Oh, so you've run into old Alastair,' said Rory MacDonald. 'Then I'm sorry. He's not very sociable.'

'Sociable,' Alyssa snapped, clenching her fists so the nails bit into her hands, reminding her with an unpleasant shock of the large splinter. 'He's downright dangerous and should be locked up. If that dog had caught me I'd have been torn to ribbons.'

Rory came closer. His fingers gripped her arm as he studied her, and then he brushed a finger lightly across her cheek. 'My God, the dog's certainly gone at you. You'd better come inside, and let me take a look at these nasty scratches on your face. And that splinter really seems embedded in your hand.'

Alyssa was confused by her unexpected response to his nearness. He was wearing a blue check shirt with short sleeves and his forearms were muscled and tanned, but the underarm skin was white and slightly vulnerable. She turned her head away and raised her hand to touch her cheek gingerly. A few more spots of blood came away on her fingers.

'What are you doing here anyway?' Rory persisted.

'I've come to see the house that my great aunt has left me.' Alyssa moved away from him into the shade of a tall tree, seeking support from its trunk. She found it hard to get enough air into her lungs.

'Lady Grizelda,' Rory looked at Alyssa consideringly. 'Was she your great aunt? I thought the house had been left to a nephew. Or perhaps sold.'

Alyssa didn't answer for a moment. She felt uneasy, touched by hidden currents that disturbed her. She wasn't prepared to discuss her great aunt's will with Rory yet. She knew nothing about him, and besides too many questions kept popping up. Who was this nephew that everyone was talking about? She wasn't going to say another word before she had spoken to the lawyers.

She squared her shoulders and put on a show of confidence. 'Then you thought wrong,' she replied. 'I'm thinking of moving to Scotland. The air is so beautiful and I feel like relocating. London is so overcrowded and stressful.'

'Relocating!' Rory looked stunned. 'You don't just decide on a whim to relocate. You'll be hot-footing it back to London within a week. Life's much too hard up here for a gently reared London girl.'

Alyssa was puzzled at his response. There was a slight hostility in his words. Why should he be reluctant for her to stay up here? She'd only just arrived. She pushed his arguments aside. She'd surprised herself by even thinking about moving up to the island. To buy a holiday home up here would be fine. But what about the long dark winter evenings when it was freezing cold and nothing was going on?

A young woman appeared at the open door of the house, and stood staring. Her fine, dark hair was pinned up high on her head, and she wore a neat skirt and blouse. Her smiling gaze was fixed on Alyssa.

Seizing the initiative, Alyssa said: 'Do introduce me to your wife, Rory.'

He wheeled round and caught sight of the young woman. 'She's not my wife,' he said easily. 'Meet Barbara. Barbara, meet Alyssa.'

The two women shook hands. 'Hello, Alyssa, where have you sprung from?' said Barbara, her touch cool against Alyssa's palm. 'You don't live round here.'

'Oh, I just dropped in,' said Alyssa smoothly, hoping she hadn't left a smudged mark or piece of grit from her encounter with the garden, on Barbara's soft pink fingers. So the delectable Rory was spoken for. It was only to be expected. Barbara was beautiful, and well made up with a delicately tinted complexion and professionally applied lilac and green eye shadow. Her reddened lips were carefully outlined with lip liner, and she studied Alyssa with a friendly expression.

In comparison, Alyssa felt herself a dishevelled mess, her hand swollen and grit-embedded, and her hair full of leaves. Her shoes were scraped and she'd managed to rip her jeans in her impetuous flight over the wall.

'Come in and meet my father, Alyssa,' said Rory. 'He used to be minister of the local church here and he likes unusual visitors. You who come from the big city can bring him up to date with the London news.' He winked at her teasingly.

Barbara moved aside in the front porch. Suddenly the air seemed to crackle between them as Alyssa passed through the small space Barbara left for her as she held open the door to the sitting room.

The room was stifling as the heat rose from a low fire burning in the grate even though the May sun was blazing outside. An elderly man sat in a lug-backed chair with a tartan rug over his knees. He was poring over some papers and making amendments with an old-fashioned fountain pen. On the table beside him lay a heap of important look- ing papers and a pile of books. At his feet lay the ubiquitous Ginger, the collie dog.

So this kindly-looking old man was Rory's father. There was a clear resemblance in the lock of pure white hair which tumbled over his brow just like Rory's untameable jet black hair.

The old man swung round and caught sight of Alyssa. He rose carefully, and walked towards her, holding out his hand courteously to her.

'So you are the lady who's come to see Balvaig Farm,' he said. 'Welcome to our island, Miss Alyssa. Are you staying long?'

Alyssa was taken aback. Rory must have been talking about her to his father since the old man knew her name. She hadn't expected such a warm welcome after Rory's off-putting manoeuvres. She'd expected a highland minister of the church to be buttoned up and very correct. And here was this sweet old man with a twinkle in his eye, apparently ready to share a joke with her.

'Well, you're quite a beauty, my dear,' he said in his soft highland voice. 'It's good for Rory to think about something else than lambing ewes or swine fever. I'm afraid his conversation isn't always so varied.'

Alyssa burst out laughing. The old man was flirting quite outrageously with her. And behind her, Rory started laughing too.

'You're a bit hard on me, Dad,' he said mildly. He turned to Alyssa: 'I've only been back on the island for a few months, you know. It's very hard work building up a veterinary practice that's been so long neglected since there hasn't been a vet on the island for years.'

Barbara looked from the one to the other. Like a mischievous child dropping a large stone in a tranquil pool, she asked: 'When will you be going back to London, Alyssa?'

Why wasn't she welcome here? Alyssa wondered. Why did they keep harping on and asking her when she was leaving? Rory, his father and now Barbara. But they needn't think they could push her out so easily. 'Did you know my great aunt, Mr MacDonald?' she asked the old minister, deliberately ignoring Barbara.

'I knew her very well,' he said. 'She was a few years older than me, but a great catch, as we used to say. All the young men wanted to walk out with her, but she wouldn't look at any of them. She believed they were after her farm,

21

not herself. Yet she was such a beauty and not unlike you with her lovely red hair.' He settled back in the depths of his armchair and smiled. 'I was in love with her myself.'

He turned to Barbara. 'Could you bring in a cup of tea for Miss Alyssa?'

'Of course,' said Barbara with her ready smile and disappeared from the room.

She reappeared five minutes later from the kitchen bearing a tray with a teapot, some cups and saucers, and a pile of floury scones. She set out the china on the low table beside Mr MacDonald.

Alyssa felt uncomfortable with her scraped and earthy hands and tangled hair. 'Will you excuse me so that I can clean myself up a bit?' she asked.

'Talk about being dragged through a hedge backwards, poor Alyssa,' said Barbara, her voice sympathetic.

Upstairs, the bathroom was freezing cold and dominated by a huge bath with clawed feet. At one end of there was a strange looking hood with all sorts of gleaming taps and nozzles. Alyssa peered inside and was lightly sprinkled by drops of water. Probably an old-fashioned Victorian shower, she thought.

She inspected herself in the mirror above the basin. Stark against the red of her hair, her face seemed bloodless, with two long scratches running down her left cheek. She looked at her long slim hands, scraped and dirty with two broken nails. She washed her hands with the pine-scented soap, and then dabbed cold water on the scratches on her face. She splashed more water briskly on her skin, trying to revive herself.

An imperceptible movement in the corner of the room startled her. A slight disturbance in the air. A new wave of grey mist threatened to descend on her. What was wrong with her? Was there someone else in the room? Someone watching her? She strained her ears and gripped the basin to steady herself. Someone seemed to murmur her name. *Alyssa, Alyssa, Alyssa*. The whispers re-echoed round the white walls of the bathroom. Sounds below sounds. Was she hearing something or was it only her imagination working overtime?

Confused and shaky, she sat down on a small white stool. She cradled her throbbing hand against her breast and looked down at her scuffed shoes, rubbing them together, loosening the laces. Recovering after a few moments she got up and examined her scratched face in the mirror again. A dark silhouette moved behind her, the contours clearer now. She wheeled round to look, but jumped as there was a sharp rap on the bathroom door, and a deep voice called: 'Alyssa, I have some antiseptic for that cheek of yours.'

Straightening up, Alyssa went to unlock the door for Rory. He entered carrying some ampoules of antiseptic and a package of bandages. The bathroom seemed to get smaller as he stood close behind her at the mirror over the basin. Alyssa's breath caught in her throat. The blood pumped through her veins, and in a panic she just stopped herself from pushing him away.

'Turn round,' he said, and dabbed her cheek. The smell of disinfectant was pungent in the air as Alyssa tried to hold herself still and avoid jerking away from him. His eyelashes were long and dark as he bent down to study her sore cheek, and his hands were deft. Gradually she relaxed under his gentle ministrations.

He looked at her hand. 'That splinter doesn't look too good. I'd better extract it for you, or you'll have trouble.'

His dark head bent over her hand, and Alyssa resisted the impulse to stroke the unruly silkiness of his hair.

'There you are.' He swabbed her hand and gave her a little pat.

'Have you removed it already?' Alyssa was surprised because she hadn't felt a thing.

'Yes, ma'am. I'll leave you in peace. Come down when you're ready.' He picked up his package of bandages and pulled open the bathroom door.

Alyssa watched his tall figure as he ran downstairs. She shut the door again. With a small comb she tried to remove the tangles from her hair and the sprinkling of leaves that adorned it. She looked like a battered wood sprite, but unlike Barbara, she had no make-up with her to camouflage her appearance. She pinched her cheeks to put some colour into them, and found a lipstick in her pocket. She slicked it quickly over her lips and then was ready to face the party. With luck she had a chance to learn some more about her great aunt.

They were all waiting for her, seated round the low table, where the tea was set out. She took her place and smiled at the old minister. 'Have you always lived on the Island of Mora?' she asked him.

'Oh, yes, my dear, my family, like your great aunt's family, have lived for generations on the island,' he said. 'And in our family one of the sons from each generation has usually gone into the church. Rory is the exception, but he does a lot of good in the community, so we're all very pleased to have him back. He takes such good care of me too. In fact he's like a shepherd with one sheep.' Mr MacDonald smiled at Rory to take the sting out of his words. 'I have a little heart problem, you know.'

'I tried to break free of the strong family bonds and branch out in a new direction. I had a big veterinary practice in Edinburgh,' Rory explained. 'But when my father turned ill, I felt it was the right time to come back.'

'And you don't regret it do you?' Barbara sat on the crimson velvet chair next to Rory 'You fit in so well with us all. And if you can set up the surgery in the house next door, that will be perfect.' She stretched out her hand and touched Rory's arm, holding his gaze with hers.

Alyssa's antennae worked overtime. So Rory was keen to get his hands on the old house next door. *Her* house.

Barbara was wearing a pretty ring of sapphires surrounded by diamonds on her engagement finger. She must be engaged to Rory. Certainly up here on the island there wouldn't be any living together in a casual fashion. In such a small community young people would have to conform.

Rory patted Barbara's hand. Turning to Alyssa he asked again: 'Will you stay long up here, or will you have to go back to your job?'

Alyssa took a long drink of the reviving tea, and began to feel less shaky. A spurt of adrenaline spurred her on to tease them all a little. She lowered her lashes and smiled deep into Rory's eyes. 'I haven't really decided yet,' she said. 'I've never been up here among the mountains and the lochs before, so I've got to look around a bit.'

Rory drew his eyebrows together, frowning. 'But what would you do up here? What kind of work do you do anyway?'

'I'm a management consultant. I manage people!' Alyssa's mouth curved in a smile.

Barbara leant forward: 'Well that's not much good up here. Would you really like to live here? There isn't much work and certainly not the kind of professional work you do. It would be very difficult for you.'

'Perhaps she could help out at the museum, but I can't see her making up beds at the hotel,' Rory didn't sound very enthusiastic either.

'Why ever not?' said Alyssa. 'I can turn my hand to most things.' The tea had restored her strength, and her courage was returning. Rory and Barbara's opposition made her all the more determined to stay.

Rory looked doubtful, and Barbara butted in. 'We've enough people without jobs on the island, without incomers taking away the few jobs we have.'

'And what do you do, Barbara?' Alyssa's lips were stiff with the effort of keeping a polite smile on her face, after Barbara's sharp remark.

'I've a very busy job,' said Barbara. 'I'm Rory's assistant and I'm also housekeeper to Mr MacDonald, so they couldn't possibly do without me.'

Mr MacDonald leaned forward and patted Barbara's hand. 'You do a very good job, my dear,' he said. 'We'll all miss you when you get married.'

'Oh I'm not going to leave you, Mr MacDonald. Who would type out your sermons for you? You know your handwriting is very hard to read.' Barbara was staking out her territory. 'Besides what would Rory do without me to help him with the animals in the surgery?' Then playing the perfect hostess she turned to Alyssa: 'Would you like another scone, Alyssa?' Her face was friendly and open as she pushed the plate towards her.

Barbara was a good cook. The scones were floury and delicious and the raspberry jam was home-made. It was unlikely that either Rory or his old father could produce such delightful jam. Or perhaps it was a present from one of the parishioners.

'You certainly had a narrow escape from that dog,' said Rory, his blue eyes fixed on Alyssa, and another jolt of electricity passed between them.

She dropped her eyes from his intent blue gaze. 'Yes, it was terrifying. But I can't give up now. I've got to get a good look at the house, at least from the outside. Later on I'll get the key from the lawyer.'

'I'll walk back with you,' said Rory. 'He'd never dare to set the dog on me. So you'll be quite safe.'

Alyssa was relieved, but tried to hide it. 'I can just as well go alone,' she said.

'I insist,' said Rory.

Barbara was clearing the plates, her face inscrutable.

'Thank you so much for the tea and scones,' said Alyssa and jumped up from her chair. Saying goodbye to Mr MacDonald and Barbara, she followed Rory out of the house.

She crossed the fingers of her undamaged hand.

Please let everything go right this time.

CHAPTER THREE

Rory and Alyssa left the colourful flowers and leafy calm of the manse garden and walked the few yards along the road to the old, neglected house. Alyssa's heart sank at the sight of its blank staring windows. It would need a lot of time and money invested in it to make it habitable, let alone comfortable. The gate still lay where it had fallen when Alyssa tried to get through for the first time. But Rory heaved it up and left it leaning against the stone wall.

'I can't see a city girl like you settling down in this primitive place,' he said looking down at her.

She was annoyed. Why did he want to push her away? What was behind it? He kept harping on about her being so feeble that she couldn't manage to get a mere house licked into shape? She squared her shoulders and looked at him. 'You underestimate me. I love the countryside and I grew up on a farm. If I really decided to live up here I could do it.'

Rory laughed and took her good hand, swinging it easily. 'I'm sorry. It's just you look more suitable for town life. Look at your designer shoes. They've really taken a battering.' His fingers were warm and comforting, and Alyssa felt an answering warmth spread through her.

A deep-throated growl sounded behind them. Alyssa

whirled round and saw that the ugly black dog had slunk along the wall of the garden. It stood there barring their way, its teeth bared and hackles raised.

'Get off!' shouted Rory. The dog retreated a few steps, but held its ground, its stance full of menace, and flecks of foam on its jaws.

Alyssa snatched her hand from Rory's and looked for a quick getaway route. It was only a short time since she'd escaped from the animal, and it wasn't looking any friendlier. It continued to growl and took a few steps forward. It seemed only just to hold itself back, like a black cannon ball ready to explode.

Rory approached the dog slowly, holding its eyes with his own. Alyssa's legs were about to give way, and she was dissolving inside, her fear was so great. Now she felt a fatalistic acceptance that the dog would attack them and there was nothing they could do about it.

Rory talked soothingly to the dog. He stretched out his hand to seize it by the scruff of its neck. But there was a shout from behind the dog, and the old man from the trailer came hobbling towards them, an old Glengarry perched askew on his head. He let fly a string of wild curses, probably in Gaelic.

'Get off my land,' he shouted. 'This is ma hoose and ma sheep, get off and away. I ken ma rights!'

The dog looked back at its master. Then like a spring uncoiling, it leapt up and snapped at Alyssa's arm, but fell back at the first attempt. Rory shouted and moved forward as the bundle of black muscle flew at Alyssa again. This time its teeth caught her jeans and ripped a jagged tear from knee to ankle. The old man aimed a flying kick at the dog, and almost tumbled backwards himself.

Rory grabbed the dog by the scruff of the neck, but it slipped through his fingers and honed in on Alyssa again. Rory missed it again and with a howl it sank its teeth into Alyssa's already injured hand. She screamed in pain and collapsed on the ground.

Rushing forward, Rory managed to seize it this time and pulled it away from Alyssa. Out of his pocket he took a dog's neck chain and slipped it round its neck. He drew it tight and clipped on a lead. Tying the dog to the gatepost, he ran over to Alyssa.

She lay on the ground, her hands over her ears. Beyond fear, she tried to block out the roaring anger of the dog. She turned on her side and drew her knees up to her chest in a foetal position. Then after some time she focused on Rory. She swallowed and tried to mouth something, but no words came out. Then breathing deeply she looked up at him quite calmly although her lips were white. 'It's over now isn't it?'

'It's over now,' he said bending down on one knee and drawing her to him. She relaxed against him, savouring his strong body against hers.

'Is it safe now? Please take me back to the hotel,' she whispered. 'I'll have to come back another day.'

Cold anger swept over Rory at how she'd had been mal-treated. He felt gently along her arms and legs. Her jeans were torn, and he could see where she'd tried to wipe them clean, but he couldn't see any mark of a bite on her exposed bare leg. Perhaps she'd had a lucky escape after all. She didn't seem to be suffering any pain, but then he noticed some drops of blood on the sleeve of her white shirt. He looked at her hand and saw the dark purple marks where the dog's teeth had penetrated deep into her skin just beside the scar where the splinter had been.

He looked up at old Alastair who stood rooted to the spot like an evil black rock, his eyes blinking nervously. It was obvious that the old man realised the situation was very serious.

Rory tried to think clearly and calmly, and to stem the turmoil of emotions flooding over him. 'This is the end of the road for that brute of a dog,' he said curtly to Alastair. 'You didn't even *try* to keep it in check. A dog like this is too dangerous to roam free. It attacks anyone who passes.'

He turned back to Alyssa who was now trying to get up and creep away from the scene. He helped her to her feet. She swayed against him and his arms tightened round her. He resisted the temptation to draw her head against his chest.

He cursed inwardly, furious that he'd failed to stop the dog from getting at Alyssa. Things had run out of control so fast. But he should have acted quicker. She didn't deserve the attack. She was so plucky, so full of life with her fiery red hair.

Still supporting Alyssa, he towered over crabbed old Alastair. 'In my capacity of veterinary surgeon in the district, I'll be reporting you to the police and arranging for the dog to be put down.' He turned back to Alyssa. 'How do you feel now? I'm going to take you to the local hospital and get your hand seen to. Dog bites can cause bad infections. You could easily get tetanus. Can you just sit at the side of the road for a moment and I'll run back and get the Land Rover.'

Alyssa bit her lip and resisted the desire to clutch Rory and beg him not to leave her alone. Struggling for calm, she asked: 'Are you sure you've tied up the dog tightly enough. I don't want to take any chances.' She tried to conceal that she was shaking with reaction. Waves of cold chills swept over her. She didn't want to be abandoned even for a moment to the mercy of old Alastair and her hairy black enemy.

'Look, I'll manage to come with you,' she said. She pulled herself to her feet and staggered along a short stretch of the road, supported by Rory's strong warm arm. 'Oh, my legs are like cotton wool,' she whispered and collapsed onto the ground.

She could hear Rory speaking to her, but enclosed in a veil of faintness she couldn't make out what he was saying.

At last his words broke through. 'Alyssa, Alyssa, how do you feel? We've got to get you straight up to the hospital, your face is sheet white and you've got a very nasty gash on your arm as well.'

With a gasp of horror Alyssa examined at the jagged tear in her flesh, the pain arrowing down her arm. 'I thought it was only my hand the awful dog grabbed!'

'Sit here just a second,' said Rory, depositing her carefully at the side of the road. 'The danger's over now and it'll be much quicker if I go myself to get the car.' He tore off to collect the Land Rover, glancing back quickly at her as he ran, his long legs covering the ground at breakneck speed.

Alyssa leaned back against the bank and breathed deeply. The fresh, clean air and the scents of the wild flowers in the grass cleared her head a little.

The Land Rover skidded to a stop beside her and Rory helped her to climb up into the passenger seat. He reached across her into the back of the vehicle and drew out a bandage. Tearing off the packaging, he bound a neat bandage round first round her arm, and then round her hand. Then he got into the driving seat and they set off down the winding road.

'I'm fine now. I don't need to go to any hospital and I can't sit around waiting in casualty for hours,' said Alyssa.

'You have to get a tetanus shot, and you definitely need stitches. Anyway this is not one of your big London hospitals. We still keep some country standards,' said Rory. 'I know the doctors there, and I'm sure you won't have to wait long.'

A grey square building loomed before them and Rory drove up to a main door with a large 'Accident and Emergency' sign above it. Together they walked straight in.

'Hello, Master Rory.' The receptionist from behind the brown reception desk smiled at him. 'How's yourself?' She sent them onwards down a dim corridor lined with doors. The lingering smell of disinfectant was stronger here and it stung Alyssa's nostrils as she clung on to Rory with her good arm. She focused on his face. He had a beautiful well-shaped mouth. She'd love to trace it with her finger. What would he be like to kiss?

Stupid, stupid! He was engaged to Barbara, and Alyssa had no right to think such thoughts.

Rory's blue eyes searched her face, and she felt the stain of a hot blush rise up from her neck. Damn the man, he was getting under her skin, just when she was most vulnerable. She was here at this hospital to get patched up, not to engage in idle dalliance with good-looking highlanders.

The sharp tang of antiseptics stung her nostrils combined with the smell of yesterday's dinner. She forced herself to look around her. The waiting room was painted a dingy brown to halfway up the walls, when it became a tired-looking cream. The whole style was as outdated as if she had been transported thirty years back in time.

Two or three people were sitting on the leatherette benches in the waiting room, one of them staring intently at the swing doors that led to the doctors' consulting rooms. A pile of coloured magazines with tattered pages lay on a table.

'Not a big queue waiting for treatment this evening,' Rory said with awkward cheerfulness. 'Looks like we're a healthy lot up here.'

A stout, bustling woman in a blue and white uniform, with trousers straining at the seams, barged through the swing doors. 'Hello, Rory,' she greeted him with a beaming smile. Then a worried look crossed her face as she asked: 'How's your father?'

'No, no,' said Rory. 'We're not here because of him. Miss Mead is the patient. He pushed Alyssa gently forward.

The woman faced Alyssa. 'What's wrong?' she asked in a loud, clear voice. Alyssa cringed. She didn't want the whole world knowing what had happened to her.

'She's got bitten by a dog,' Rory said, filling in for her. 'It's a really nasty wound.'

The nurse bent over to look at Alyssa's puffed and swollen hand. 'You'll probably need some stitches in it. You'll have to wait for the doctor.' She gave Alyssa a form to fill out. 'Lucky it's not your right hand.'

Alyssa's hand throbbed, but her head was clearing. She looked around her. Could this be the hospital that had looked after Great Aunt Grizelda before she died? Could she ask a few questions about her aunt? But despite her feeling of strong attraction to him, she didn't want to talk about anything in front of Rory before she knew whose side he was on. What if his plan was to buy Balvaig House and settle down there with Barbara?

He seemed to realise she wanted to be alone. To her relief he told her: 'I'll just go out and park the car properly, and I want to find a phone to tell them I'll be late for evening surgery. Mobiles don't always work in here. But I'll be right back.'

Despite her reservations about him, in a mixture of conflicting emotions, Alyssa felt very much alone as his tall figure walked out the door. What madness, she hardly knew him! She was independent and she didn't need a minder!

The bustling staff nurse returned and told her that the doctor would see her in ten minutes. Summoning all her strength and concentration, Alyssa asked 'Did you know my Great Aunt Grizelda, Lady Lovat? Was she brought to this hospital when she could no longer take care of herself at Balvaig House?'

The nurse started and looked strangely at Alyssa. 'Are you really related to Lady Grizelda? I thought she only had one relative. She was a very lonely old lady.' She looked accusingly at Alyssa. 'She died alone here, you know. Nobody seemed to bother about her, except that nephew who came out of nowhere.' Her small red mouth clamped tightly shut, and she left the room.

Alyssa sat back exhausted. She closed her eyes and her thoughts blurred. Leaning her head against the wall, she didn't feel equal to playing detective any more. All she wanted to do was to crawl into her bed and sleep and sleep.

She had no sense of time passing until she heard brisk footsteps approaching. The staff nurse spoke in her ear, and Alyssa jumped. 'The doctor will see you now,' she said.

She ushered Alyssa into a white-painted room. A stern-looking man wearing steel-rimmed glasses and a white coat strode in. He extended a cool dry hand to Alyssa, and sat down without a word behind the large desk. He pulled forward some papers and began writing. Alyssa sat down in the chair he indicated, and her eyes fixed on the shiny steel lamp that stood on his desk, directing a sharp beam of light on the papers he was working with.

The nurse spoke to her. Her voice seemed to come from a long way off… further and further away. The white room was spinning jerkily, the walls see-sawing around her. Alyssa put a hand to her head as webs of dazzling colour reflected off the lamp. A silvery shadow slipped in front of her eyes.

'Find the truth, find the truth,' the shadow whispered. 'I died before I came in here.'

Alyssa grasped the hard wooden chair she was sitting on. *Hallucinations! I must really be in a bad way. For God's sake come back, Rory, and take me home.*

The nurse's voice was tinny. 'Show doctor your arm, Miss Mead.'

Alyssa's lips moved soundlessly. She tried to lift her arm toward the nurse, but grey clouds were rolling over her. Her ears buzzed like a jet plane taking off. She slipped to the floor.

'Oh my God, the woman's fainted,' The doctor's un-sympathetic voice brought Alyssa back to consciousness. She was cold, so cold. He pulled her up firmly and helped her back into her chair. The nurse brought her a glass of water, and they left her for a moment to recover. The nurse walked around the surgery collecting bandages and a sy-ringe. Her accusing voice floated across to Alyssa's ears as she told the doctor: 'She tells me she's Lady Grizelda's niece. Why didn't she come to see her before she died?'

Alyssa straightened up on the chair. The doctor raised his eyebrows showing a modicum of interest. 'Lady Grizelda had her nephew,' he said. He spoke to Alyssa directly 'If you are as you say Lady Grizelda's niece, you know she did have lucid spells and she could have talked to you if only you'd taken the time to come and see her.'

Alyssa concentrated on trying to drag air into her lungs. But adrenaline began pumping through her body at this unexpected attack. Who was this nephew that everyone talked about? How dare the doctor treat her as if she was a non-person with no feelings, and to crown it all, begin to scold her. She almost jerked her arm out of his hold, but his grip was firm. He swabbed her skin, inserted the needle of the syringe into her arm and then began to stitch her wound.

When he had finished stitching, he swept out of the room without saying goodbye. It was left to the nurse to help Alyssa out into the waiting room.

Rory came rushing in, red-faced and breathless. 'Sorry it took so long. Are you okay? Have they fixed you up? God, woman you do look a bit pale! What've you done to her?' He turned accusingly towards the nurse.

Alyssa's lips moved soundlessly. She tried to move her arms towards him, but the grey clouds were rolling over her again.

'Rory,' she whispered despairingly. *Grizelda, Grizelda* called the black-winged birds beating around her head. *'Lady Grizelda.'*

*

Rory drove Alyssa back to Inverdarroch Hotel. 'You could come back and stay at my father's house, if you like,' he said, but she sensed a kind of hesitation in him. Was it because of Barbara? In any case she didn't feel up to meeting Barbara again.

'I'll be okay. Mrs Nicholson will give me a light supper and I'll go to bed early,' she told him. She wanted to get away from everyone to ponder what'd happened to her. She longed to lie down in cool sheets and shut out the world. She couldn't tell Rory about the strange voice that had whispered in her ear, and the dreamlike and floating sensation that had made her faint at the hospital. She'd never been a fainting sort of person. She supposed it was delayed shock after the black dog's attack, and the injections the doctor had given her hadn't helped.

She crept into her bed, and shut her eyes trying to block out the images of the black dog springing on her. She slept badly, slipping in and out of dreams where she was being pursued by shadowy figures.

CHAPTER FOUR

Rory was nothing if not efficient. The next morning Mrs Nicholson came to tell Alyssa that a man had brought her a replacement car and it was parked outside the hotel. Alyssa ran down the stairs and looked out. Goodness that was decent of him. She'd have to settle up with him later and make sure that she didn't owe him any money on the repairs to the Land Rover.

Today she planned to visit the lawyer who had sent her the letter about her inheritance. She hoped it would be straightforward to take over the house. But there was a huge problem because it was so dilapidated, and how on earth would she find the money to renovate it if she decided to keep it. She was jobless now that the little management consultancy she'd worked for had folded. She had joined three of her old university friends in starting it. They'd had such high hopes and worked so hard, but the competition was tougher than any of them had estimated. With the re-lentless vision of hindsight she realised that they hadn't marketed their services enough. Just worked hard at making it a respected consultancy, but not widely enough known. Now it was all for nothing.

She wrenched with her one hand at the steering wheel of the car, but was too late to avoid a large pothole in the road. As she bounced painfully on the hard springs of the car seat, she forced herself to concentrate on the road ahead of her. But she groaned inwardly as she thought of all the money, not to mention the hours she'd invested in the consultancy. Perhaps she'd been too impetuous rushing up here, but since the company was no longer in existence, the lawyer's letter offered her a way out, and she'd jumped at the chance of getting away from London and all her worries. A new start that's what she needed.

The sea was restless and hungry as she drove across the island's causeway, towards the mainland. The grey swell of water on either side tossed around pieces of flotsam like small matchboxes. A boat silhouetted against the sky, bobbed aimlessly as Alyssa passed. To the west of the island, the peaks of the hills stuck up like jagged teeth, making her hand throb as she thought of the vicious dog.

The fresh white bandages on her hand and arm forced her to make an awkward change of gear, and she fought to suppress a feeling of nausea which still lingered at the back of her throat. Gradually she began to relax, following the road as it coiled around the multiple bends, and passing the ancient peat bogs still in existence where the damp, brown squares already cut, lay exposed to the air to allow them to dry. The drier mounds of peat were stacked neatly alongside. She took a deep breath as a childhood memory of the aroma of burning peat rose in her mind. A memory of her mother and… her father, visiting an island when she was very young. Which island, she couldn't remember. Her mother was now dead and her father always away on some trek or other, up in Amazon river or in the depths of Peru. Sadly she'd never been really close to him.

She brushed aside her dragging thoughts, reminding herself that she managed very well. She was used to being solitary. She wasn't dependent on any one. Least of all Jeff, who'd failed to support her when things began to go pear-shaped at the consultancy. In fact Jeff – and his expense account – was probably one of the most cogent reasons for the company's failure. Her partner and her lover. Their break-up had been all the more devastating when she found it he'd been tricking her all along. Her heart was crumbling as she remembered the good times they'd had before she'd found him out.

Then she pulled herself up. God, she was stupid and trusting allowing a honey-tongued man to take over her life. Well she'd learnt some useful lessons. She'd never be a blue-eyed innocent again.

The road dipped sharply down past some silver birches and she shot too quickly over a narrow stone bridge, rounded a corner and found herself on the outskirts of the west highland town of Oban. Taking a right-hand fork she drove into the centre of the town, and with a quick turn of the wheel, slotted the car into an empty parking space. In the small town of Oban it wasn't hard to find a space. What a relief from the congested streets of London.

Walking along the pavement further into the town, her gaze caught a round colosseum-like tower at the top of the hill. In a benevolent way it dominated the town.

The coastline ran parallel with the road and as Alyssa walked along she could see two or three large black and white ferries riding at anchor in the Port of Oban, ready to transport passengers and as well as a few cars to the outlying islands. Islay, Jura, Lewis, Iona. Alyssa stopped for a moment savouring the ancient names of the romantic

Hebridean islands. Maybe she would take the ferry to one of the islands one day.

The air was fresh and salty, and a brisk breeze blowing off the sea ruffled her hair. She stopped for a moment and looked around her for the offices of Balfour, Fraser and Shaw, the legal firm who had written to her with the news about her unexpected inheritance.

A softly spoken highlander in a well-worn kilt directed her to a red sandstone building. A highly polished brass plate outside the entrance displayed the name of the firm and Alyssa raised her hand to push open the oak-panelled door.

Now she sat opposite Graham Shaw, the most junior partner of Balfour, Fraser and Shaw. Between them was a highly polished mahogany desk larger than a billiard table, covered with neat piles of papers, some of them tied up with pink tape. In contrast to the heavy Victorian furniture of the office, a computer blinked on the left-hand side of the desk.

Graham Shaw smiled at her, his eyes keen and penetrating behind his trendy spectacles, and Alyssa felt immediately in tune with him as he was almost as sharply dressed as her colleagues down in London. He was wearing a dark suit with a faint stripe and his dark crimson tie was stylishly knotted. Conflicting emotions rose inside her as she realised she was missing the familiar cut and thrust of her London life, although goodness knows life on the island was fast-paced enough. She never knew what to expect. Next thing she'd be savaged by one of the sheep or gored by a large white boar from one of the farms. She smiled ruefully to herself.

She leaned forward on the edge of her seat to avoid being engulfed by the immense puffed-up leather armchair she was sitting in. It was destined for sturdy farmers much broader than she.

'Your hand, Miss Mead – have you had an accident?' Graham Shaw looked at her sympathetically.

'Just a silly run-in with a dog. It's nothing at all,' Alyssa dismissed it airily.

Graham Shaw looked as if he would like to ask her some more, but Alyssa compressed her lips and looked at him fiercely so that he let the matter drop, merely asking, 'Would you like some tea or coffee?'

Alyssa moved restlessly, struggling to escape the clutches of the too accommodating chair without knocking her injured arm. 'No, thank you. I'd like to get straight to grips with the situation around my great aunt's will.'

Graham nodded and drew out a file from among his stacks of documents. 'It's a complicated matter. That's why we're so pleased that you could come up here and discuss it with us,' he said. 'Up until recently there was no question about it. You were the residuary beneficiary as Lady Grizelda's husband had predeceased her, and her closest kin – her two brothers – also died before her. But now I'm afraid the situation has now changed drastically.' The word sounded almost shocking coming from his precise lawyer's lips.

'Drastically?' repeated Alyssa, a cold hand of apprehension squeezing her heart.

'Yes, after Lady Grizelda's death, another contender to her property came to light. Unknown to our firm, a second will was drawn up by a firm of solicitors. Indeed as far as we can understand, this person was unknown to Lady Grizelda herself except during the last months of her life. The new will was drawn up at the instigation of a

Mr Michael McDermott, who claims he is closely related to your great aunt. He is now the sole beneficiary under the terms of the new will. Do you know this person, Miss Mead?' Graham Shaw paused and scrutinised her as if assessing her reaction.

'I didn't even know of my poor great aunt. And it was only yesterday that someone told me that my great aunt had a nephew,' Alyssa said cautiously. She sat forward: 'Is this true? Does this McDermott have a stronger claim than me?'

Graham Shaw shifted his position in his chair. He adjusted his spectacles.

Alyssa's uneasiness increased. 'But when you wrote to me it all seemed clear-cut,' she said. 'You told me I had inherited Balvaig House. Now you tell me there is someone else involved.'

'Lady Lovat had not changed her will for many years,' said Graham Shaw. 'Then suddenly after her death, just as we were preparing to get confirmation of her will, we were informed that a new will had been drawn up for her during the last weeks of her life as she lay in hospital.

'But how could this happen? Wasn't Lady Grizelda your client? It seems very strange that your firm hadn't ever heard of this man before.' Alyssa's head whirled. Now it seemed that she had travelled all the way up to the Scottish highlands for nothing. She felt her cheeks flushing with annoyance that Graham Shaw hadn't informed her earlier about the new developments.

He moved some of his piles of papers around, his eyes unfathomable behind his spectacles. 'At the time we wrote the first letter we believed you were the sole remaining heir to Lady Grizelda Lovat's house and the small piece of land surrounding it. We were very taken aback too when this McDermott showed up and the new will came to light.'

'Is he any relation to Lady Grizelda?'

'He calls himself her nephew… that is grand nephew.'

'As far as I know I don't have any first cousins,' Alyssa said.

'We are checking out what his relationship was to Lady Lovat. He's apparently friendly with a Miss Brodie who lives on the island of Luan. She was a close friend of Lady Grizelda, although several years younger than her.'

'I'm really shattered by this.' Alyssa felt more trapped and uncertain by the minute. 'I thought everything was cut and dried, even though I was surprised that my great aunt left me her house. From what you wrote in your letter I certainly didn't expect to face any opposition to my claim. I've even been to look at the house from the outside but I was shocked to see how rundown it is.'

'Yes, it was allowed to fall into disrepair in the last few years of Lady Grizelda's life,' Graham said. 'She wouldn't allow anyone to do anything about it. Then latterly she was away in hospital.'

'I believed that you'd sorted everything out and that it would be plain sailing to take over the house.' Alyssa sat forward in the chair and looked at him accusingly.

He held her gaze firmly. 'We've done our best, and we've had the court grant an injunction so that McDermott can't yet gain access to the house, until the court decides which will is valid. We held the keys for Lady Lovat after she went into hospital. We haven't let them out of our hands. The keys are still here if you wish to look around inside the house.'

'The biggest problem I expected to face was to decide whether to keep the house or sell it.' Alyssa sighed.

'These are the not so pleasant facts,' Graham Shaw said in a conciliatory tone. 'But don't give up. We are determined to do everything in our legal power to ensure that your rights under your great aunt's will are upheld.'

'Who is this Miss Brodie?' Alyssa spoke mechanically as she contemplated what her next move should be now that Graham Shaw had thrown this devastating news at her. She looked out of the window at the cars whirring past in the street, and felt a tide of frustration welling up inside her. She fiddled with her bandages and flexed her fingers stiffly as she tried to absorb what he had told her.

'Miss Brodie seems to have helped Mick McDermott gain access to your great aunt as she lay in hospital.'

'She brought a complete stranger to visit an old woman as she lay dying? What about the hospital? How could they allow this?'

'McDermott made out he was Lady Grizelda's nearest relative.'

'It all sounds very fishy to me,' said Alyssa. 'But perhaps I should go and talk to this Miss Brodie.' She twisted her hair round the fingers of her good hand, more shaken than she cared to admit. Then she stiffened her spine and asked, 'How strong is my position?'

'That's what we're investigating now,' said Graham.

Alyssa pushed back her hair which felt heavy and hot round her face, and wondered if it was a drawback that she'd never heard of Lady Grizelda's existence until she received Graham Shaw's letter.

'Do you know anything more about this Michael McDermott?' she asked.

'Mick McDermott, as he is known here, is an auctioneer who lives in the south of Scotland. Over the past few years he has had dealings with some of the farmers up here when the big cattle or sheep sales are on,' Graham told her. 'Thanks to Miss Brodie, he began to visit Lady Grizelda very regularly during her last weeks in hospital.'

'But never before that? Do you know Mr McDermott?' asked Alyssa.

'Not well at all,' said Graham. 'He appeared very suddenly. Our senior partner here, Mr Balfour, was a long-standing friend of Lady Grizelda and her husband. He was a very regular visitor to Lady Grizelda in hospital. It was he who first noticed this new visitor.'

Alyssa nodded. 'Was poor Lady Grizelda in hospital long?' She felt inadequate and guilty that the poor old woman should have lain there alone, without Alyssa knowing anything about her.

'I suppose for about four or five months,' said Graham. 'Mr Balfour kept on visiting her, even when she became so muddled that she didn't seem to recognise him. Nor did she remember his visits. She was extremely disorientated latterly.'

'Poor Great Aunt Grizelda. She had absolutely no family left. Only me and I didn't know anything about her. Yet it's so strange that no one ever told me about her until after her death.'

'Apparently there was a bitter family quarrel many years ago, and Lady Grizelda cut herself off from the rest of the family for some reason. Because she seemed to have no family around her, we were all astounded when the second will came to light after her death,' said Graham. 'McDermott is only up here sporadically, and no one paid any special attention to him. Why should they?'

'Surely the hospital must have noticed him,' said Alyssa.

'Yes, probably,' said Graham. 'But for one thing they're so busy. If they did notice they'd be only too glad that the poor, lonely old soul did actually have a visitor.'

Alyssa's thoughts were churning like shoals of fish in the sea. Graham Shaw had certainly given her a lot to think about. She felt a deep sympathy for poor, lonely Grizelda, cut off from her family. But one thing was clear, Alyssa decided. She needed to stay on the island for some time and she couldn't stay in the hotel long term. With her job gone, she had nothing to rush back to London for. She might as well stay here and try to find out what had happened. She had an instinctive feeling that she must stand and protect her rights, however tenuous. Somehow it seemed the right thing to do – for Grizelda.

Her thoughts flicked back to the delectable Rory. What of him? Did he know anything about what was happening in the house next door to his father's? Could he be involved in the plot with McDermott? If Rory and Barbara were to get married, it would be the ideal place for them to live, right next door to his father. Barbara had even suggested it.

Alyssa's thoughts drifted from her present situation. Even though Rory was so at home in these isolated surroundings, Alyssa was sure that he'd easily manage to navigate the London scene. She tried to imagine him at one of the drinks parties. It wasn't hard to picture him holding sway, a wine glass in his hand, while the other guests listened intently to his stories of the isolated island of Mora and the thriving community there.

Alyssa realised Graham was speaking to her, and came to earth with a bump.

'Have you got somewhere to stay up here?' he asked. 'It may take quite some time to get things sorted out.'

'I'm staying at the little hotel on the island at the moment,' she said. 'But I've just left my job in London, so I'd be glad to get somewhere cheaper to stay for the time being. She raised her head. 'I'd like to stay on the island for a few weeks or until things get sorted out. If you do know of somewhere to rent that'd be a great help. A little cottage for example.'

Graham got up and pulled open the drawer of one of his filing cabinets. 'I might just have something for you,' he said.

Alyssa watched his strong fingers riffling through the files, then turned and looked round the spacious and airy office. She admired the expensive-looking watercolour which hung on the wall behind Graham's desk, showing the tide rushing in over the causeway which she'd driven over this morning. She pushed her hair back out of her eyes. Had she done the right thing by dropping everything in London and rushing up here? How long would her depleted finances hold out without any regular earnings coming in?

Graham placed a file on the big mahogany desk. He pulled out a sheet of paper. 'There's a little cottage for rent on the island quite near to the seashore. It's very small, just a but and a ben – that means just two rooms, but there is a small kitchen and bathroom as well of course. The cottage has water, electricity and gas laid on. I think you'd be quite comfortable. It's owned by a widow and her daughter who have recently moved to Glasgow, but they don't want to sell the cottage, at least for now.'

'When can I see the cottage?'

'Any time,' Graham said. 'I have the keys here if you would like to take a look around.'

'What sort of rent will they charge?'

'I don't think they'll charge so much. They just want someone to live there and keep it aired.'

'Perfect,' said Alyssa. 'And when could I move in?'

'I'll have to make a phone call, but perhaps more or less straight away if you like.'

Alyssa sank back into the plushy chair. Phew… at least something was going right.

With the keys to the little cottage as well as the keys to Lady Grizelda's house in her pocket, she left the lawyer's office and started on her return journey.

Crossing back over the island causeway, she followed Graham Shaw's directions, and found herself at the end of a narrow track leading to a small cottage with white-washed walls. It stood solidly by itself, overlooking the ever-changing sea. At the bottom of the small garden, a stone wall dropped down to the sandy beach as a protection for the cottage against the high tides of winter.

Looking round inside the cottage, she saw it was quite small, but clean and tidy, with everything she needed in the kitchen, which fitted neatly into a corner of the living-room. The second room was a small bedroom almost completely dwarfed by a large comfortable bed.

Straightaway Alyssa felt the ancient cottage welcoming her. She touched the solid walls, which must be at least two feet thick. They certainly knew how to build to keep out the cold in those days.

She was drawn to the large modern window in the sitting room, which overlooked the seashore. She watched the seabirds whirl and swoop, then skim with outstretched wings over the blue waters. She would have to get herself some binoculars to follow all the pulsing activity going on. She must try to learn the difference between the different types of gulls, so alike in a whirling flock, but so varied as individuals. She supposed the sinister black birds perched on the rocks were cormorants. She admired their skill as one or other kept dropping into the sea, suddenly to rise again with a fish in its beak. Mick McDermott must be like that, she imagined, always ready to plunge and grab a prize.

The air was exhilarating and fresh, quite different from the drained grey skies of London, if indeed the sky was visible between the tall buildings of the city.

Alyssa collected her bags from the hotel where she'd been staying. She drove half a mile along the road to stock up with basic supplies at the small supermarket, which in addition to food, seemed to provide everything from pins to pitchforks. Fresh vegetables were in abundance. Fresh fish too with the salty tang of the sea rising to tantalise her nostrils.

The faces at the check-out were friendly, showing a barely suppressed curiosity. 'You'll be the lady that's renting "Seal Cottage",' said the cashier who took her money. Alyssa smiled. It was the old story. News travels like lightning in small communities.

She settled down quickly in her new quarters and set about preparing her supper with her new groceries. Standing in the small kitchen in the corner of the living room, she paused continually to look out of the window at the ever-changing panorama of birds. The sky turned from blue to pink and to orange as the day moved on to evening and the sun sank down into the sea. For the first time for many months she felt at peace with herself. She hadn't thought of Jeff all day. She wouldn't let the bastard get her down. She was finished with him. Now she'd only rely on herself. 'It was the right thing to do to come here!' she said aloud, her voice stirring the quiet air, and the cottage walls seemed to echo in agreement.

Tomorrow she would make a new attempt to get into the old house. She must make a closer inspection. Even though it looked so horrible from the outside and would probably need an awful lot of time and money invested in it, she was convinced it was meant to be *her* house. Was that why Lady Grizelda haunted her dreams?

Her visit to Graham Shaw had revealed some tough stumbling blocks ahead, but she wouldn't let that deter her. She had the keys to the door in her hands and could examine the house at her own pace, fully accredited by the lawyers. She'd make sure that she'd get in this time. On her own, without Rory's help… or interference.

But for the time being she'd shut Grizelda out of her mind. She was determined to get a good night's sleep with no dreams or visions.

CHAPTER FIVE

Am I brave or foolhardy? The words beat around in Alyssa's head as she let in the gear of the car. The bandages on her left arm and hand still hindered her movements, but the throbbing pain had lessened. She set off in the direction of Balvaig House. Turning the last corner, the steep gables of the house came into view. She gritted her teeth. This time she was determined to find her way into the house, which she now regarded as her property. No one, animal or human, was going to keep her out this time.

She drew up and parked the car carefully in front of the ramshackle gate with the intention of blocking the path up to the house. She reached behind her for the stout stick she'd placed on the back seat and which she hoped would provide protection against the dog if it appeared.

Gritting her teeth, she climbed out of the car, and edged herself and her cumbersome stick through the gate. She took a cautious look round. There was no sign of old Alastair or his fearsome companion, although a puff of grimy smoke spiralled out of the chimney of the battered red caravan behind the house. The two beasts were still in residence. Alyssa's mouth curved in an ironic smile.

Next time she spoke to Graham Shaw she would have to ask more about old Alastair. Why was he camping on Lady

Grizelda's ground? She had been so taken aback at finding out about Mick McDermott's rival claim that she'd quite forgotten old Alastair.

In the distance a curlew rose with its bubbling cry, and Alyssa took it to be a good omen, spurring her onwards up the overgrown path.

The old house crouched low, slumbering in the morning sun. The boarded up windows stared at her with blind eyes, and a tangle of brambles impeded her way. Yet in a mysterious way the house beckoned her closer. This tumbledown house, with stones missing from its crumbling walls, had been Lady Grizelda's home for so long. The house seemed to be holding its breath… full of expectancy to be stirred again back to life.

Alyssa drew out the set of keys that Graham Shaw had entrusted her with. Fumbling in her haste, and hampered by her bandaged hand and arm, she inserted the largest old-fashioned key into the keyhole. The lock was stiff and the door swollen, but after turning it back and forward, it suddenly yielded to her efforts and she almost fell into the dim interior. She pushed the door shut behind her, and leaned against it to allow her heartbeat to slow.

She waited for a moment allowing her eyes to become adjusted to the darkness of the hall. The place smelt dank and musty but she walked steadily across the hallway. Her footsteps echoed hollowly as she climbed up the bare wooden staircase, drawn upwards by the sound of faraway voices. She wasn't sure if they were real or if she were just imagining them.

The large window halfway up the stairs was partly boarded up from the outside and shed only feeble light. It was a dusty stained-glass window which pictured long-haired maidens drawing water from a well. The surround was of blood-red glass. How strange to find something so elegant in this primitive house.

The voices continued to whisper and call, just low enough to make her uncertain that she was hearing anything at all. Steeling herself, she walked over to one of the doors on the landing and entered a bedroom with a huge iron bed in the middle, draped in dusty sheets. The sunlight filtered in glowing shafts through the boards on the windows, but threw the corners of the room into deep shadow.

Movement swirled to her right and then dissolved into empty darkness. Now Alyssa was struck by the feeling that she was an intruder, disturbing the dust of ages. The movement came again, and Alyssa turned her head from side to side trying to pinpoint the movement. Again a dizzy feeling swept over her. Was there someone else in the room?

Stumbling against the old iron bedstead, with its sagging mattress, she sank down beside it on a high-backed wooden chair with a faded cushion. A hazy white cloud seemed to shift and drift across the room.

Alyssa put her head between her knees, to blot out the sight. Her legs felt like shaky ribbons. She couldn't have stood up to save her life. But after a couple of minutes she forced herself to look up. The gauzy shape seemed to float toward her and she could just make out a woman's face. Alyssa rubbed her eyes. Was there… could there be… a young woman in a wedding dress with a flowing white veil? The room whirled and then righted itself. Alyssa shut her eyes again. She breathed steadily through her nose in a stress-busting technique just as she'd regularly taught the participants on her courses in London, but now it didn't seem to help.

She caught the sound of a bagpiper playing a light strath-spey. The room was dark, dark as a cave in a rock. Alyssa's heart pounded. It was as if she had two hearts in her breast, struggling to burst out. Terrified, she leant back in the chair, her breath choking in her throat. She heard someone beside her gasping for air. Could it possibly be herself?

She bit down screams to stop them tearing from her throat. Daggers of light filtered through the boarded-up window and blinded her vision.

Who was she? Where was she?

Still struggling to breathe, she put her hand to her head and touched a crisp, net material, which seemed to stream forever down her back. She touched it again with her fingertips, and her hand brushed against her hair which was piled up heavily on top of her head. Her fingers caught on a large hairpin and the petals of a flower.

Her limbs felt leaden. Was this a dream or a horror movie she had somehow managed to fall into? A nightmare where nausea came in waves? The room wheeled once more and she sucked in a life-giving lungful of air. Dazzling colours shimmered around her, gradually fading until she became aware that she was in a bedroom with pretty wallpaper decorated with pink and red roses. The scene came sharply into focus. She was sitting on a chair staring into a mirror.

*

June 1950

'Miss Grizel,' called a voice, and she heard the heavy tread of someone coming up the stairs. The room brightened and steadied. Her heart beat quietly and rhythmically. Her head ached a little, probably from excitement about the day to come.

What day to come? But, of course it was her wedding day! Really she must have fainted for a moment. She felt so bemused.

Behind her, the door pushed open and someone came in. Grizelda turned to see dear old Mrs McMorran whose earnest face was red and flustered in contrast to the unrelenting stiff black frock she wore. On her head was an elaborate hat, which had not seen the light of day since her poor husband's funeral three years ago.

'Come, Miss Grizel,' she puffed. 'Ye canna keep the minister waiting in the kirk. He'll be fair put out at your shenanigans.'

Grizelda looked at her faithful housekeeper and smiled. 'And my future husband too? Don't worry, Mrs McMorran, you go ahead and sit in a good pew in the church. I shall manage.'

She wanted to be alone to savour her last minutes as a single woman. She, Grizelda Finlay, owner of Balvaig Farm on the Scottish island of Mora… no longer would she be just a spinster of the parish.

Now she was carefully gowned in white silk ready to be the bride to the slaughter, prepared as if for a ritual sacrifice. Was it really as bad as that? In a way, she supposed. She didn't love Peter. She felt no fast-beating heart or pounding of hot blood as she had done for Robin before he had so cruelly left her. No, she just felt a strong liking for Peter. They had a mutual respect for each other.

Grizelda scanned her unmarried face in the mirror. Had she changed? Or would she see a change after the wedding? Certainly she supposed she would no longer be a virgin. Would a new worldliness show in her face? Would she smile as if she had some secret knowledge marking her as different from the young girls still unwed? Would Peter be kind? Could she stand the bestial panting and coupling which she had seen her cows submit to out in the field? Or was it somehow different for humans?

Outside her window two ponies stamped restively as they stood harnessed ready in their traps. They had been waiting for the best part of half an hour. The heart-stirring sound of the bagpipes rose clearly from the bottom of the hill. She reminded herself that it was her day. She was the queen. She looked down at her silk dress, smoothing it over her hips. It had taken Mrs McMorran and her three helpers over two months to sew it painstakingly by hand. The stitches were so cobweb fine that she could hardly see them. The purity of her dress reflected her own virginity. Her bridal veil streamed down her back like a white waterfall.

She wasn't so young in marriage terms. Nor was she sure that Peter Lovat was in love with her. But this was certainly her day. Today she would assume a new, more authoritative identity. She would be a married woman. People would listen to her opinion, no longer dismissing her as poor Miss Grizelda who couldn't find a man.

Robin had hurt her deeply, when he'd left with Catriona Grant to start a new life in America. It was hard to forget that betrayal.

Yet she had been running the farm for five years now since the death of her father. Unusually, her father had left the farm to her as the oldest child, a mere woman. He had made the stipulation that her two younger brothers would have their home and employment on the farm. And they did. She managed her brothers well, guiding them with such a subtle hand that they believed that they made all the important decisions.

Her fifty head of cattle meant that she owned the largest herd on the island. Her dream was to make Balvaig Farm one of the most important milk producers for miles around, but for that she needed money to invest. In the village they thought her unladylike to know so much about money and doing business. In truth she was getting married for love of the farm, not for love of a man.

Did Peter understand that?

Outside her window, she heard the piper tuning up his bagpipes again. A frisson of excitement swept though her. She, Miss Grizelda, the plain one, as she had always thought herself, was getting married. She would show them. This was the emergence of the butterfly from its chrysalis. A billowing, frothy, light butterfly in her beautiful dress, ready to fly freely over the hilltops. It was a pity that Mamma and Papa couldn't see her now. They would have been so proud.

She could hear her mother's soft voice saying 'Grizelda, how pretty you are. I'm so proud of you!' And Papa? Well he wouldn't say anything but he would harrumph and nod his appreciation of his only daughter as he chewed on his pipe. Perhaps he might even light one of his very special cigars in celebration.

She came back to the present with a start. Her brother, John shouted up the stairs, using the pet name of her childhood: 'Hurry up, Grizel. We have to leave in fifteen minutes. The pony is waiting.'

She ran over to look out of the window. The pony in the front trap shifted its hooves impatiently. It was freshly groomed with white ribbons on its bridle. John stood outside, keeping a firm hold on the reins. Someone had tied bunches of pink roses on the trap and spread a silken shawl over the seat so that her beautiful dress would be kept clean and perfect.

Margaret, her dearest friend and a married lady herself, rushed up the stairs and into the room. The flowered headdress on her hair was askew, but the blue satin dress she wore, was elegant and understated. She took her duties very seriously as Grizelda's matron of honour. 'Aren't you ready Grizel? We must be off or you'll arrive late at the church, and frighten the life out of Sir Peter, because he'll think you aren't coming.'

Grizelda's blood surged in her veins. She took one final glance at herself in the mirror on the dressing table.

'Don't do that,' screamed Margaret. 'You know it's bad luck for a bride to look at herself fully dressed in the mirror.' She tried to move Grizelda away without ruffling her dress.

But Grizelda was staring at how her cheeks bloomed a delicate pink that no amount of careful artificial colouring could have given her. 'Silly superstition,' she said. 'Just old wives' tales.' She resolutely bit her lips to redden them, while Margaret fussed and tweaked her veil becomingly round her face.

'Will I do, Maggie?' she asked, suddenly tentative. After her thirtieth birthday she had never expected to be a bride. She believed herself firmly placed on the shelf, the spinster sister of her brothers. It didn't seem to matter if a man wasn't married. He would always command the same amount of deference and respect as any married man.

'Of course, Grizelda. You'll do very well. You look perfectly enchanting.' Margaret gave her a very careful hug so as not to disturb her beautiful wedding dress or to get tangled up in the long veil. 'Come, the ponies are waiting, and can't you hear the bagpipes tuning up?'

The discordant sounds outside struck Grizelda as a reflection of the music of her soul. Not yet in harmony with herself.

'I feel like those bagpipes,' she confessed, shocking Margaret.

'Grizel, what are you saying? A beauty like you comparing herself with the squawking bagpipes?' And both of them dissolved into laughter, which gave Grizelda the necessary courage to finish pinning her veil.

'Should I put a white rose in my hair or will Peter think I'm too fast?' She looked questioningly at Margaret.

'You must be careful not to frighten the minister in the kirk or you'll never be wed,' Margaret giggled.

Grizelda tossed back her veil and picked up the tightly clustered fresh white rose, which lay on the dressing table. Defiantly she stuck two extra pins into it and fixed it firmly on her white veil, which covered her luxuriant red hair. 'That's for my Jacobite ancestors,' she said. 'I'm ready to go now.'

Margaret turned and hurried off downstairs, leaving Grizelda to look around her bedroom one last time. She tried to quell the fluttering in her stomach as she knew she wouldn't come back here again as an inexperienced maiden. She studied the polished floorboards, worn in places, the pretty wallpaper with its coloured roses, the single bed with the white counterpane, the dressing table with chintz material discreetly covering its legs.

She felt sad and elated at the same time, sad to be leaving the old familiar ways and elated because her new life as a married lady was about to start. But what did she know of

Peter Lovat? He was fifteen years older than she, and he had already buried one wife. Would that be her fate too? Dead in her early thirties? Surely not. She felt young, strong and full of vitality. She could out-dance all the young girls of her age, her heavy auburn hair swinging loose as the reels grew more frenzied. No one had smaller feet or more nimble, they told her, but often she felt they were just teasing her with their flattery.

John and Margaret with Mrs McMorran hovering in the background helped her into the pony trap. Margaret lifted Grizelda's long silken skirts and folded them neatly beside her. Then she got in carefully and sat down beside her.

John swung his whip, just touching the pony's hindquarters and they set off at a brisk trot. They moved swiftly along the familiar road and Grizelda felt her past floating away behind her leaving her only the unknown future.

John pulled up the pony outside the church. Through the doors she heard the harmonium creaking out a hymn. She was glad she'd pinned the rose in her hair and she held her head high and proudly, clutching her bouquet of white roses firmly. Margaret had insisted on inserting a sprig of white heather for good luck. Grizelda paused for a moment to survey the scene before she proceeded up the aisle on John's arm.

The wedding guests sat regimented in the church pews, and the scent of flowers wafted towards Grizelda. Through her veil she could see the women dressed in their best finery. The older ones were mostly encased in stiff black frocks like Mrs McMorran while the men in their bright kilts were the peacocks of the scene.

Now her breath came in gasps as if she was climbing a steep, steep hill. She caught her foot in her train and stumbled slightly against John, who gripped her arm firmly and turned his ruddy wind-burned face towards her. 'Are you all right?' he whispered.

Mrs McMorran's head bobbed forward as she peered at her anxiously from her seat in the pew nearest the aisle. Could it be symbolic? Grizelda wondered. A bad omen, tripping at your own wedding. Luckily she hadn't fallen. 'A fallen woman', they would have called her forever after. She stifled a nervous giggle.

The harmonium wheezed on sturdily, but Grizelda couldn't have told anyone what tune it played. All she knew was that she was compelled to proceed onward up the aisle to the steps of the altar.

There he was: Sir Peter Lovat of Jamaica. A stranger waiting for her. She hadn't noticed that his hair curled slightly below his ears. And what was the colour of his eyes? What was his favourite music? Or what kind of books did he like to read? She only knew that he was a very strict churchgoer. Did he like children. Did he miss his first wife? Could he milk a cow?

She almost stopped in her progress. How foolish she was! She knew nothing at all of this man. Only that his family, like hers, had lived on the island since the mists of time. And then Peter himself had been away in Jamaica for many years. He was the owner of a large sugar plantation where he had lived until the death of his wife. Now free again, he had returned to the island of his birth.

Her brother detached his arm from hers, and she almost stumbled again. But she managed to step into position beside Peter and take his arm. He looked down at her, his eyes shuttered and enigmatic, but his lips were curved in a small smile.

The minister in his black robes, lightened by the white Geneva tabs at his throat, began to intone a jumble of words.

'Doest thou, Grizelda, take this man…' She felt the bile rising in her throat. She simply mustn't scream: 'No.' Not here in the respectable portals of the church, with everyone looking on.

She forced out a dry-lipped 'I do.' Peter Lovat lifted her left hand, and struggled to push a gold circlet on her stiff and reluctant finger.

Then they were in the vestry, signing away her old life. Distantly she heard the harmonium squawk out a more cheerful hymn as the congregation awaited their return as freshly-minted man and wife.

Back down the aisle, they progressed. Grizelda's arm was clamped firmly against Peter's side, making her feel like a trapped bird.

The open church door loomed ahead and the sun streamed in from outside. Now Grizelda's spirits lifted. She smiled brilliantly at Peter and quickened her pace. She gripped his arm like a vice as if she would never let it go.

They passed through the arched church door. A man, wearing a tattered kilt slipped out from the shadows at the side of the building. He stood barring the way for Grizelda and Peter as they turned towards the waiting pony and trap.

'Safely married, Grizelda? And a fine lady too,' he sneered. 'Let me be the first tae gi' the bonnie bride a kiss!' He pushed his face into Grizelda's and forced his lips against hers, dragging her veil askew. The alcoholic fumes of his breath made her want to faint.

Sir Peter pushed him aside, and from behind them John shouted, 'Get off, Fordyce. You've no business to be here.'

The man snatched a rose from Grizelda's bouquet, scattering petals and leaves. Laughing he loped off. He vaulted over the stone wall at the bottom of the churchyard and disappeared into the pine trees.

'Who the devil was that?' Sir Peter's voice was stern. But Grizelda stood transfixed in front of the church door, unable to move forward. The guests milled and peered behind her, trying to see what the commotion was about.

Grizelda looked at the torn roses and straggling leaves of her beautiful bridal bouquet. She looked at the petals on the ground. Her brief feeling of happiness dissolved. What kind of omen was this for her new marriage? She shivered in her white silk gown.

CHAPTER SIX

Alyssa stirred. The wooden seat of the chair was digging into the backs of her legs. A scent of roses wafted through her nostrils. She yawned and stretched. Had she have fallen asleep? And where was she? She opened her eyes cautiously and surveyed the dusty room. For a moment she didn't recognise her surroundings. Then slowly the mist in front of her eyes cleared and consciousness returned.

She gazed round the unfamiliar room, and smoothed her hand over her unruly hair. Where was her veil? Gradually it dawned on her where she was. Yes, she must have fallen asleep. The dream was still starkly vivid in her mind... if it was a dream.

I feel most peculiar. That awful dog has damaged more than my hand. Clinging onto a tall chest of drawers, Alyssa pulled herself up from the chair. She walked across the creaking floorboards peering into the dark corners of the room. Was this Grizelda's room? It was large and spacious, but dusty and neglected.

A pricking at the back of her neck made her feel she was being watched. She turned towards a black-framed wedding photograph hanging on the wall. An old-fashioned bride with a long flowing veil, her hand resting on her bridegroom's arm seemed to observe her from the photograph.

Her eyes followed Alyssa's movements around the room. With a jolt of recognition Alyssa stared back at the bride. It was the young Grizelda of her dream, her eyes bright and her hopes intact.

The oval photograph was faded and brown-tinged but the Grizelda of the picture looked out at Alyssa with a strong, confident gaze and a graceful smile on her lips. A jaunty white rose was pinned onto her tumbling hair at one side of her veil, flamboyant in its contrast to her demure, stylised demeanour. Alyssa stared back at her, still gripped by the remnants of her dream.

Deliberately she turned away from the bridal photograph and started examining the old chest of drawers more closely. She tugged at one of the lower drawers and it slid out with a protesting groan. A rank smell of mothballs assailed her. Heavy knitted cardigans in black and navy blue still lay there, mutely awaiting the return of their owner. In the third drawer from the top she found some dainty white silk knickers, slightly yellowed and still packaged carefully in tissue paper.

Alyssa felt as if the girl in the photograph was urging her on. She seemed to be saying, Look at my things. This was my life. Get to know me.

So Alyssa moved on and pushed open the heavy doors of the dark brown wardrobe. Two or three black frocks hung there forlornly, as well as a dainty rose-coloured one with a tiny waist, but Alyssa saw the delicate silk of the dress was rotted. 'She's gone you know.' Alyssa's words were loud against the silence of the room. 'She'll never be back, so you must stop waiting for her.'

She felt a strange pity pass through her as the frocks seemed to sag and diminish. But they were only old clothes after all. They couldn't have feelings. She mustn't allow the lonely old house to overwhelm her.

She left the bedroom and continued her tour of the house. There were two other bedrooms on this landing and no bathroom. Trying to regain her courage, Alyssa spoke aloud into the empty air. 'Where did they wash themselves? What a harsh life with no water on tap.'

There was no answer. Now the only movements in the silent house were the dust motes she had stirred up, and in one of the shadowy corners she saw a spider scuttling for cover. The hushed room pressed like a heavy weight on her shoulders and the white floating girl of her imagination was gone.

A thunderous knocking at the front door downstairs made Alyssa nearly jump sky high. Her pulses leapt and the blood pounded in her ears. A jolt of annoyance ran through her. Was it Rory? Had he walked over from his neighbouring house when he saw Alyssa's little red car parked outside? But wouldn't he have called out?

The knocking came again and an angry voice roared, 'Is there anybody there? Come out! You're trespassing on private property.'

Now it was Alyssa's turn to be angry. Adrenaline coursed through her body. She ran quickly down the stairs as the thumps on the front door grew louder. She picked up her heavy stick from the bottom of the stairs where she had dropped it, and buoyed up by anger, she pulled open the front door.

A stout man stood there blocking out the light. What he lacked in height he made up in breadth. He stuck forward his chin, and his moustache bristled.

He fell back a step in astonishment. 'Who are you?' Then moving quickly forward he seized the stick from Alyssa's startled grasp. He grabbed her by the arm and almost lifted her back into the house, his chest unpleasantly close to hers.

She wrenched her arm from his hold and stepped back. 'Who are you? How dare you push your way in here. You've no right to be here and no right to touch me.'

'I've every right to be here,' he thrust at her in a coarse accent completely unlike Rory's softer tones. 'I'm the owner of this property.'

Alyssa tore the keys out of her pocket and waved them at him. 'I'm the owner of the property.' Her fear made her exaggerate her claim. 'Get out at once yourself or I'll call the police.'

The man was the first to get hold of himself. 'Go ahead, call the police,' he sneered. 'It'll take them at least half a day to get here from Oban. So what'll you do while you're waiting?'

Alyssa faltered for a moment. From habit she felt in her pocket for her mobile phone. Would 999 work up here? The man had just underlined how far she was from her orderly life in London.

But then his hectoring manner changed and an ingratiating smile spread over his ruddy face. 'You're a pretty girl,' he said. 'What's your name?'

'What's yours?' countered Alyssa.

'Michael McDermott, but you can call me Mick.'

'I'm Alyssa Mead,' Alyssa's tone was reluctant.

The man's face lit up. He stuck out his large meaty hand to engulf Alyssa's. 'Alyssa Mead? I'm your cousin Mick and friend of Rory MacDonald. You and I have things to talk about.'

This was not good news to Alyssa's ears. Friend of Rory MacDonald, the man said? Did it mean that Rory was involved in the plot about the rival claim? If so she didn't want anything more to do with Rory. And she certainly didn't like the blustering man in front of her claiming kinship with her.

They stood in the dark hall until Mick moved sideways and pushed open a door on the right letting in some light. With his hand on her back, he propelled Alyssa into what seemed to be a sitting room. By the pale light filtering through the boarded-up windows Alyssa could just make out the humped shapes of furniture covered by ghostly white dustsheets.

The man licked his lips. His bulk filled the room. 'Understand one thing. The island of Mora is nae for townies like you. Just pack your la-di-da clothes and go!'

Alyssa almost burst out laughing at the absurdity of his words. He couldn't think the ancient cardigans and moth-eaten clothes upstairs were hers, could he? That would also mean he had been in this house before.

She didn't answer, but stood her ground and scrutinised him sternly. His jacket of loud checks made her teeth ache. His khaki breeches were torn and shabby and his mud-splashed rubber boots left dirty wet prints on the dusty floor.

'Get back to London and your friends there,' he said with a sweeping wave of his hand. 'Haven't you got a little job there too?'

Alyssa was furious. Mick McDermott was even worse than she had expected. And how could poor Lady Grizelda ever have succumbed to such a person, totally without kindness or charm? How could she have signed a new will in his favour when it was obvious he was simply out to get her money?

But, of course, Lady Grizelda couldn't have done such a thing. She couldn't have known what she was signing anything if she'd been as confused as Graham Shaw said. Or maybe she had been pressured by this bully.

Mick was lighting a cigarette without as much as a by-your-leave. Alyssa stepped forward and looked him straight in the eye. 'You didn't ask my permission to smoke, Mr McDermott. Please put out that cigarette at once. You're on my property.'

Mick's face purpled and his big nose became even redder. He was almost spitting as he tried to get the words out: 'You'd better get back to your fine London life. We Scots don't like incomers. You don't belong here. Look at your fine English clothes, they won't last a week here. What do you know about the countryside? You'll never have done a hand's turn of hard work. You don't know what that means. Besides we didn't know about you. Why did you have to come now?' He took a step towards her, his arm raised. 'Go home, miss, we don't need you here!'

Alyssa dodged under his arm, her mind working fast. She took up a position as far away from Mick as possible and looked him in the eye. She wasn't going to creep away from him like a scared cat leaving him in possession of the house. Mick McDermott had seriously underestimated her if he thought that she was such an easy touch. She wondered if she had the strength to push him out through the door, if she caught him unawares, but he stood with his legs planted apart. Outside, old Alastair's dog set up a fearful barking. Could she lure Mick to go and take a look?

A strange calm swept over her and a warm feeling enveloped her like feathered wings as if an unseen presence watched over her. Suddenly she heard a cracked ringing from a doorbell. Mick whirled round and strode out of the room into the hall. He pulled open the front door and Rory, who had been leaning on it, pushed his way in.

Mick dropped back in surprise. 'What are you doing here, MacDonald?' His tone was rough. 'Interfering neighbours are the last thing we need.'

Rory paid no attention to this. 'Where's Alyssa Mead?' he demanded, staring past Mick.

To Alyssa, Rory had never looked so delectable. She forgot that she suspected him of belonging to the rival camp. She had never been so pleased to see anyone ever before.

The two men began to circle each other like cocks spoiling for a fight, their faces red.

'Leave now, McDermott, you have no right to be here, intimidating a young woman.' Rory now stood his ground firmly, chest to chest with Mick.

Mick was the first to step back. He didn't stop to pick up his discarded cigarette. 'You haven't heard the last of this,' he threatened. 'I'll get an injunction to keep you off my property.' He strode out slamming the front door with such force that it burst open again.

Alyssa looked at Rory, and Rory looked at Alyssa. Their eyes locked and held, speaking volumes of words yet unheard. Slowly Rory held out his arms and like a homing bird, Alyssa rushed into them. His hand came up and brushed her cheek.

He was even more stunningly virile than she remembered. His brilliant blue eyes were concentrated on her. His hands on her shoulders drew her close to him, and a quiver surged through her veins. She felt the cold tension draining out of her body as she relaxed. Warmth was creeping back like a tidal wave. She slipped closer her soft curves moulding to his lean body.

She turned up her face to look at him. He bent his head, his eyes fixed on her mouth. The caress of his lips on hers set her heartbeat skyrocketing as he pulled her firmly against him. The hardness of his body pressed urgently against her thighs.

Pressing closer, she inhaled the smell of him. A combination of new mown hay and leather, with a dash of peppermint from his fresh breath. Her senses reeled as his tongue explored the soft recesses of her mouth.

He coaxed her closer, teasing her, making every nerve in her mouth tingle. Never had she been kissed like this before. She had an inexplicable urge to lie down on the dirty floor, drawing him with her.

Bang! The front door left ajar by Mick's swift departure, swung shut on its hinges.

Alyssa jumped and became aware her back was hurting where she was pinioned up against the wall by Rory. She pushed him away. Desire had come all too quickly She must be mad. She didn't know this man at all. He could well be her enemy since Mick had claimed friendship with him.

She began smoothing her hair, and tucking her blouse down into her trousers. She brushed a hand over her swollen lips. 'I'm sorry,' she said, straightening up and turning to face him. 'We got a bit carried away. I'm so sorry. I was just so grateful that you came as you did when that awful man was hassling me. We were just a bit quick for each other.'

'Grateful,' said Rory looking stunned. 'Is that what you call it? You certainly could have fooled me. You participated very eagerly.' His eyes were dark and his voice cool.

'I'm so sorry,' said Alyssa again. 'I hardly know what's happening to me.'

'Don't worry, I'm leaving,' said Rory. He walked out of the room and Alyssa heard him slam the front door. That must be a record, she thought, slumping to the floor like a washed out rag.

Two men have walked out on me in anger and slammed the door all within half an hour. This island isn't good for me. I don't understand the people, and they don't understand me. Maybe I should just go back to London.

She brushed her dishevelled hair out of her eyes and found an unopened refresher tissue in her pocket. She rubbed it over her hot face and tried to relax again. Would she be letting Great Aunt Grizelda down if she gave up now? Would it matter? Or should she start searching for other people who had known Grizelda in the latter months before her death.

Loneliness crept over her. She took a shuddering breath. Could she go back to London with nothing accomplished except that she'd got bitten by a vicious dog. What had she to go back for anyway? Jeff was out of her life, and she certainly didn't want him back. Wasn't it only fair to Rory to find out if he really was involved with Mick and the drawing up of the second will. He had been so good to her and she had overreacted twice, first by letting her feelings overwhelm her and then by rejecting him so abruptly.

Her people management skills had gone right out of the window.

Get up, she told herself. *You've got work to do. You've got to talk to some more people who knew Lady Grizelda.*

It's only fair. And you can't let that horrid Mick McDermott get the better of you.

CHAPTER SEVEN

It was a quarter to three in the afternoon when Alyssa shut the door of her temporary home, not bothering to lock it. She walked toward to the narrow strait of water dividing the island of Mora from the smaller island of Luan. The salty tang of the sea blew sharp and pure in her nostrils.

Down on the shore, she took off her shoes. She curled her toes enjoying the feel of the polished sea-washed pebbles and the sand. The seabirds whirled, calling and mewing to each other like flying cats above her head. She strolled along for a few minutes allowing the waves to lap over her bare feet and picking up a few well-washed shells. Then looking at her watch, she realised she couldn't put off her visit to Miss Moira Brodie any longer, so she turned back and climbed up onto the small jetty to wait for the little ferry. She waved vigorously to the man standing in the ferry on the other side of the narrow strait.

Catching sight of her, the ferryman cast off the small motor boat, and set course for Alyssa's side of the strait. The small craft skimmed over the tops of the waves. Ten minutes later the boat drew alongside the jetty.

Alyssa was struck by the ferryman's resemblance to Rory, although he was probably about twenty years older. He had the same strong figure and tumbling dark hair. As if feeling her scrutiny, the man looked at her and smiled, and she saw his eyes too were the same piercing blue as Rory's.

As he manoeuvred the small ferry alongside the jetty, Alyssa called out to him. 'Hello, are you Neil? Can you take me across to Luan, I want to visit a Miss Brodie there.'

'Aye, I ken her weel,' he answered and extended his hand to her, almost lifting her aboard with one flick of his wrist.

'I'm told she lives by herself in a little cottage. She was a friend of my great aunt, Lady Grizelda. I'm not sure where she lives. Perhaps you can point her cottage out to me.' Alyssa looked enquiringly at Neil.

'Yes, I can show you the way,' said Neil. Now it was his turn to study Alyssa. 'So you're Lady Grizelda's grand niece. Poor thing she had a very hard life in the end.'

He'd given her a great opening. 'Yes, I'm her grand niece, Alyssa. Did you know Lady Grizelda well?' Alyssa was pleased to meet someone friendly that had actually known her great aunt. At last here was a direct link to Lady Grizelda's latter days. The lawyer had only been able to tell her about Lady Grizelda second-hand.

She scrambled into the seat in the stern and sat down, only to jump up again. 'Oh God, I've forgotten my shoes and my rucksack,' she cried. 'I'm so sorry.'

Neil simply laughed and ran down to the pebbly beach to pick up her rucksack as well as her trainers, which were embarrassingly new and shining. He dropped them all neatly into her lap.

The small boat was on its way surging through the white-topped waves. Alyssa began to relax. Under her lashes she admired the pleasant looking ferryman so like Rory. He looked up and caught her staring.

Alyssa flushed with embarrassment. Rory was taking up too much of her thoughts. She didn't want him there. She was attracted to him physically, but she shouldn't have let down her guard with him at the house yesterday. He'd been just too quick to press his attentions on her when she was in a highly emotional state. Where did Barbara fit in? And what about Mick? Mick had told her he knew Rory. Although Rory had come to her rescue in the old house, now in the cold light of day she wasn't sure how far he was involved with the devious Mick. Besides she didn't want to be disturbed by other men. She was here on business and not to play around.

'Where are you staying on our islands?' Neil asked. 'Not at Lady Grizelda's house? Nobody could live there now.'

Alyssa thought it was time to underline her claim to Balvaig House. 'No of course not,' she said. 'But Lady Grizelda did leave the house to me.'

He nodded his head but his eyes were questioning.

'Tell me about Lady Grizelda,' Alyssa coaxed.

'Och I kenned her well,' he said. 'Such a beauty and a such a hard life. Although she was away with the fairies long enough.'

'Away with the fairies?' Alyssa gripped the side of the boat as it was seized as if by a giant hand. Her stomach lurched as the boat slipped sideways in a rush. The waters churned with white-capped waves and Neil opened the throttle of the engine for extra power against the driving currents of the water.

'What's happening?' she cried in a panic.

Neil laughed as he caught the boat, swinging the tiller hard over. 'That's old Thor, as we call him, trying to grab us. He's always on the lookout for unwary boatmen, but we know how to deal with him!'

Alyssa exhaled the breath she was holding. Fairies, underwater spirits, whatever next?

The little boat sped swiftly across the narrow strait. Alyssa began to be afraid there wouldn't be time to ask all the questions that were burning inside her. She leant forward. 'Tell me how my great aunt was before she went into hospital? Was she very confused?'

'Poor thing, she was very wandered, long before they took her in to the hospital,' said Neil. 'She used to walk round, searching, searching for something.'

'What could she have been searching for?'

'First we wondered if she was looking for the cows they took away from her. Or perhaps it was her long dead husband. Or even her two brothers. But when we asked her if we could help her, she couldn't tell us.'

Alyssa pictured an old woman with long flowing grey hair, who wandered around weeping and shaking her head hopelessly. 'She must have been very unhappy,' she said, her voice full of sympathy.

'She couldn't rest.' Neil manoeuvred the boat round a dark rock sticking up from the water. 'It was a sore thing to watch the poor body. My mother often tried to help her, and sometimes she would take washing away from the house to do it for Lady Grizel. For in the end the poor old lady took no care of herself. When the last cow was sold she lost heart entirely. That's when they had to come and take her away. You never heard such a screeching and crying as when they came to take her away from her beloved home. She understood that at least.'

Alyssa drew in her breath with horror.

'Rory MacDonald and his father were there. And that Barbara. Probably they'll take over the old house. Rory needs more space for his veterinary surgery. The manse isn't very big.'

Alyssa struggled to digest his words. How Lady Grizelda must have suffered. There seemed to have been no one to take care of her. She must have felt that she was being kidnapped when they took her away. Did Rory and his father just stand by? Were they helping Lady Grizelda or were they after their own ends? A quick and cheap deal with Mick McDermott and then they could take over the property just next door to the MacDonalds' own house. How convenient.

Alyssa felt an intense need to find out what'd really happened. To find out if Lady Grizelda really meant her, Alyssa, to have the house because she was her closest relative. Or had the poor old lady felt that Mick McDermott was the only one who'd bothered about her. Was that the real reason for her changing her will?

Alyssa's heart burned with sympathy for poor Lady Grizelda. 'How dreadful, poor Lady Grizelda! She must have been so lonely.'

'Or maybe she was waiting for someone,' said Neil. 'But we never knew who. If we went over to speak to her she would grow quiet and silent and just look worried and upset. Her eyes would go all blank. But one thing was certain, she didn't live in this world anymore. There was no sense to be got out of her in the last few months before they took her into the hospital.'

The boat bumped gently against the jetty on the other side of the water. Neil sprang out and threw a rope round the stanchion. He drew the boat close in and helped Alyssa up onto the wooden structure.

Safely on shore Alyssa followed the path Neil had pointed out. This smaller island was not as pretty as the

Island of Mora. There were very few flowers, only rough grass and clumps of greedy bracken which encroached on the overgrown path. The grasses and scratchy undergrowth grabbed at her bare legs. She'd been foolish enough to wear shorts instead of trousers which would've protected her, but the day was so warm and the air so gentle. She wanted to let her skin breathe.

The path was steep and in places Alyssa had to scramble over huge protruding rocks. She wondered how Miss Brodie, whom Graham Shaw had described as an elderly woman, managed to get down to the ferry, but perhaps there was another easier way.

The cottage was long and low. From a distance it looked quite attractive, but close up she could see the cheap white harling on the walls was flaking off.

She walked across the grass, which had been roughly scythed in front of the cottage. A black cat with luminous yellow eyes stared out of the window as she searched for a bell to ring, but there wasn't even a brass knocker, so she pounded with her knuckles on the heavy door.

Through the window she saw a face, which came closer. Someone wearing a man's hat peered curiously at her and then disappeared. After a couple of moments the door was opened and a large man emerged wearing a deerstalker hat, and a heavy jacket and trousers. How strange! Where was Miss Brodie?

'Yes?' the tall figure looked inquiringly at Alyssa. 'Take your boat round to the far side and I'll come out and catch the moorings.' Alyssa was astonished and confused. She found herself rooted to the path. Although the person facing her had quite a deep mannish voice and wore men's clothing, Alyssa's instincts told her that she was confronting an elderly woman. There was something about the swell of a large Valkyrie-like breast that the heavy tweed jacket failed to conceal.

This was probably the woman Alyssa wanted to see.

'I haven't got a boat to moor,' Alyssa said. 'Are you Miss Brodie?' she rushed on, 'I'm looking for you because you were a friend of my great aunt, Lady Grizelda.'

'And who might you be?' The large woman took a step forward. She towered over Alyssa, and glared at her, her eyes full of thunderclouds.

'I'm Lady Grizelda's great niece, Alyssa Mead.' Alyssa stood her ground. Then she tried a shock tactic. 'I'm trying to find out what happened to her before her death. 'Did someone play a trick on her? There seems to be some doubt about the validity of the will.'

Her blunt tone made Miss Brodie step back and she seemed to deflate. Her face under the deerstalker hat went a dull red. Her chin, which sprouted several long grey hairs, trembled.

'So you do know who I am,' said Alyssa, seeing she'd won an advantage.

Miss Brodie, who must have been in her seventies, half turned away from her. Over her shoulder she said, 'You'd better come in and have a cup of tea. Not that I really want to talk to you. But I can't deny that you are who you say you are. You are exactly like your great aunt in her younger days. But tell me, why did you never came to see Grizel before she died? That was a cruel thing to do. How do you have the gall to come now?' She moved behind Alyssa, agile as a much younger woman.

To her surprise Alyssa felt herself propelled by Miss Brodie's hand on her back through the front door into a dim hall. The dank air was chilly on Alyssa's bare legs. The old lady seemed very strong for someone of her age. She was probably a good ten or fifteen years younger than Lady Grizelda had been.

Miss Brodie continued to shove Alyssa forward into the sitting room. Abruptly she removed her hand and pointed to one of the green plush armchairs. 'Sit there,' she ordered, as if speaking to a dog.

Alyssa obeyed, amused by the woman's actions. What if the old lady got violent? Miss Brodie was almost a head taller than she was, and much more bulky.

Alyssa tried to psyche herself up. She breathed deeply to calm herself. The most important thing was the information she'd come for. At least she'd been invited indoors, like in the story of Hansel and Gretel! She'd rather have sat outside in the sun because there was a distinct odour of shut-in cat throughout the cottage.

'I'll bring the tea,' said her hostess, lumbering out of the room.

'Thank you,' Alyssa said, not admitting she'd counted on highland courtesy which dictated she couldn't be turned away and that she must be offered refreshment. She'd gambled on these customs still being adhered to in these remote islands. She hoped the cat wouldn't help to brew the tea.

The old lady trundled out to what Alyssa supposed was the kitchen, because she could hear her opening and shutting cupboards. Well now she'd been given a chance to find out something. Stifling her guilty feelings, she stood up and began to look around the sitting room. Could she find any letter or anything, which might throw light on what had happened in the preparation of the will? Had Lady Grizelda been coerced into signing something? Had she known what she was doing? And where did Mick McDermott fit in? And Rory? Alyssa pushed that last thought quickly aside.

If Mick was fond of old ladies, it wasn't really so surprising that he had thrown his lot in with Miss Brodie. Perhaps he had designs on her money too, although she seemed in good health and able to take good care of herself at least for the time being.

Alyssa heard a door bang and looked out of the window. Miss Brodie was striding along the path, carrying a kettle. There must a well or a burn where she got her water. Was there no running water in this house either? How could these old ladies survive without water and electricity? But then Alyssa caught sight of an electric light fitting in the ceiling and a standard lamp behind the sofa, so at least Miss Brodie must have electricity installed in her cottage.

A strange compulsion outside herself drove her on. *Get on with it*, she urged herself. *Don't stand here hesitating, wasting time*. She forced herself onward even though it seemed very mean and underhand to poke through another person's belongings. She'd never done anything like that before in her whole life.

Well she'd only have a quick look at the things in this room and she didn't have much time. *Go on, go on,* a voice murmured in her ear. Alyssa moved reluctantly over to the mahogany desk positioned under the window. Taking a quick peep outside she saw Miss Brodie bending down, filling the kettle from the small waterfall of a rushing burn. Alyssa only hoped the water was untainted by dead sheep or other decaying matter.

She was counting on Miss Brodie having to boil the cold water for the tea, giving her a few minutes more to carry out her unorthodox search. If only the old woman didn't suddenly appear again in the sitting room to chat with her unwelcome guest.

Alyssa kept her body crouched below the window, so that her reluctant hostess couldn't see her. With trembling hands she drew out the top right-hand side drawer of the desk. Only a bundle of used crayons, some old pens and an eraser. She tried the top drawer on the left-hand side but it was empty except for a small tin box marked 'drawing pins' and another marked 'safety pins'.

She pulled out the deep drawer below. This was more encouraging. Here was a heap of old papers, some yellowed, some more recent. Still crouching, she peered again through the window. Now Miss Brodie was walking briskly back to the cottage, carrying the kettle. Any important papers had to be here in this drawer, otherwise Alyssa would have to give up. Time was running out.

The papers were slightly torn round the edges. There were a number of bills, which Alyssa leafed past quickly. But here was an interesting long brown envelope. 'Balvaig House' was written on the outside. Peering rapidly inside, Alyssa inserted her fingers and drew out several folded papers and a letter signed in a very shaky hand with a black pen – Grizelda Lovat. Inside the envelope there were several other papers with nothing on them except similar wavering signatures as if someone had been practising how to write the name.

There was no more time. Alyssa could hear footsteps approaching. She took a last peek at the papers in the drawer and pulled out a roughly sketched-out family tree. Shock almost blinded her, causing her ears to ring and her head to spin. She blinked rapidly, trying to decipher the letters, which danced in front of her eyes. She retained just enough sense to shove the brown envelope and the family paper with her name on it into her small rucksack, swiftly shut the drawer, and threw herself back into the armchair with a bump.

The door opened and in came her hostess bearing a tea-tray. She set it down on the small table in front of Alyssa, and regarded her with a stern eye. 'I am receiving you only because you are Lady Grizelda's great niece,' she said. 'For no other reason. You should be ashamed that you never once came to see her all that time when she was ill and lying in the hospital.'

Alyssa shook her head from side to side, trying to shake off the heart-pounding experience she'd just been through. Her feeling of guilt rose several degrees. How shameful that she'd rifled through a complete stranger's desk. But the rough family tree? What of that? If it were correct, her whole life was founded on a lie. Yet the dates seemed to fit. She bit hard on her fist to stop herself from crying out loud.

Alyssa realised that Miss Brodie was waiting for a reply from her. Her cheeks became hot under Miss Brodie's stern gaze.

'You should be ashamed,' repeated Miss Brodie.

Ashamed of what…? Alyssa's head wasn't working. Then her mind cleared. 'I'm sorry,' she said, forcing herself to speak normally. 'But I truly did not know I had a great aunt until I got the lawyer's letter, and then it was too late. My poor great aunt was dead. And Mick McDermott had appeared from nowhere and taken over.'

Miss Brodie looked taken aback. 'Didn't you know about Lady Grizelda?' She huffed through her nose. 'Mick was a good nephew to Grizel. He visited her regularly in hospital and brought her flowers. There were only the two of us who bothered to visit her in the end.'

'Did you know about Mick before he came to Grizelda's deathbed?' Alyssa deliberately dropped the harsh word in front of Miss Brodie. 'Or more to the point, did Lady Grizelda know him? Did she ever tell you anything about him? He wasn't her nephew, you know.'

'How do you know that?' Miss Brodie's tone was hostile. 'He told me he was her nephew.'

'Have you not seen the family tree?' said Alyssa, scrutinising Miss Brodie's reaction. 'I thought you knew everything about this family. Mick was an outsider who forced his way in. I am a much closer relative.' Again she watched Miss Brodie's face.

'You weren't there, my fine girl,' said Miss Brodie huffily. 'Mick cared for his poor Aunt Grizelda.'

Alyssa sighed. Should she disillusion Miss Brodie and explain her suspicions that Mick was an opportunistic trickster? No, she decided she'd not say anything at this stage and see what the lawyer could come up with. And she still had to digest the meaning of the birth certificate which nestled so secretly in her rucksack. At the thought of it, Alyssa's heartbeat surged with anguish, but she couldn't let Miss Brodie see what she was feeling. She had to keep control of her emotions.

'Poor Lady Grizelda was very confused,' said Miss Brodie. 'Sometimes she didn't even know me. And I had been friends with her for the last ten years. I never let her down. Not like her family, except for Mick of course.' She glowered like an ancient bulldog at Alyssa.

'But you say she didn't recognise Mick at all,' said Alyssa. 'That's because she never had seen him before in her life.'

'Well, we couldn't be sure,' said Miss Brodie, taking a gulp of her tea. 'I thought it was nice for Grizelda to have one of her own family to visit her. Besides Mick was charming and he brought that nice lawyer to visit her too.'

'Nice lawyer indeed. Did Lady Grizelda know the lawyer?' Alyssa pressed on. 'Was he her usual lawyer?'

'Oh, no, she'd never seen him before,' said Miss Brodie. 'But you must see she needed a lawyer to make her will.'

Alyssa jumped up from the armchair. Her tea stood untouched on the small side table, a feeble trail of steam rising from it. 'You mean that you and Mick brought in a completely strange lawyer to an old woman who didn't know what she was doing. A person who didn't understand anything of what was happening. It's almost criminal what you did.' Alyssa's heart pounded with indignation. She paced across the room, looking down at Miss Brodie.

Miss Brodie flinched. 'Mick said we had to get her affairs in order.'

Alyssa's cheeks flushed as she grew angrier. 'Did you ever check Mick's credentials? For one thing he's not her nephew. Her close relatives are all dead, except for me. I'd like very much to know where this McDermott came from.'

'Grizelda was alone for many years. Her husband and brothers were dead. But what about you? Where were you?' There was scorn in Miss Brodie's voice.

The old woman was trembling, the grey hairs on her chin again prominent. Alyssa reminded herself that this was an elderly woman who had probably acted from the best of intentions. She'd tried to be a good friend to Lady Grizelda, but she had taken no precautions and she seemed to have put poor Grizelda in jeopardy.

The room was getting darker. Now Alyssa could just distinguish a faint voice in her ear saying: 'Don't be so angry with her, she was only trying to help. But you, Alyssa, must put things right.'

Was she hallucinating? Alyssa asked herself, trying to control the now familiar dizziness that threatened to overwhelm her. Or was it really Lady Grizelda's voice? Could she believe that? She sat down quickly and took several large sips of the strong tea. If she'd never left London, she'd never have got involved with these other-worldly experiences. And worst of all, she was unsure whether she'd heard or seen anything at all. Was it her imagination playing tricks after all the stress she'd been under, or could she really slip between two worlds?

Voices whispered in her ear. She rubbed her hands over her eyes, trying to clear her vision. A heavy weight pushed down on her chest. *No, Grizelda. No, Grizelda. Don't come here!* Alyssa's lips formed a silent scream. *Leave me alone!* But the mist swirled and engulfed her and she was falling, falling...

CHAPTER EIGHT

At the wedding feast in the town hall, fatigue was sweeping over Grizelda as she sat in the high-backed chair at Peter's side. She didn't think she could bear to listen to another interminable speech. Supporting her head with her right hand, she wished that these pompous men in their kilts and tight and stuffy black suits would get tired of hearing their own voices. She wasn't impressed by their bragging, or their need to be the centre of attention, and they did make her head spin.

To keep herself alert she began to count the guests at each table, starting at the top table where she and the bridal party were sitting. To her horror she counted thirteen at the table. Margaret's superstitious words about the mirror had upset her and made her remember the old country beliefs. If she started counting starting with herself first, Peter became number thirteen. And if she started with him, then she became the thirteenth person at the table.

Together with her and Peter at the same high table were her two brothers, John and William, along with Margaret and her husband as well as Peter's younger sister, Elvira, and his aunts and uncles. Grizelda pleated her long veil between her fingers, and told herself to ban such foolish superstitions.

Elvira, looking like a bird of paradise in her elegantly tailored red and yellow gown, easily outshone most of the other women in their subdued black silk dresses. Grizelda caught her trying to hide a yawn behind her delicate fingers. She wore bright red nail varnish. The villagers would think that shocking, but Grizelda thought it was rather daring and fun.

She looked across at the other wedding guests as they sat at long tables covered with snow-white tablecloths. A group of women helpers from the church had taken three days to iron the cloths to perfection. Bunches of heather mixed with wild flowers and tied with festive tartan ribbons decorated each table.

Grizelda felt the red cushioned chair she was sitting on become harder as time dragged. She was sure her beautiful white dress was crushed into permanent folds. She sighed. At least three hours had passed since they sat down to the rich food and copious wine. Not that she'd had more than a glass, but the men of the party hadn't been so abstemious. They drank deeply from the wine provided. The mounting collection of empty bottles was proof enough of that.

Grizelda's eyelids drooped. The heavy wedding fare was weighing her down. First the Scotch broth, a soup far too hot for the heat of this day. Then followed the huge legs of roast lamb, fatty and substantial served with huge heaps of potatoes. The only light part of the wedding breakfast had been the mounds of fresh raspberries, which the women of the island had taken two days to gather. Lashings of fresh cream was being poured over the fruit.

The low hum of the guests' chatter nearly lulled her to sleep. She forced herself to sit up straight on her chair, and survey the scene. The male guests were beginning to throw off their inhibitions after all the wine they'd drunk, and they constantly refreshed themselves with ill concealed draughts of whisky from their hip flasks. Her eye caught yet another hip flask passing no-so-discreetly between John and another man, fuelling the festivities.

Despite it being her wedding day, Grizelda had got up at six o'clock this morning and worked with her brothers to milk the cows, after they'd been brought in from the lush summer grass of the fields. At least today, John had relieved her of mucking out the cow shed once the cows had returned to their daytime pasture.

She looked down at her hands. They were strong and supple and much too brown from the sun to be ladylike. She twisted the shiny gold ring encircling her finger. Would it bind her or free her?

Peter leant forward and smiled directly at her, his face flushed with the red wine. His hand crept down and squeezed hers under the table. She felt her fingers being pinched against the gold ring and she moved restlessly as she tried to free herself.

'I'm just going out for a minute,' he whispered. 'Wait for me!' His heavy kilt swung bravely as he moved away from his chair.

Grizelda admired the soft green colouring of his brand new kilt. He must have bought it specially for the wedding as he seemed a man more at home in dark well-tailored suits. She smiled back at him, letting some of the tension float away from her. He was a very attractive man, and perhaps she would make a good wife after all. Her thoughts swept to the coming night. How would it feel to be a married woman in the full sense of the word? Would she be able to please him, to delight him? Or would she find it so painful that she would scream so that everyone would hear her?

Peter had still not returned when a small boy in short trousers, hanging down below his knees, crept up behind her. Grizelda wondered how on earth he had got in. He certainly wasn't one of the wedding party. He stood there uncertainly, wiping his nose on the sleeve of his holey jersey.

'Missus, Missus,' he cried, his dirty hands pawing at her veil. 'Your man wants you. You must come to him now. He canna wait.'

Grizelda pulled her veil smartly out of the wee boy's hands. 'What's all this?' she asked. 'Is something wrong? Is Sir Peter hurt?'

'Come on, Missus, hurry, hurry,' the boy said, trying to pull her silk covered arm.

'Careful, careful, keep your dirty hands off me.' Grizelda pushed him back and almost knocked over her chair as she rose hastily from the table.

She gathered up her veil, hooking it up over her arm, and flicked the long train of her white dress neatly behind her. She whisked through the door, as the guests stared after her in horrified surprise.

She hurried through the dark hall with the darting small boy dancing in front of her. She reached the outside porch of the town hall, and two kilted men, woollen scarves tied over their mouths, emerged from the gloom. Stepping on each side of her they seized both her arms.

They were unsteady on their feet but their grip was firm. 'Ow – let me go at once!' screamed Grizelda shocked and frightened. She fought to break free of their tight hold on her. 'Who are you?' she demanded. 'Where's Sir Peter?'

One of the men laughed triumphantly, and his scarf slipped down so that he blew whisky fumes in her face. 'What a prize! The brand new Lady Lovat!' he said. 'Your man's waiting for you and we're going to take a nice little drive.'

Grizelda stared at him trying to recognise who he was, but he was a complete stranger to her. She tried to resist and escape from his rough hold. A third man appeared out of the shadows, a dirty scarf hiding his face, and thrust her forward away from the wedding party inside. 'Help me, help me,' she cried, struggling frantically, hoping that some of the guests would hear her. In the scuffle, the third man trampled on her long dress, which ripped with a loud tearing of silk.

A battered old lorry stood on the other side of the road, and a stream of vile smelling exhaust poured out into the cool evening air. The three men propelled her quickly across the road to where it stood. The tallest man loosened the back of the lorry, letting it fall with a clank of metal. All three of them hoisted her into the back, and she fell forward scraping her face on the rough boards. Her beautiful wedding gown billowed up like a sail full of wind and then slowly collapsed.

'You've torn my veil,' she shouted defiantly, struggling upright and fighting against feeble tears. 'You've ruined my wedding. Oh, the humiliation of it. My future is spoiled. What a disgrace on my wedding day. Oh my beautiful dress!'

She stared boldly at the three men. 'Where's my husband?' she demanded fiercely. With a raucous laugh one of the men pointed at the back of the lorry. There was a black shape lying sprawled there. No, no, it couldn't be! The nightmare was getting worse. Realisation swept over

Grizelda: a few feet away from her in the dark space, her brand new husband tried to sit up. Grizelda crawled over to him across the dirty wooden boards, hampered by her long dress and petticoats. The most recent occupants of the truck must have been sheep and they had left horrid smelly traces as well as scraps of white wool that became entangled in her veil. As she crept across to Peter a few petals dropped from the brave white rose in her hair.

With a jerk the lorry started moving down the narrow road.

Peter groaned. He managed to pull himself upright into a sitting position, and leant unsteadily against the outer board of the lorry.

'Peter, speak to me,' implored Grizelda, grasping the side of the vehicle as it rattled along. 'Are you all right? What happened? Who are these people?'

'It's your wild highlanders playing a prank,' Peter's words were slurred. 'I'm to blame. I should've looked after you better, my new wife. How could I let us get caught by a trick like this!' He slumped back. 'Oh my head!' He clutched his head and groaned again.

Grizelda could see a lump fast developing on his forehead. 'Can you sit up?' she asked, moving beside him and putting her arm around him to support his back.

The old lorry roared round the sharp bends of the narrow road, bumping and shaking its reluctant passengers. Grizelda dashed away angry tears, trying to decide if she recognised any of the men who'd abducted them. It was hard to be sure when their faces were concealed by the heavy scarves.

Now they were tearing along the road that led to the deep hill loch. The truck slowed and Grizelda's mind raced faster. What would the abductors do with them? Had none of the other guests seen what had happened?

Gently releasing Peter, she rose up on her knees, and heedless of her torn and filthy dress she moved toward the back of the driver's cabin and began banging on it. The dank air spread chills through her whole body and her torn silk dress held no warmth. The lorry continued to rattle through the night.

'Please God,' she prayed. 'Don't let them push us into the loch.'

CHAPTER NINE

Alyssa left Miss Brodie's cottage. Walking like an automaton, she placed one foot carefully in front of the other. A cloudy blur floated around her and she found it hard to see straight. She couldn't remember saying goodbye to the old woman, or even how she'd managed to find the strength to get out of Miss Brodie's sagging chair. She stumbled down the path to the ferry, grabbing at the branches of trees to help her stay upright, and wavering from side to side as if she'd drunk too much wine.

Neil, the outline of his figure unclear, was waiting for her at the ferry pier, and she clung to his hand to steady herself as he helped her aboard.

'Are you feeling quite well, Miss Alyssa?' he asked her in his courteous highland tones.

Alyssa realised she must look very white and shaken. 'I'm feeling fine, Neil. There's nothing wrong with me.' She was bending the truth, more for her own sake than his. 'I'm just a little tired.' She tried to smile reassuringly at him as he regarded her with a worried air.

Quickly she sat down in the boat and fought to push down her queasiness as they sped over the narrow strait between the islands. She let her thick hair form a curtain between her and the outside world. Hazily she wondered if Miss Brodie had put something in her tea.

Some time later, she woke up in her bed in the cottage, feeling limp and exhausted. Her shorts and tee shirt were crumpled and she couldn't remember removing her trainers. She sat up in the bed and looked at her watch. Seven o'clock. Was it morning or evening? She was completely disoriented and must have slept for hours. There was a cup of cold tea standing on the bedside table. Had someone been to visit her? Was it Rory? Or Neil? Surely not Mick? Who entered the cottage when she lay there in a deep sleep? She shivered. She didn't like the idea of someone coming in while she lay there helpless.

Shadows hovered in the background, but she refused to let them come close. She'd had enough of Grizelda's troubles. How was she able to see these visions of the past as clearly as if she was actually standing there? And even enter Grizelda's mind so that she actually knew what she was thinking and feeling. That was the most inexplicable part. She wondered if she could she have fainted again, back at Miss Brodie's cottage. These dizzy spells came over her so suddenly that she was getting really worried that there was something seriously wrong with her. Should she see a doctor?

She pushed back the bedcovers and got slowly out of bed. She stripped off her clothes, and went into the small bathroom to immerse herself in a long hot shower. She let the needles of water drum on her back, and kept her mind blank. After towelling herself dry, she put on a light green dress as the evening was still warm. She felt like wearing something frivolous and carefree to try and pretend she hadn't any worries.

She couldn't remember when she'd last eaten and now her stomach rumbled in complaint. She went into the kitchen and looked in the refrigerator. She lifted out some eggs and some butter. Breaking two of the eggs, she tossed them into the frying pan with some herbs for an omelette. She cut some bread from the loaf she'd bought yesterday, and put the kettle on to boil. At least she didn't have to go out to the stream to get water.

She sat at the kitchen table with her plate of omelette, steam curling up from the fresh cup of tea in front of her. Memories of her visit to Miss Brodie came flooding back.

She was consumed with guilt. How could she have stolen a letter from an old lady? *But they were stealing from me,* a little voice murmured in her head. *They were trying to manipulate me.* Alyssa put her hands over her ears to try and block out the sound. Was she hallucinating again? The envelope! Had she brought her little rucksack back with her? Stifling a feeling of guilt, she went back into the bedroom and to her relief found it lying on from the floor beside the bed. She retrieved the brown envelope… and the other document she'd taken from Miss Brodie's desk, her guilt churning inside her.

Outside the evening stretched, long and light. It beckoned her out of the cottage and down onto the deserted shore. She put her hand in her pocket to touch the papers lying there and they seemed to burn against her thigh.

She sat down on the beach, took off her shoes and curled her toes in the warm sand. A small white ship far in the distance traversed the blueness of the sea as if on a painted canvas. The sweep of the horizon stretched to infinity, making her feel a very small element in the grand scheme of creation. The soft sound of the sea lapping at the shore soothed her tumultuous thoughts. She closed her eyes, and let the late evening sun caress her face.

After some time her head felt clearer. She got up and began to walk along the beach as her mind worked furiously. What would she do now that she had proof that Lady Grizelda's will had been tampered with and the signature forged? Would the lawyer believe her? He might ask some awkward questions about how she came to be in possession of the letter and the signatures, but she'd face that problem when it arose.

A picture of Mick and his angry red face rose before her. No, he was not going to win! She wouldn't let him. Besides she was convinced that Great Aunt Grizelda would've applauded what she'd done. Was it Grizelda who had urged her to take the envelope? Certainly a presence outside herself had compelled her to behave in a way that was entirely out of character for her. Snitching documents – how could she have done that? But there had definitely been an unseen presence there in Miss Brodie's cottage. And all in all it was hard to believe that Miss Brodie could ever have been a friend of her aunt's.

The sea whispered over her feet, reminding her that the tide was rolling in. She moved back up the beach to sit on a huge grey rock, sculpted by the sea. She had to decide what to do next. Could she trust Rory? He was a very attractive man, but maybe he was playing the field. Was he involved with Barbara? Was that why she was so hostile to Alyssa? If he and Barbara were engaged, it was strange that he could put Alyssa, the newcomer, before his fiancée. No, Alyssa couldn't ask him for advice. There was no choice. She'd have to go back to Graham Shaw. He'd be able to look at the legal aspect of the situation.

She was very alone. Her home in London seemed far away. It wouldn't help to telephone any of her friends. They wouldn't understand anyway and she just couldn't tell them about the massive crime she'd just committed. Compelled by a ghost! They would laugh their heads off at her nonsense!

Jeff was out of her life, and she certainly didn't wish him back. He'd become only a distant shade, and she could hardly recall his face or his voice. Now when she thought of it at all, their life in London seemed empty and monotonous. Nothing but a steady round of visits to galleries, to the theatre or sitting in restaurants or wine bars. A far cry from the clean champagne air of the highlands. She inhaled the fresh ozone smell of the sea and her cares slipped away on the gentle breeze. New strength came to her and a new determination to fight for her rights, and for Grizelda's.

Only then was she able to draw out the strange scribbled extract of her family tree that had so stunned her. She had tried to block it out of her thoughts, but she knew she'd have to confront it. She spread it out on the rock. 'William Finlay, married Morag MacKay.' So far, so good. That must have been Great Aunt Grizelda's brother. But he had had a son, a second "William Finlay" married... yes no doubt about it, it was her mother, Frances Russel. The dates were correct. Frances Russel, her mother had been married before. Of course Alyssa knew that, but she hadn't thought much about it. But now it seemed that she, Alyssa was not Howard Mead's daughter as she'd always believed. Not her father's daughter, but daughter of a stranger, this William Finlay, first husband of her mother. Her cry of anguish mingled with the sea gulls flying high above her head. And she'd believed that her connection with Lady

Grizelda came through her mother's side of the family. Her head was spinning as her whole world shifted. Her father wasn't her father. How could she ever come to terms with that?

*

A few lonely sea birds circled the vast expanse of the horizon emitting melancholy cries, as Rory walked along the beach.

His eyes studied Alyssa as she sat on the grey rock above the restless sea, intent on the pages she was holding. He walked toward her, the faithful Ginger following at his heels. He stood quietly for a moment in the shadow of the pine tree, drinking in the spell of her soft auburn curls and slender body.

His hand went out towards her. God, she was appealing. He felt a strong surge of desire and tried to suppress it. He was finished with women. His entanglement with Magda in Edinburgh had made him wary of women. What a fool he had been allowing himself to be seduced by her charming wiles, just until the next guy with more money in his pockets came along.

Alyssa was a city girl. She seemed rather fragile and she'd never settle down here. The winters would be too cold, the storms too harsh. Besides what would she do here? Was there any point in embarking on a hasty sexual liaison, which would be broken off just as quickly as it began when she went back to London?

No, he had enough on his mind. His veterinary practice was building up nicely. It had lapsed badly because the previous vet had only retired after reaching the age of eighty. Then there was the problem of his father's ill health. He owed it to his father to keep a close eye on him. Anyway life was good here on the island, and he was doing an interesting and worthwhile job.

Rory brushed against the pine branches and Alyssa looked up, startled. She'd been so intent on the paper she held in her hand. Her face was white and strained and she looked cold and shocked. Then her lips curved in a rather lopsided welcoming smile. His resistance to her attraction faded swiftly as he gazed at her. Her green silky dress was rucked up like a child's revealing her long bare legs and rose-painted toes. She was like one of the fairies in the Celtic myths, mesmerising him so that he couldn't take his eyes off her. He held her gaze and the minutes stretched forever. Then he reached for her hand and drew her up. Something intense flared between them. But sudden wariness flashed in her eyes and she stepped back, ready to dart away from him. She gently freed her hand from his warm clasp and backed off like a startled deer.

'Rory,' she whispered, her voice low and husky. 'Rory, did you stop by and make me a cup of tea earlier?'

He nodded, not telling her that he'd been worried when he called at the cottage and found her sitting white and still in her sitting room. He'd helped her into the bedroom and made her lie down, removing her shiny new trainers and pulling the bedcovers over her. He'd wanted to kiss her, to hold her, but he'd held himself back, only brushing her cheek so very gently with his lips.

'Are you okay now?' he asked her, stroking her shoulders. 'Did you drink the tea I made for you?'

She smiled at him brilliantly. 'So it was you, Rory, who took care of me. I've never felt so faint before. How feeble, I don't know what came over me. But don't you think I look better now?'

She sat up and straightened her dress, tugging it down as if to conceal herself from him. The long golden rays of the late evening sun illuminated her face and the whiteness of the papers in her hand. Her lips were red and full. Again her eyes sought his. He could hear her rapid breathing.

Deliberately she pushed the pages into an envelope and picked up a piece of quartz to hold it down and prevent them from fluttering away. She rose, careful in her movements, but drawn by the silver cord between them, she stepped forward to grasp his outstretched hands.

Ginger began to bark sharply and fiercely.

A loud tooting shattered the peace of the summer evening, Both Rory and Alyssa swung round towards the road some fifty yards away as a large, white van skidded to a halt. A man jumped out. Ginger was beside himself, growling and blustering as the newcomer strode toward them.

'What the hell do you want, Mick?' Rory took a firm hold of the dog's collar as the unwelcome visitor closed in on them.

'I want a word with your lady friend here,' Mick said, puffing with the exertion of walking a few yards. 'I know she's got something belonging to me. She's a right wee thief. You ask her what she's done!'

Hot blood pounded in Rory's ears, as irrational anger rose, almost choking him. He stepped forward and seized Mick by the back of his collar. He shook him like a dog.

'Back off, back off, f*** you!' gasped Mick. 'Why are you attacking me? You haven't heard anything yet. Your fine girlfriend here has stolen a letter from a poor old lady. Now what do you say to that?'

Rory let go of Mick so suddenly that he collapsed on the sea-washed rock. 'Prove it, is what I say!' he snapped.

Mick stumbled up and regained his footing. The air was blue with his cursing. He raised his fists like a prize fighter. 'Come and get me, MacDonald, and I'll give you a bloody nose!'

Rory towered over him, not bothering to raise his fists in retaliation. 'Just hit me first, McDermott, and you'll regret it.'

Mick dropped his hands to his sides. He turned toward Alyssa and thrust out his chin. 'What was that envelope you took from Moira Brodie? Tell us. It wasn't your property. I'll report you to the police for stealing.'

Alyssa flushed with guilt. But Rory stepped forward, frowning. 'What sort of wild accusations are these?' he said to Mick.

Mick jabbed his finger at Alyssa. 'Ask her.'

Alyssa's cheeks were hot with embarrassment, but she said nothing. The very rocks seemed to form a ring of disapproval round her. What would Rory think of her now? But it wasn't the right time for explanations when Mick had barged in as an uninvited third party. The two men held their ground, eyes locked, neither giving an inch.

Alyssa gritted her teeth. Her papers! Her eyes searched the ground until she found the envelope under the stone where she'd placed it. As the two men tried to face each other down, she quietly gathered up the envelope from its hiding place, and slipped it back into her pocket. She exhaled in relief. This was her most important piece of evidence in her efforts to build up her claim to Great Aunt Grizelda's house, and she wasn't going to let it fall into the wrong hands. Then she whirled round and sprinted off back to her little cottage leaving the two men staring after her.

CHAPTER TEN

The warmth of Rory's lips on hers was cooling. His body became insubstantial. The vision of his face as he stood with his hands outstretched toward her, wavered and faded. In her large comfortable bed in the cottage, Alyssa lay in a drowsy state of transition. Then as she surfaced from sleep, she squirmed in embarrassment, remembering how she had abandoned Rory so abruptly the evening before.

Her eyes opened. A faint scratching sound penetrated the interior of the old cottage. She jolted upright in the bed, now fully awake. Could there be mice running around the wainscotting of the house, even behind the bed head?

She swung her legs over the side of the bed and stepped onto the cold hard floor. Where were her shoes? Suppose the mice nipped her toes? Then she straightened up. She wasn't afraid of a few mice, for God's sake. But the rustling in the wall was getting louder, and now it seemed to be coming from outside. She tiptoed through into the sitting room to look out of the window.

She felt isolated in the lonely night as she tried to hold her breath, listening for sounds, but apart from the steady tick of the pendulum of the old grandfather clock in the corner of the room, all was now silent. She glanced at the clock face, gleaming white in the moon's rays. Its hands stood at five to three. Tick, tock, the sound seemed to magnify in the stillness of the room.

Cold shivers trickled down her back when she remembered that she hadn't bothered to lock the door of the cottage last night. She'd had the foolhardy idea of being like the natives of the island who left their doors trustingly unlocked. It didn't seem such a good idea after all. Not now as she stood twitching the curtain of the window trying to decipher the dark shadows thrown into stark relief by the moon sailing across the sky.

A foot scraped on a loose stone outside. Alyssa tensed, straining her eyes until they blurred, but failing to make out anything. A minute later her acute hearing picked up a stealthy movement outside the unlocked door. She clenched her fists. The brass knob turned slowly, and with a small creak the door was pushed open by an unseen hand. Alyssa's breath caught in her throat as she waited to see what kind of intruder would come round the door.

A slim shadow slipped inside.

Alyssa hesitated for a moment, poised on the balls of her feet. Then molten fury sped through her veins and galvanised her into action. Without stopping to think she rushed forward and grabbed the intruder's wrist. The white light of the moon's rays illuminated the face of young girl of about twelve or thirteen, trying to conceal herself in her grey hooded top. Curly, carroty hair stuck out on each side of the hood.

'Who are you?' demanded Alyssa, almost dropping the girl's wrist in surprise. Somehow she'd expected a large, swarthy man. 'What are you doing in my house at this time of night?'

Unexpectedly the girl hissed and spat at her like a vicious cat. Alyssa recoiled, but managed to keep tight hold of her arm. The girl's hood slipped further down revealing a thin, fierce face covered in freckles, and none too clean. Alyssa gave her a little shake, and the girl wriggled and twisted sharply almost breaking Alyssa's hold.

'No, you don't, you little eel,' said Alyssa. 'First you tell me what you're doing here, and then I might think of letting you go. Or perhaps I should call the police.'

The young girl began to whimper.

'First, tell me your name.' Alyssa looked at her sternly.

'Let me go, damn ye. I've no' taken anything of yours.' The girl looked back at Alyssa defiantly, then her eyes shifted and she looked away from Alyssa's steady gaze. She heaved a deep sigh. 'I'm no' telling you a damned thing.'

'You're not getting away until you tell me your name and why you're here in the middle of the night.' A thought struck Alyssa. Could the child have a knife? She took a firmer grip on the girl's arm, and led her over to a chair, and pushed her down. With her other hand she patted down each side of her, but she didn't seem to be carrying anything dangerous. Though she couldn't really be sure. She wondered what to do with her. She hadn't actually had a chance to do anything or steal anything from her.

'Tell me your name,' Alyssa persisted.

'It's Libby, missus' said the girl, with an ingratiating smile. She appeared suddenly docile. She sat quietly in the chair looking up at Alyssa.

'Well, Libby, now you can tell me what you're doing in my house in the middle of the night.'

'Och, missus, I'm awful sorry, I ken I've done a bad thing. Thon man told me tae do it.' The girl's head drooped.

'Do what?'

'Come here and get the envelope.'

'What envelope? From whom?' Alyssa's mind reeled. Could it be Miss Brodie's envelope?

'Who sent you?' she asked, quickly summing up the position. 'Tell me, was it Mick McDermott?'

A tear slipped out of the girl's eye, and she sniffed, wiping her nose with the back of her free hand.

A guilty feeling swept over Alyssa. This was just a child that she was gripping so firmly. If Mick was behind this, the child was just a pawn in his game. Well she was glad she had seized the envelope from Miss Brodie's house even though its contents were so devastating. She relaxed her hold, and immediately Libby snatched her arm from Alyssa's hand. She gave Alyssa a sharp kick on the shins. In an instant she was out of the door.

Alyssa raced to the door and tore after her, but was hampered by her lack of shoes. She ran a few steps down the path, but the stones cut into her bare feet and she stopped. Libby had got a good head start. Within minutes she'd been swallowed up by the night.

Alyssa turned back to the cottage and locked the door carefully behind her. She fastened the chain for good measure. She leaned against the door trying to collect her thoughts. Could Mick really have sent a child in the middle of the night to steal the envelope? It must be vitally important to him. She went over to the kitchen drawer where she'd put the envelope last night. Still there, but from now on she would keep it well hidden until she could show the papers to Graham Shaw.

Alyssa felt driven. There was no point in going back to bed. She'd never be able to sleep again. She pottered about in the kitchen making a hot cup of tea for herself.

The mountain of problems with the inheritance was growing. Could she be even more closely related to Grizelda if she were the granddaughter of her brother, William. But she couldn't really base what appeared to be a whole new relationship on a scribbled piece of paper. But it hurt, it really hurt. Had her parents deceived her? Had she lived almost her whole life with someone that wasn't her real father? Was the paper based on genuine facts? She pushed the painful thoughts away. Perhaps she should just forget the piece of paper. Or should she take it to the lawyer and let him sort it out?

Grizelda... and William. Apart from *them* getting under her skin, Mick McDermott elbowed his way into wherever she turned. First he'd interrupted the sweet idyll that she might have spent with Rory yesterday. Thanks to Mick, Rory probably now regarded her as a basket case as well as a dishonest person. The only comfort was that Rory had taken her part against Mick yesterday, but then in her confusion she'd stupidly run out on him. Then Mick had sent an innocent child to rob her. Well not exactly an innocent child, and not exactly a robbery. But he'd invaded her feeling of security on the island. From now on she'd find it hard to sleep peacefully at night.

The sun rose outside the picture window in the sitting room. A delicate canopy of lemon and palest pink spread across the sky. Alyssa decided she needed some physical exercise to clear her mind and resolve her thoughts. Even though it was still very early she went out into the small garden shed and excavated the old hand-pushed mower. There were no neighbours to disturb so she could do as she liked. It was hard work pushing the mower back and forward across the small square of grass in the garden, but thanks to her efforts neat swathes of evenly cut grass began to emerge.

Gradually, the need to speak to someone grew so strong that she relinquished the small mower, and sat down for a moment on the stone wall. Who could help her? Questions tumbled over in her mind. Should she stay on the island? Or abandon everything and drive back down to London? Who could give her impartial advice, and yet really care what happened to her? Was there in fact anyone?

She had a flash of insight. Rory's father would fit the bill. He was involved, yet not involved. This afternoon she would go and talk to him. Maybe he could tell her more about William Finlay. And perhaps Rory would appear after he'd been out on his rounds. That would be a good way of getting in contact with him again. She couldn't expect him to come to see her after she'd had rushed off so quickly yesterday. Damn, Rory, he was becoming an obsession.

*

It was again a beautiful day. The birds were singing their hearts out as Alyssa climbed the hill to the MacDonalds' manse. What about all these stories about swift downpours and non-stop rain in the islands? She had been lucky except for a couple of times. The highland summer stretched endlessly full of butterflies, bees and lazy hours, and as she walked, her spirits began to rise.

She arrived at the manse, mentally girding her loins. Really she was getting quite biblical. She would chase Barbara off, and get the old man on his own. She rang the bell and after some minutes, Mr MacDonald himself appeared, wearing a very dark old-fashioned suit and a shirt with a high stiff collar.

'Why, Miss Alyssa,' he said. 'I'm so pleased to see you. Come in. I'm sitting in the garden at the back.'

They walked through the house to the walled garden, which seemed quite private.

'My housekeeper's off today,' Mr MacDonald gave Alyssa a mischievous smile. 'She chivvies me around just a little too much. But she's left us some nice scones and some tea.' He indicated the thermos on the table.

Alyssa heaved a sigh of relief. With luck Barbara wouldn't be back for a bit so she wouldn't be able to eavesdrop on Alyssa's conversation with the old minister.

Alyssa and the old man sat together comfortably, Alyssa in the hammock swinging gently to and fro, and Mr MacDonald in a solid wooden chair supported by stuffed cushions, with his red tartan rug over his knees even in the warm and sunny weather.

'Now what can I do for you, my dear?' he asked.

Alyssa hesitated. It wasn't easy to know where to start, but the heady scent of the summer roses and the rhythmic swinging of the hammock served to calm her thoughts.

'Do you think I could ever settle down on this island? Everybody seems to think I'm some sort of fly-by-night, who will up and leave at the drop of a hat.'

'Everybody including my son, Rory?' said the old man shrewdly.

Alyssa felt her cheeks reddening, and bent over quickly to take a sip of tea.

'Just don't forget, my dear, that you have strong roots on the island. Your family came from here, and your great aunt was an important person in the community. I'm sure you could settle down here. Just fight for your rights.'

Alyssa leant forward in the hammock to choose a scone from the plate. 'Can you tell me anything about Lady Grizelda?' she asked. 'I've been having such vivid dreams about her, that it's quite frightening. It's as if she can't leave me alone. It sounds silly, but do you think she really wants me to stay and live in her house?'

'I think there's some unfinished business there,' said Mr MacDonald. 'Lady Grizelda's life was incomplete. I think that was why before her death she began to wander around the island searching for something. Something which nobody could find for her.'

'Yes, Neil the ferryman said that she was always out searching for something,' said Alyssa. 'What do you think that could be?'

'I think she was searching for her own lost happiness or something like that. I don't know. Perhaps you can find happiness for her on this island. Maybe that is your God-given task, to help her find peace,' said Mr MacDonald, his hand going out to pat the black and white collie, which had appeared from round the side of the house to thrust its nose into his hand.

Alyssa was surprised. If Grizelda was a ghost or a transient spirit, how did that combine with the faith of a minister of the church?

Mr MacDonald looked at her quizzically. He seemed to be able to read her thoughts. 'You must remember that most of us on this island are a wee bit fey. We like to believe we're in touch with things beyond the concrete realities of this world. Our souls... now that's a complicated matter.'

'What do you think about Grizelda? Do you believe she's really there?' Alyssa felt a need to confide her fears. 'I have tried to help her, but now she won't leave me alone.'

She looked at Mr MacDonald. Would he think her out of her mind?

'Yes, I do believe she's in touch with you because she's not able to rest. But you must be careful or she may take you over completely and *you* won't be able to shake her off.' Mr MacDonald studied Alyssa's face. 'You must do your best to help her and then you must block her out of your thoughts. Strong will power is needed, for the danger is that these unquiet spirits are very tenacious, and they're not always aware that they're dead.'

Alyssa's heart began to pound. She felt the colour leave her cheeks and she shivered in the afternoon sun. 'I didn't realise it was so dangerous. I thought I was helping her and trying to right old wrongs. In the beginning I didn't understand what was happening. I thought it was all a dream or imagination.' She clutched the old minister's hand in relief that he understood what she was talking about. 'Now I'm thinking of visiting her grave. Do you know where it is?'

'It's in the churchyard down the hill from Balvaig House.' Mr MacDonald patted her hand and then gestured towards the sea, where in the distance Alyssa could just make out a stone church surrounded by a small graveyard.

'But you mustn't go there.' Mr MacDonald's face was suddenly haggard. 'You might give her extra strength to influence you, even to take you over.'

Alyssa raised her head. Not visit Grizelda's grave? But some inner compulsion drove her on. Surely Grizelda wouldn't have that kind of power? 'I have to go,' she told Mr MacDonald firmly. 'Just to pay my respects. It's something I have to do.'

Mr MacDonald struggled to his feet, the rug slipping from his knees. He knocked against the table in his agitation, scattering the cups and saucers. To Alyssa's astoundment he seemed to grow in height, towering above her, his eyes glittering. He shook his finger at her. Hoarsely he shouted: 'Beware, Miss Alyssa. You are playing with fire. You may be damned to walk this earth for ever, with no resting place. Beware, Alyssa. Heed my warning. Do not go near Lady Grizelda's grave.' In his old-fashioned black suit and with his pointing finger, he was like an old style hell-fire preacher, striking the fear of death into his congregation.

Alyssa was stunned. Whatever had happened to Rory's mild-mannered father? He seemed to have turned into a menacing stranger as he stood, gesticulating in front of her, his stark silhouette blocking out the sunshine.

She swallowed nervously, but held her ground. 'I will heed your words, Mr MacDonald,' she said, taking his arm and trying to calm him. 'Please sit down and I'll pour you another cup of tea. Please don't get upset.' She rushed around setting the upturned cups to rights and picking up the silver teaspoons that had fallen to the ground. She filled up his cup again and put it in front of him.

Trembling, the old man sank back into his seat. He took out a handkerchief and wiped his lips, his laboured breathing disturbing the stillness of the garden. After some time, he seemed to relax, and his head sank forward on his chest and his eyes closed.

Feeling shaken, but now even more determined to find Grizelda's grave, Alyssa straightened the old man's rug and piled up the teacups. He mumbled something and she bent closer to him.

'Don't go near the grave,' he whispered sternly, and then seemed to slip into a peaceful sleep, his breathing easy and untrammelled.

Feeling that he didn't need her any more, and guilty at having upset him, Alyssa left the garden and went out onto the road again. Clutching her arms around herself protectively as she felt so shaky, she climbed the slope which passed Balvaig House. Conflicting thoughts tumbled through her brain. What should she do? The old man had given her a serious warning. Should she just ignore it? Grizelda was powerful enough without Alyssa allowing her to get closer and more possessive. But no, she couldn't let Mr MacDonald's fears hold her back. Alyssa sighed. She felt drained and exhausted, her resistance weakened.

The sun's rays flashed against one of the few remaining panes of glass in one of the upstairs windows. Alyssa's eyes hurt. A swirl of cold air kissed her cheek. She turned away quickly, fighting against the sensation of falling... falling... into darkness. She clutched desperately at the tufts of grass on the bank at the side of the road. Was that a plume of smoke rising from the tall chimney of the house? Two figures moving about in the garden? Her vision clouded and the depths of darkness received her.

CHAPTER ELEVEN

The night was as black as an unlit dungeon when the moon slipped behind the clouds leaving only the faintest glimmer of light from the loch. As helpless prisoners in the fast-moving lorry, Grizelda and Peter continued to bucket down the road, the lorry lurching in and out of the ruts. The trees became taller and more densely packed, and only the occasional gleam of light slipped through as the road grew narrower. Grizelda realised that soon they would have to stop, and a spurt of hope went through her.

Realising that banging on the driver's cab was not going to help them, Grizelda gathered up her long wedding dress, and crawled back over the dirty boards of the lorry until she reached Peter and bent over his still form. What a way to spend her wedding night! Hot tears seeped unchecked down her cheeks. She cradled her new husband's head in her lap trying to protect him from the worst jolts of the rough track. His eyes were tightly shut revealing long dark lashes against his white and drawn face. Grizelda longed for him to speak or to give her some sign that he hadn't lapsed into a coma.

'Peter, Peter, wake up,' she urged him, her veil falling over him. 'Speak to me.' But he remained silent. Her heart skipped several beats. Had they killed him?

The lorry jerked to a stop, the door slammed and the driver came round to the back shadowed by his two broad-shouldered henchmen.

He let down the back flap. 'This is as far as we go,' he said. 'Out you get!'

Peter stirred and muttered. His eyes opened and he tried to release himself from Grizelda's protective arms. He struggled free of her hold.

'Grizelda, allow me to sit up,' he said in a cool voice.

Relief swept over Grizelda. She prayed that the lump on his head wasn't so serious. Perhaps he wasn't concussed after all.

She felt the breeze lift her veil. Bundling up her skirts in one hand she jumped down. Landing unsteadily, she was seized roughly from behind and wrestled to the ground, the weight of a man pinning her beneath him. A scream burst from her throat as he flipped her onto her back, and her heart plummeted to her toes in fear. She grabbed desperately at the man, and the scarf slipped off the lower part of his face. Recognition struck her like a blow.

'Fordyce!' she cried.

The ringleader of the cruel abduction was none other than her second cousin, Fordyce McDermott. She was furiously angry that anyone of her blood, however distant, could play such a vicious trick, yet in a conflict of emotions, she felt slightly safer.

'Fordyce, you dirty cheat!' The words choked in her throat as she struggled to rise from under his weight. 'How could you do this to me?' She lunged at him, her fingers scraping across his face. He turned sharply from her and pushed her away, breathing heavily. Grizelda tried to seize his arm and force him to speak. 'You won't get away from us.' She tossed her head defiantly, refusing to let him see how afraid she was.

He gave her a brutal and unfriendly stare. 'A married woman, Grizel. I never thocht I'd see the day.' His derisive laugh hit her in a blast of alcohol.

Rage almost overwhelmed Grizelda at his calculated insult. 'Why can't you leave me alone? You're always hanging about me, causing trouble. And today of all days. You've ruined it, my special day.' Her voice was full of bitterness. 'You've always been jealous of our family. You've always tried to make mischief for me, and for John and William.'

How she hated the way he'd sneak into the byre when she was alone, and try to steal an unwary kiss. He'd pawed her, touched her where she didn't want to be touched, always trying humiliate her. He made her feel defiled, although she always held him off. She never told anyone. It was too shameful to tell her brothers. They might not even understand. They might have accused her for leading Fordyce on, but she'd time and time pushed him away. She loathed and despised him, and feared that one day he'd catch her where she couldn't escape. She was exhausted by rejecting his advances, brushing them aside, pretending they were of no consequence. The constant attrition wore her down, like the sea forever sucking greedily at the shore.

Now her anger boiled up like a red haze in front of her eyes, bringing her renewed strength. She stuck her elbow in his stomach, so that a groan burst out of him. She turned sharply and broke free of his hold. She scrambled to her feet, dragging her silk skirts away from him.

Swaying slightly as she gathered her veil around her, she pointed at Peter, still incarcerated in the lorry. 'Lift him down, lift him down, you filthy curs,' she cried to Fordyce's two henchmen who were standing idly with their arms drooping by their sides. They seemed subdued and uncertain. At a nod from Fordyce they dragged Peter with rough hands from the lorry and set him down on a rock, which protruded from the clumps of grass and heather growing at the side of the road. He slumped sideways but didn't fall any further.

It seemed to Grizelda that the gang of men had sobered up and become less intimidating. She heard one of them shout at Fordyce: 'We're awa' hame. It's gang tae far. It's no' right.'

Fordyce argued with them in a rumbling voice. But one of the henchmen shouted angrily, 'This is a bad day for us all, Fordyce. Do your own dirty work!'

The two younger men slunk off into the heather, leaving Fordyce throwing curses after them. With a disgusted look at Grizelda and at Peter, drooping at the side of the road, he got back into the old lorry. With a scraping of gears he turned it round in a small clearing, and headed back the way they had come, spraying them with grit from the wheels as he passed.

Grizelda didn't care any more. She was freezing, and Peter didn't offer any comfort. The future stretched before her, bleak and dismal. Now she was shackled to this man, her new husband, who had failed to protect them both. Could he possibly be an asset to her farm? Could he really help her to realise her ambition of making Balvaig the best run dairy farm for miles around? In her distress she stared at the dark waters of the loch as it lapped at the shore. There was no answer to be got there. So she sat down beside the silent Peter, pulling her white dress around her. The two of them were alone.

What seemed like hours passed. Then the whine of an ancient car engine brought a flaring of sudden hope to Grizelda. A weak ray of light penetrated the gloom. Then round the corner, a vehicle appeared. It bumped along in the dark, its headlights only just managing to pick out the contours of the road. Mr Smith's grocery van, driven by her brother John! And wasn't that William beside him? Grizelda jumped up, fired with new energy. 'Peter, Peter, wake up,' she cried, giving his flaccid body a shake. Her hands gripped his shoulders, but his sonorous breathing frightened her. 'Wake up, the rescue party is on its way.'

She tried to raise him, but he slumped back again. Fear squeezed her heart that there was something seriously wrong with him, but she propped him up for the moment and rushed into the road waving her arms in fear and relief.

John braked hard on the van and behind him she could see two other motor cars as well as young Gavin on his carthorse, galumphing down the track. Even farther away, around the curve of the loch, she could just make out a gaggle of guests, some running, some walking and even some limping along. Many of them were still in their hot woollen, Sunday-best suits, some in kilts. The ladies moved as quickly as their skirts and high-heeled shoes would allow them, hands high, holding onto their hats.

John and William sprang out of the old van leaving the engine running and the doors wide open. They ran towards her, arms outstretched. 'Grizelda, are you all right?' John's face showed a mixture of fear and guilt. 'What a wicked thing to happen. But that damned Fordyce'll pay for it, never fear.'

Grizelda tried to keep calm, fighting back the urge to scream, cry and tear her hair. John seized her hand and put his other arm around her shoulders holding her tight. Grizelda leaned against him for a moment, drawing strength from the feel of his familiar body. Perhaps it was all a mistake to try and break away from her family and start out on a new life on her own. Her strength was returning and she raised her face from John's chest. She looked down at her torn dress and saw that both the dress and petticoats were ripped down one side, exposing one slim leg encased in its silk stocking. Horrified she tried to cover it up hastily.

She turned and looked across at Peter. Now he was standing up, stark and tall even though he was a little unsteady on his feet. The moon sailed out from behind the clouds, bathing the scene in an eerie light.

Then Margaret was there, her arms clasped round Grizelda. 'What a dreadful thing to happen,' she cried. 'Your beautiful dress all tashed about.' She took out her dainty handkerchief and tried to rub away the worst splashes of mud. That was the last straw. Grizelda began to laugh hysterically and found she couldn't stop. Margaret tried to soothe her, but Grizelda was locked in the waves of laughter that rolled over her.

Peter looked towards Grizelda, and supported by John he walked over to the two young ladies. 'Grizelda,' he said sternly. 'Stop it!'

To no avail, Grizelda continued to shake. Laughter pealed out her and still she couldn't stop. Peter freed himself from John's supporting arm.

'Please step out of the way,' he said to Margaret. 'I'm sorry, Grizelda. I've got to be cruel to be kind.' He raised his hand and slapped her face briskly.

Grizelda stopped in mid-wave of laughter. She looked at him horrified. Her breath was coming in short gasps.

Then recovering herself, she put her arms around Peter and hugged him to her. 'Thank you, Peter. You were the only one who understood what I needed. I'm all right now and I can face what's coming. Let's go home.'

Mrs McMorran, arriving long after the others in the rescue party, came bustling up to them. 'Oh, Miss Grizel,' she cried, her face streaming with perspiration and her breath coming in laboured puffs. 'What a wicked thing to happen.' She turned to John and William who stood at the side of the road looking guilty. She drew herself up with great dignity despite her hat hanging askew on her head. 'How could you two let such a dreadful thing happen to Miss Grizel and her new man,' she accused them. John and William were speechless but each of them showed a hectic red flush in their cheeks.

Peter, fast recovering, turned to Mrs McMorran. 'Grizelda is now my wife, and if anyone is to blame it is I,' he said. 'But my wife is a true lady and I know she will rise above the happenings of this evening, and will start our married life the stronger.' He stretched out his hand to Grizelda who took it bravely. 'Come, Lady Lovat. It's time to take you home.' He bowed gallantly to her.

His words lifted Grizelda up. She felt some of her self-respect returning. Perhaps after all this evening would mark her position as a married lady. Thanks to Peter she had passed from being poor Miss Grizel, the plain, ordinary one. Now she was Lady Lovat in the eyes of her husband and the world. She straightened up and dashed the remaining traces of tears from her eyes. She flicked back her torn veil and drew the skirts of her wedding dress carefully round her. She looked straight into Peter's eyes with a brave smile. 'I'm ready to go home, Peter,' she said, standing tall and proud. 'But Fordyce McDermott will never set foot on my… our farm again, nor will I speak to my other cousins for the rest of my life. They'll be as if dead for me. That door is shut. This story will go no further.'

Peter nodded and putting his arm around her, he led her to the van which John and William had brought. John ran up to help her. She and Peter settled themselves cramped close together in the front seat.

'You'll have to walk back, Willie,' said John as he got into the driver's seat and let in the clutch. 'There's no room here.'

Dawn was just breaking behind the trees. Fordyce, the fox, had long returned to his lair along with his rowdy companions to brag over the night's work. Tomorrow he would be off the island, unscathed and ready to create new havoc elsewhere.

*

Never had Grizelda been so glad to see her own home again. Leaving them outside the door, John accelerated away down the hill, and Grizelda and Peter watched the van until it disappeared round the bend of the road.

Grizelda hesitated before stepping over the threshold. It was symbolic of the start of her new life with Peter. Would her freedom be curbed? Would she always have to defer to another's wishes instead of being independent Miss Grizel?

She felt Peter impatient behind her. 'Come on, Grizelda,' he said. 'Let's get inside and have a drink. It's time for bed!'

Reluctantly she opened the front door. 'I'll make us a cup of tea,' she said.

Peter laughed. 'After all we've been through, you'll make us a cup of tea!' he said. 'That's not good enough, my girl. A drink is what we need.'

Grizelda looked at him. Her feelings were confused. The black sheen of yesterday's beard was pushing its way through his skin. He looked like a disreputable pirate, with his collar askew, his hair on end and mud streaks on his face. She didn't know if she liked him. She didn't know if she wanted him in her house. But this was the man she had married.

He came up behind her, and put his arms round her. 'Show me where you keep the whisky.' The male smell of him, a combination of rank sweat and of musk was very pungent, almost exciting. Grizelda felt drawn to him against her will. She walked over to the cupboard next to the window and took out an unopened bottle of island malt whisky and one glass.

'Will you not join me?' Peter lifted an eyebrow.

'I don't like whisky,' quavered Grizelda. 'I'll get a cup of tea.' She shook herself. Was that trembly voice really hers?

In the kitchen, she raked over the embers of the range. She filled the blackened kettle from the pitcher, the water fresh from the burn behind the house. She stood waiting for the kettle to boil, giving herself time to collect her thoughts. She unpinned her head-dress and her veil, and hung them over a chair.

She'd taken on more than she had bargained for. She didn't expect to feel the stirrings of attraction to a man, if that was the reason for this sudden heat in her cheeks and weakness in her legs. She had married Sir Peter Lovat for his money and what he could do for the farm. For nothing else, she told herself. She had expected him to meet her on her terms, to be as docile as a poodle, still bound up with thoughts of his late wife, dead and buried in Jamaica two year's past.

What a fool she was. He was a man after all, and she knew how contrary her brothers could be. They kicked against letting a mere woman boss them about, if she didn't handle them properly. But she wished she weren't alone with Peter now. She wished her boisterous brothers were here to back her up, although they hadn't been much use in hindering Fordyce and his hooligans from seizing her and Peter.

'Grizelda, come in here,' Peter's voice called her. She poured the freshly made tea into a teapot and put it on a tray with two cups and saucers. Carrying it carefully, she walked back into the chilly green drawing room.

Peter lay back in the big chair, one leg cocked over the arm, his face flushed. 'Come here to me, my beautiful, raggedy wife.' He sprang up and crushed her to him. Her wedding dress with its train trailed across the floor. She hadn't dared to go upstairs and change. She pushed back from Peter like a nervy thoroughbred, and looked down at herself. The original pristine white of her dress was muddied; one of the sleeves was torn as well as the long, jagged rip in the side of her skirt. Her graceful train was marked with black splotches of mud.

'Why don't you take off your dress.' Peter almost knocked the cup out of her hand. 'Let me get a look at my brand new wife!' He began fumbling at the tiny buttons of the dress.

Grizelda felt the heat rising in her body. She found it difficult to breathe. 'Peter, wait!' she implored.

'Why should I wait,' said Peter. 'You're my wife and I want you now.'

She felt his body strong and hard, pressed against hers. Her head fell back, and he kissed her urgently, his tongue teasing her lips open, insistently finding the secret places of her mouth. She gasped and drew him closer, closer until a blade of grass couldn't have slipped between them.

'Come to bed, Grizelda. We must be together now.' His urgent hands slipped the ruined dress from her shoulders, letting it slip to the ground in a whisper of silks.

Grizelda was nearly frantic with longing for him. She stepped quickly out of her dress. She felt reckless, ready to enter uncharted territory. She felt her legs weaken, till she almost fell down. Peter supported her with his arms round her, nudging her towards the stairs, kissing her neck, stroking her white shoulders. 'My beautiful virgin,' he murmured. 'I can't wait to have you.'

They entered the bedroom. The big bed was waiting, freshly made up by Mrs McMorran. That was Grizelda's only coherent thought. Peter drew down her petticoats and knickers revealing her soft nakedness.

Her eyes closed as he stroked her gently. His mouth throbbed on hers with the insistent heat of desire. He drew her down onto the bed and began kissing her breasts and her soft belly. His lips trailed slowly and tantalisingly down to her core where she felt hot and swollen as never before. She twisted and turned, thrashing about in the bed, until he stroked her and soothed her. She just had time to wonder, would it hurt, would she bleed, when she felt him pushing to enter her.

She drew him tighter into her, tighter and tighter, the pain was excruciating – agonising – never ending – exhilarating.

With a triumphant cry, he spent his seed, while Grizelda wept with a feeling of liberation and triumph.

He fell back and turned away, while Grizelda lay there feeling the warm seed filling her, making her a true woman.

Morning came and Grizelda couldn't think where she was. The bed was so huge, and there was a stranger beside her.

*

Alyssa stirred. Her hand went out to touch the bed beside her. Bed...? She jerked back into full consciousness. The birds were singing a mad chorus above her head. Her face was pressed against the rough grass of the bank. Her nose tickled and she sneezed. She sat up stiffly and looked around her, but all was quiet.

Waves of cold fear were rolling over her. How could she have fallen asleep in the middle of the day right out in the open air. Was she losing control of her own body? Of her mind? Perhaps it was some kind of seizure.

Or was it Grizelda who was in her head just as Mr MacDonald had warned her? Grizelda, clinging on, tightening her grip on Alyssa's mind. The torrent of thoughts pouring through Alyssa's head terrified her. She pulled herself to her feet and began to stumble down the road to the haven of her little cottage. She kept her eyes scrupulously turned away from Balvaig House.

Chapter Twelve

The early morning sun filtered through the curtains of Alyssa's small bedroom, and laid a finger of light across her face. She threw back the bedcovers. She couldn't lie here any longer, her thoughts beating like blackbirds' wings in her brain. Something outside herself told her that today she had to find Lady Grizelda's grave. Her respects to her Great Aunt must be paid by a visit to her final resting place. Perhaps that would bring a kind of closure even though Mr MacDonald's warning about Lady Grizelda getting a tighter hold on her, still rang in her ears. She tried to push the picture of Mr MacDonald's staring eyes and pointing finger out of her mind. Whatever had come over him? Was Grizelda getting to him too?

It was true she felt Grizelda draining her strength. She seemed to have no will of her own. Walking over to the mirror, she gazed at her morning self. Her thick red hair waved untidily round her pale and strained face. She grimaced. It was all Grizelda's fault. Mr MacDonald would have been shocked to hear what'd happened to Alyssa yesterday after she left him. Just as he had said, Grizelda *was* gaining power over her. Possessing her. Alyssa winced at the thought, wondering if Grizelda could actually possess her entirely. She'd read about it, but never paid particular attention to it before.

Squaring her shoulders, she told herself not to be distracted from her purpose and the inner compulsion she'd felt yesterday drove her on. She would get no peace until she visited Grizelda's grave. And now she knew how to find the churchyard where Grizelda was buried.

After a quick breakfast, Alyssa shut the gate of the cottage garden behind her and walked slowly along the road. On each side the wild flowers peeped through the grass like glowing jewels to be harvested. Alyssa picked a small nosegay of pink clover, blue forget-me-not, yellow poppies and pink ragged robin.

She reached the bottom of the hill. The small stone church rose up in front of her, ringed by an ancient stone wall. She walked up the well-trodden path leading to the church door. High up on a hill above the church a small waterfall tumbled in white cascades down into the clear pool beneath. The air was pure as glass and the churchyard was enfolded in a deep peace, disturbed only by the sweet fluting sounds of the birds, their clear calls floating through the air. She passed through the half-open gate, which she supposed was to keep out the sheep of the island, and latched it carefully behind her.

Inside the churchyard the grass was vibrant green and well tended, and most of the gravestones stood sturdily upright. Some were so battered by the winds and rains of time that the names were obliterated. Others seemed to date back to the fifteenth century.

So this was the timeless pathway leading to the church where Lady Grizelda and her forebears had trodden every faithful Sunday, probably dressed in sombre black with elaborate hats, in worshipful adoration. Alyssa stopped. She mustn't allow her imagination to run riot as goodness knows what could happen.

She stepped across the grass, allowing her instincts to guide her in her search for Grizelda's grave. She walked through the sweet scented place, feeling soothed and calm. The high notes of a reed flute called to her. She turned her head to see who was playing, and almost fell over a large grey rock, which suddenly lumbered to its feet and ran away from her, its fuzzy tail waggling. She smiled. Yet another of the ubiquitous sheep had been taking its ease in the warm sun. It must have taken advantage of the open churchyard gate.

Then her eye caught sight of an old man sitting on the ground, his cap beside him, his fingers light on a small flute. Like the spirit of the place he was playing the crystal clear notes that floated through the churchyard. As Alyssa drew near, he laid the flute aside and looked up at her. His face was as polished as a chestnut, with the skin drawn tightly over his knobbly cheeks.

'You're Grizelda's niece,' he greeted her. 'Are you looking for her grave? About time too!' He looked at her accusingly.

Alyssa stopped in surprise. 'And who are you? How do you know me?'

'You're the mirror image of herself. Thon fluffy red hair of yours. Tis a pity you didnae come when she lay in her bed in the hospital.'

'I didn't know she existed,' said Alyssa, despair in her voice. 'Of course, I would've come before, if I'd known about her. They told me she was very lonely and abandoned at the end. But I never had the chance to know her.'

The old man looked at her with his honest blue eyes and she felt guilty as if she'd committed a crime.

'Nobody told me about Great Aunt Grizelda until it was too late. Who are you?' she repeated, looking squarely back at him.

'I'm old Davy,' he told her. 'Her shepherd, ye ken. There aren't many of her flock left, but I take care of them.' He stretched out the curved head of his crook and tenderly scratched the head of one of his resting sheep.

Alyssa sat down beside him on the grassy bank. Perhaps he could tell her why Grizelda wandered about in such an unhappy state at the end of her life.

'Tell me more about my great aunt,' she invited, smiling at him. 'Did you know her well?'

'Danced at her wedding, didn't I.' He drew himself up with pride as if it was the high spot of his life. 'I kenned her when she was a young innocent girl, and I kenned her when she was an old lonely woman. I kenned her weel.'

'What about her husband?' Alyssa leaned forward and plucked a small yellow flower in the grass. 'Did you know him too? Was she happy with him?'

'Aye, I kenned Sir Peter,' he said. 'But Miss Grizel wasnae happy wi' him at first. It was sich an awfy start at her wedding.' He drifted off almost in a reverie.

His eyes turned inwards and he began murmuring to himself, as if recalling the long ago past. He didn't seem to notice that Alyssa sat riveted to every word which fell from his lips.

'Aye, she was a fine lass, Miss Grizel. She didnae deserve what befell her. But she was proud and hasty and she shouldn't have been so pernickety. Her brothers couldn't control her. She wouldn't listen to them. She was much cleverer and sharper than them. She kenned how to run a farm, she kenned how things were. These daft brothers of hers just wandered around doing what she told them, and as like as not they'd be off down to the pub in the early afternoon. She did the milking and fed the beasts all on her own. But she never complained, not once. It was the farm she loved… and Sir Peter later, near the end. But it was by far too late by then. Oh aye, she did love and respect him in the end.'

The old man's voice wavered, and he gazed into the distance, as if picturing the sadness of the past. He heaved a heavy sigh. Then he bestirred himself and with a flash of anger he continued: 'That wicked Fordyce. What he did to her. He ruined her wedding and set her off on the wrong foot. He wanted her for himself. Such a beautiful spirited lass, and such a fine heart in the farm. But she wouldn't look at him. That's why he stole her and her new man away from their wedding. He wanted to hurt and destroy her. That divil Fordyce, sich a dirty divil.'

Alyssa was enthralled. She sat quietly not wanting to disturb the old man's memories. But as the silence dragged, she prompted him: 'Who was Fordyce?'

The old man started. It was obvious he'd forgotten she was there. He drifted back into his story. 'Fordyce, the Fox,' he said. 'Fox by name, fox by nature, I say.'

The sheep stirred restlessly. Bae… bae… their tremulous bleating filled the little churchyard. Davy took no notice, intent on his thoughts.

'Why d'you say he was a fox?' Alyssa leaned forward, trying to encourage him gently. A bee zoomed toward her, the sound of summer heat. She brushed it away from her hair.

134

Davy stirred himself and plucked at a tuft of white sheep's wool lying on the grass. 'Fordyce was Miss Grizel's cousin and a right fly one.' he said. 'He often tried to get the two lads, her brothers, to have a go at one of his money-making schemes. Those daft schemes. They were nae good, and then the two daft lads'd go running back to Miss Grizel to bail them out. She always did, for she cared so much for them, it was as if they were part of the farm she had to nurture. She'd never let her folks down, of course, no' her mamma or her papa. Ach she was a proud girl, and that was her downfall.' The old man's eyes were sad as he gazed into the distance and he rubbed his face hard, seeming to wipe away a tear.

'Tell me more about Grizelda's wedding,' she coaxed. 'You said you were there.'

Old Davy's eyes flashed and he beat his crook on the ground. 'Miss Grizel's wedding was one of his meanest tricks. He stole the bride and groom away from their wedding. He took them off in a dirty truck and dumped them out in the cold down the lochside. Ach it was a cruel thing he did. Spoiling her wedding and her happiness. It took years for Miss Grizel to get over it, and she never forgave her family for not protecting her.'

'How dreadful,' said Alyssa, shivering in spite of the warm sun. 'Couldn't you have helped her?'

'I was just a young laddie at the time. Naebody listened to me. I didnae understand what was happening.' He pursed his lips.

'She must've been furious and terrified.'

Davy nodded. 'She and her brothers turned away from the rest of the family after that. It was as if the trunk and the shelter of the tree had been torn from her. And now

135

Fordyce's son is here, sniffing around like a rabid fox, just like his father.'

'His son?' asked Alyssa, her head whirling with her attempts to keep track of Davy's story. 'Who's that?'

'Why Mick McDermott, the auctioneer,' said old Davy. 'Do ye no' ken him? You mind and watch your back there. He's a right fly, twisty one, that's the only thing you can be sure about.'

Alyssa felt her mouth dry at the shock of it. So Mick was Fordyce the Fox's son! That figured! She took several deep breaths: 'But Mick's the person who says he's been left Balvaig House. Surely that's the last person Aunt Grizelda would want to leave her house to?'

Davy wasn't listening. 'You'll be wanting to pay your respects to Miss Grizel,' he said. 'She's over there. Come I'll show you. She's been waiting a long time.'

He walked across the churchyard, limping and leaning heavily on his crook. Alyssa followed, breathing in the flowery scent of the place, a mixture of wild thyme, bog myrtle and honey-perfumed clover.

She had the sense of stepping into the world of the other side. She stopped for a moment in front of the grave of a Victorian child, and read the blurred inscription. *Mary aged three years enfolded in the arms of the Lord.* The hush of the churchyard was soothing. It would be so easy to lie down forever in eternal peace. She checked herself. She mustn't get engulfed by melancholy thoughts.

Davy led her on to a newer grave. On her left, along the straight row of gravestones, she saw the lumpy outline of a newly-dug grave, not yet subsided. A few forlorn petals of forgotten flowers rested on the mound. The gravestone at the head of it was tilted and unsettled. New brighter lettering was in place following three other names. *In loving memory of Grizelda Alice Mary Lovat, beloved wife of the late Sir Peter Lovat. Died 14th April 2006.*

Another bee zoomed out of the trees barging into Alyssa's arm and swerving drunkenly away. She laid her bouquet carefully, immaculately at the foot of the exact middle of the headstone and stepped back, her hands clasped and head bowed.

She plucked away from of the faded blooms, tided up some of the dead leaves and pulled back the branches of a tree that tended to weep too heavily over the newly inscribed stone.

'Grizelda Lovat, what a pity we never met,' Alyssa whispered. 'I think we would have been great friends. Why did you never get in touch? I never knew you existed. Yet now I have to follow the trail of your life.'

In her mind's eye she could see a vigorous and vital lady smiling up at her from the flowery bed in the depths of the earth. The picture was almost frighteningly clear, Alyssa felt the lady was about to speak to her. She could see her in every detail.

'Did you have a good life, Lady Grizelda?' she murmured. 'Or were you lonely when everyone else was gone?'

What a beauty the lady was with her luxuriant auburn hair framing her face as she lay there, just resting awhile. Alyssa looked into smiling brown eyes and felt that the lady would share a secret joke with her. It was as if she was ready to spring up and walk away with Alyssa.

But suddenly Alyssa felt herself being pulled closer to the grave. Unseen hands seemed to grip her. She tried to step back and resist the powerful impulsion. The pull from the grave grew stronger. The now familiar misty sensation crept over her, enveloping her, weakening her.

'No, don't touch me. No, let me go,' Alyssa's cries became shriller as the red-haired lady's arms rose and her hands clamped themselves round Alyssa's neck. In a desperate struggle to break free, her breath choking in her throat, Alyssa sank downward and everything became dark.

CHAPTER THIRTEEN

Grizelda yawned and stretched. Despite Peter's loving caresses last night, she now felt trapped, her youthful freedom taken from her. She looked at the sleeping man lying in the big bed beside her. Was he an intruder in her life or could she possibly be happy with him?

His eyes were still shut and she marvelled at his long lashes. This was the first time she could study him properly, her husband of one night. His fair hair was blond-streaked and his skin was burned brown from the sun of the Jamaican colonies, where he'd lived before returning to the Island of Mora.

She laid her hand on his cheek, stroking it gently. Even her hand, work-roughened from all the time spent out in the cow shed seemed almost lily-white compared with the deep tan of Peter's skin.

She knew she had to get up early. She couldn't leave John and William to do all the work and she didn't know how Peter was going to fit into their familiar routines, where words and lengthy discussions were unnecessary. She and her brothers knew by instinct what had to be done. At least she did, and then she told her brothers what to do. She knew which cow was due to calve, when the sheep had to be clipped and when it was the right time to start harvesting.

Would Peter fit in with them? Her brothers were easy enough to get on with in a rough and ready way. Usually they were too tired in the evening to talk much with her, disappearing behind their newspapers and refusing to come out again until it was suppertime. That was if they didn't disappear down to the pub.

John and William knew exactly when they could slope off down to the pub, sometimes leaving Grizelda to finish the tasks around the farm. She knew she wasn't welcome down in that sacred interior where the men smoked their heavy pipes and let off steam to each other.

Well, perhaps she was glad Peter was there. She hoped she'd be able to talk to him. Perhaps he would tell her all about Jamaica and she could ask his advice on the running of the farm. He'd sold up his very prosperous farm when he left Jamaica to return to Scotland. Really she was surprised that he had come back to Scotland when he was doing so well in the Tropics. But perhaps he really needed a change after the death of his wife.

This was the hard part. Whom would he love the most? His first wife or her, his new second wife. Would she be second best? It was going to be hard to compete with his departed first wife, so sophisticated and full of social graces.

Grizelda knew that Marina, his first wife, had been a well-known hostess, holding balls in the local society of Jamaica, and mixing with the Governor and his family. Grizelda cringed when she thought of the terrible fiasco of their wedding day yesterday. What a complete disaster! Grizelda bit her lip. What did Peter think? Probably he regretted the whole thing, for not only was the wedding spoiled, but Grizelda didn't know the first thing about arranging a ball for the local cream of society, or the lack of it, here. She was much too gauche. But she used to enjoy dancing at the ceilidhs held from time to time on the island, although the thought of a wild party made her shudder after the shambles of her wedding day.

Now Peter was stirring. He reached up and pulled her to him. 'How's my beautiful wife today?' He kissed her full on the lips, imprisoning her with his masculine warmth.

Grizelda drew back, fighting the delicious feelings that were flooding through her. 'I've got to go out and help John in the byre. It's milking time. Can't you hear the cows lowing?'

And indeed angry bellows could be heard coming from the direction of the byre. 'They're getting very edgy,' Grizelda said, disengaging herself from his warm arms.

'Just like you, my dear.' Peter turned away pettishly and flung himself back against the pillows. He rolled over and began groping for his clothes where he had dropped them last night.

CHAPTER FOURTEEN

A bird fluttered across the churchyard, emitting a mournful cry. Alyssa opened her eyes and sighed. She was exhausted. She wasn't sure who she was any more. Alyssa or Grizelda? Tears were running down her cheeks and she wiped them away with the back of her hand. She jumped as a voice spoke. Rory! He stood looking down at her so she sat up quickly.

He looked at her, enquiry in his face. 'Well what are you doing here? I thought I saw you wandering around. Aren't you a little morbid, getting so close to Lady Grizelda's grave?'

Alyssa's feathers were ruffled. She'd just returned from a frightening experience and hadn't yet returned to full consciousness. She really wasn't ready to face Rory. She looked around for old Davy, but he was nowhere to be seen. Davy had a special other-worldly quality as if he was linked to the everyday world and to the other side as well. Alyssa pictured him as the messenger sent by Great Aunt Grizelda to uncover some of the secrets of the past.

But now here was Rory, probing and asking questions. 'Why shouldn't I be beside the grave?' Alyssa retorted. 'I've come to pay my respects to my aunt.' There was no way she could explain to Rory what she'd just experienced.

Rory's voice was sharp. 'Why the hell were you lying by the grave?' he repeated. 'You're taking your great aunt's death much too hard. There's grass all over your clothes.'

'I was just taking a rest in the sun,' Alyssa tried to cover up the intense experience she'd been through. 'It made me sleepy.' She brushed at the leaves and grass clinging to her shirt.

Rory looked as if he'd like to question her some more, then let it slide. 'In fact your great aunt's funeral was one of the last services my father ever conducted before his illness. I was there too.'

Alyssa took Rory's proffered hand and scrambled to her feet. There was still no sign of old Davy, and the church-yard lay calm and still. Only a few sheep were cropping the grass round the tombstones. It was time to move on.

Down at the roadside, Rory held open the door of the Land Rover for her and she jumped in to be greeted by an ecstatic wagging of tails by Ginger and the two other dogs in the back. Ginger gave her face a hearty licking before Alyssa managed to push him off.

'I'd like to show you the high spots of the island,' said Rory. 'There's a ceilidh down in the Clachan hall tonight. Barbara will come along too.'

Alyssa wasn't over-enthusiastic at the thought of Barbara, but a sociable, carefree gathering and some wild Scottish dancing might bring her out of her preoccupation with the past.

So Rory really was attached to Barbara. What a pity! A manipulative type like Barbara certainly didn't deserve Rory! Alyssa caught herself. Rory was nothing to do with her and it didn't matter who he was involved with. All she was looking forward to was a fun evening.

*

At seven o'clock sharp Rory drew up in front of Alyssa's small cottage. He was driving a large unfamiliar black car. When he got out of the car Alyssa saw he was wearing a red tartan kilt. Her breath caught in her throat at the sight of him. He was so superbly masculine. Barbara, elegantly coiffed, sat beside him, looking superior. For the first time there were no dogs milling around him.

What a pity! A mildly malicious thought flicked through Alyssa's mind. *The dogs could have stirred up Barbara's elaborate hairstyle.*

The car reeked of heavy perfume quite knocking out Alyssa's light flowery scent. A good smell of dog would've helped too. She pushed down her mischievous thoughts and smiled conventionally at Barbara who nodded coldly to her.

Alyssa felt annoyed and a little spurt of anger rose in her. Well she would give Barbara a run for her money.

She smiled intimately at Rory. 'Hello, Rory, darling,' she said. 'I'm really looking forward to dancing with you.'

Rory smiled deep into her eyes, then walked round to get into the driver's seat. Barbara's frown marred her smoothly made-up face.

About fifteen minutes later they arrived at the village hall, which was built in Scandinavian style, wooden, long and low. It looked like an old-fashioned army hut, well-weathered by sea storms.

As Alyssa stepped out of the car she could hear the pibroch drone as the pipers tuned up their bagpipes. The men were the peacocks tonight, their kilts swinging and the colours muted but glorious against the deepening blue of the evening sky. The proud highlanders were out in full and devastating force. Alyssa could see that they knew they looked good. From young to old they wore their kilts with pride. The younger ones were almost unrecognisable after they had shed their everyday uniform dress of jeans, cheap synthetic sweaters and worn trainers. The older ones straightened their weary backs and puffed out their chests, their pride making them youthful again. There were a few hip flasks being passed discreetly around.

Inside the hall Alyssa could almost hear the tables groaning under the weight of the enormous buffet. There were great bowls of salad, while huge haunches of glazed hams lay sliced succulently and ready to eat. The variety of fish was delicately prepared, probably freshly caught that morning. Alyssa's mouth watered as she looked at the mighty legs of mutton, and some of her favourite childhood desserts beckoned invitingly. Jewelled jellies and pink castles of blancmange vied with up-to-the minute tiramisu and crème caramel. It was a stupendous feast. The five-star hotels of London weren't even in the running.

Rory, with Barbara attached to his arm as if manacled, stood behind Alyssa. He was so close she could smell the clean fresh soap scent of him with a light undertone of antiseptics.

She smiled to herself, thinking of all the lambs he had saved, the calves he'd delivered, and the horses he had struggled to bring back to health.

'What would you like to drink, Alyssa?' he asked.

'A glass of white wine.' Alyssa looked at him sedately from under her lashes.

'Come on,' said Rory. 'You're not in the society drawing rooms of London now. Try a very small malt and a dash of soda, if you must. Go native!' And he disappeared into the pulsating throng in front of the makeshift bar, which was stocked with a huge array of bottles.

Alyssa was left standing with Barbara, feeling the cold flick of her displeasure. Barbara continued to ignore her, her eyes sweeping the hall for someone more interesting than Alyssa. It was obvious to Alyssa that she was the wrong sex in Barbara's eyes.

Two men came up to Barbara, one in a red and green kilt and the other conventionally attired in trousers, which against the backdrop of the jewel-coloured kilts seemed rather drab. Each of them gave Barbara a warm kiss. She pouted her lips sexily. The cleavage of her slinky blue dress was enticing. By an intimate touch on the kilted man's arm, and by leaning back seductively on the trousered man she turned them into a tight group of three, neatly excluding Alyssa.

Rory was still at the bar. Joking with his friends, his head thrown back in laughter, Alyssa could see he was one of the popular scene, completely at his ease.

Feeling a little like Ruth amid the alien corn, Alyssa looked round for a friendly face. All of a sudden a heavy arm was slapped round her shoulders and a loud voice hurt her ear. 'If it's no' ma wee cousin, Aleesie!' Mick's voice broke through the chatter, and made her name rhyme with greasy.

Alyssa started like a nervy thoroughbred.

'Hello, dearie.' Mick blew the sour fumes of many whiskies in her face. His own face was red and moist, like uncooked beef. He had managed to force himself into a red and yellow kilt that was straining at its side straps, and looked in real danger of bursting. The cross-over fold of

146

the garment did little to contain the insistent push of his paunch.

Now he was pawing her neck, his sausage fingers sweaty and sticky. Alyssa was wary of the predatory gleam in his eye. What was it about his corner teeth, so sharp, yellowish and pointed?

'Nice one, Mick,' said one of his mates with a crude wink. Mick guffawed and took a swig from his glass of whisky.

Alyssa felt that she was out on the sea in a leaky boat with a daft skipper. The social skills of London drawing rooms, as Rory had put it, were no use here. With a swift movement she removed Mick's limp hand from her neck. It felt as if she was shaking off a slimy but hot fish. He staggered a little as Alyssa pushed him away. After a quick look around the hall she made a beeline for a pleasant looking woman dressed in flowing ethnic clothes in a soothing laurel green colour.

'Hello, I'm Eithne, who are you?' said the woman, smiling at Alyssa.

Alyssa introduced herself. 'With a name like that you must have been born here,' she told Eithne.

'Absolutely not.' The woman's eyes shone with friendliness. 'I'm what they call a ferry louper. An incomer, a non-native. But I love it here. People are kind and I'm now accepted for what I am.'

'What are you then?' said Alyssa fascinated by this soft-spoken young woman of about her own age, who seemed to be an intrinsic part of the place.

'I'm a healer, an aromatherapist, counsellor, friend,' said Eithne. 'It wasn't easy at first, people were a bit suspicious of me, but now they come to me for help and I to them. For without their support, I'm nothing.' She looked curiously at Alyssa. 'I suppose you're the pretender.'

'Pretender?' Alyssa felt puzzled. 'Pretending what?'

'The rival claimant to Lady Grizelda's house,' said Eithne. 'We were so surprised when it came out that Mick McDermott was to inherit. We called him the man from nowhere. He appeared so suddenly on the scene and no one knew anything about him. We wondered about you too, arriving well after Lady Grizelda was dead and buried. They have a worse name for you!'

Alyssa was stunned. So they were gossiping about her on the island. No wonder everyone seemed to know about her in advance.

CHAPTER FIFTEEN

The music of the ceilidh grew louder and more insistent. The fiddlers were red-faced with their efforts. Their bows crossed the strings of the violins in a frenzy of fiddling. Enthralled by the music the dancers wove in and out of each other, swinging and turning in the intricate steps of the Scottish reels and strathspeys, their kilts and dresses aswing.

Alyssa moved away from Eithne. She'd escaped from Mick's pawing only to be upset by Eithne's remarks. She stood on the sidelines longing to take part in the dancing. It was all so lively and different from the social structure she was used to back in London. There the literary jokes and the verbal illusions were sophisticated and fun with people being careful not to get too close to each other.

Rory strode toward her, two tumblers of tawny liquid in his hands. He thrust one of the glasses at her. 'Here you are. Our national drink. You may as well get acclimatized to our rough and ready ways. *Slainte!* Your good health!' He toasted her solemnly, his eyes twinkling at her over his glass.

Alyssa took the goblet of whisky, light brown and enticing as a highland burn. Uncaring and heedless, in a spirit of liberation she swallowed it down in three gulps.

Rory's jaw dropped in horror. 'Alyssa, you'll regret what you've just done. Are you out of your mind?'

Alyssa struggled with the fire in her throat and tried not to cough. She'd never been so reckless before. She was turning into a new person, inhibitions wafting off her shoulders like faded flower petals.

Her lips spread in a wide smile. She held out her arms to him. 'Rory, let's dance as you've never danced before!'

She caught the answering sparkle in his eyes as he held out his arms to her and whirled her away.

Out of the window went the careful dance steps taught to her in her schooldays, the rigid practising with her old dancing teacher at the piano. Alyssa could still hear her voice 'And a one, two, three. And a one two three,' while the young children scrambled and postured to keep up.

Out of the window went all thoughts of doubtful inheritances, graveyards and aged aunts. The dance was the music and the music was the dance. Alyssa had never felt so light, so airy, so in tune with herself, and with the sexy attractive man holding her in his arms. He released her and swung her outward in the pattern of the reel. Her feet sped faster, she was thistledown, she was the insistent melody of the fiddle, she was the rhythmic swing of the kilt.

'You're a great dancer.' Rory was light on his feet like large men often are, turning her neatly in the wild skirmish of the reel. 'I'd never have thought it, and you from England too.'

'I'm not English.' Alyssa twirled joyously round him. 'I'm a pure bred highlander like you. Only more so. I'm in close touch with the fairies, with the wee people, the landscape and the everlasting sheep.' Her breath was coming in short spurts, but her feet were just as quick in following the intricate steps. Her head was high and proud. Rory's appreciative gaze travelled over her short green dress as they twisted and turned in complete harmony. His eyes were dark and slumberous.

The reel ended and a slow waltz began. Rory gathered her close to him. His sporran rubbed her thighs in the most sensual way. The rough wool of his kilt, against the soft slither of her silk dress, excited her. Closer he drew her, and closer she crept into his warm arms, as instinctively her body arched toward him. There was a tingling in the pit of her stomach as she let herself float on the music, keeping perfect time with Rory.

Dimly she saw Barbara dancing past with a tall, severe looking man who wore glasses. He looked familiar. Of course, it was the doctor from the hospital. She noticed Barbara's eyes following Rory, as he laid his cheek next to hers. But she was cocooned in his arms like cottonwool. Nothing could touch her now. She felt herself smiling, a smile that turned her into a Cheshire cat, so broad and happy that it felt as if it was fixed forever on her face.

Even Mick stumbling round with a rather nice looking blonde girl, didn't needle her any more. The dance was the music and the music was the dance. She and Rory were out on their very own island with no room for anyone else.

The waltz ended as the fiddlers wielded their bows over the violin strings in the final chords. The spell was broken as Rory dropped his hands from Alyssa's arms. Abruptly she was propelled back into the real world.

'Come and have something to eat,' he suggested and they strolled over to the buffet. He picked up a plate and handed it to her. 'Help yourself. The ladies of Mora have surpassed themselves this time. They've been preparing all this food for at least a week.'

Alyssa surveyed the seemingly endless choice. She picked up some slices of the delicious meat and some fresh green salad. The music was still in her soul with the rhythm running through her head. Rory looked at her, his eyes holding hers for a long moment of eternity. She saw his lips move and strained to hear what he was saying, but the chatter and movement around her drowned his words. She was afraid she'd missed something important. Something that would change her life. She bent forward to ask him to repeat his words, but Mick appeared and slapped Rory on the shoulders in an unwelcome show of bonhomie.

'And how's you getting on with ma wee cousin?' Mick's voice boomed for all to hear. 'She's quite a girl. I'll have to look after her better.' He gave one of his loud guffaws.

The bagpipes tuned up, taking over from the fiddles. Rory set down his plate and glass. 'Our dance, I think,' he said to Alyssa, neatly cutting Mick out. The wailing music beckoned. With a twirl and a swirl, he and Alyssa were off again, feet flying, treading the complex measures of the reel.

Barbara stood behind Mick, left high and dry too, her mouth opening and shutting, while Mick spluttered. They stared at Alyssa and Rory as the dance ebbed and flowed around them, the eerie music getting more frenzied.

Alyssa's emotions were stirred up by the eldritch sounds. She was enchanted by an unsuitable highlander, and an un-suitable island. What could she offer this island, when her skills were purely urban? Who had need of a management consultant in the Scottish highlands? Although as a teen-ager she'd learned to milk the cows with the best of them at her uncle's farm in the Yorkshire dales, it had only been on a fun basis. Nobody wanted those sort of outdated skills when everything was done by milking machine. There was so little grazing land left round Balvaig House. There was no hope of her following in her great aunt's footsteps as the largest milk producer of the western isles of Scotland. Those days were past, and she certainly didn't have the capital to invest. She sighed. Her euphoria had dissipated. Now she'd slipped back into the real and troubled world of problems.

The ceilidh carried on with songs and dancing. Although Alyssa continued to dance and laugh, her gaiety of the beginning of the evening had dimmed. She dreaded the next day when she would have to visit the lawyer again to see if he had managed to straighten matters out further. Certainly she had some new information to give him. The envelope, she'd borrowed from Miss Brodie, lay safely hidden in the rented cottage where not even a mouse would find it.

The last waltz was playing. Once more Rory gathered Alyssa into his arms. She threw off her mental burdens again and thrust herself into his arms, feeling again the sweet safety. Slowly, slowly the music pushed them closer to each other, their limbs becoming more and more langorous.

'You're mine tonight.' Rory looked into Alyssa's eyes. There was no quibbling. No polite gestures such as *Will you come up for a last drink*, as there would be in London. Just *You're mine tonight.* So simple and honest.

The ceilidh was over. Alyssa joined hands with the others as they all sang Auld Lang Syne lustily. It was time to go home and what would the night bring, she wondered? She was still flushed and glowing with the exertion of the dancing.

'We'll leave the car,' Rory said. 'It's a beautiful night. Look at the stars.' He moved over to say goodnight to some of his friends.

The skirling bagpipes were stilled. Alyssa looked across at Rory. Did he really mean they should walk home? But what about Barbara? Where did she fit in? Could she really be left behind or would they have to take the car to drive Barbara home, gooseberry style along with Alyssa? Alyssa would rather walk the five miles across the island alone than sit in the enclosed space of the car with Barbara and her gibes.

Her eye caught Barbara being handed carefully into a dark green car by the severe-looking doctor. That's settled then, thought Alyssa as she stood at the door of the hall, listening to the islanders calling goodbyes to each other. Maybe Barbara and Rory weren't an item after all. He certainly hadn't bothered with her at the ceilidh.

She felt a light tap on her arm, and there was Eithne in her green water-frond dress smiling at her. 'I'm sorry,' said Eithne. 'I think I upset you. I certainly didn't mean to, but I was clumsy and perhaps you reacted a little too strongly. We're far too blunt up here, we don't always think before we speak.'

'You're right.' Alyssa smiled at her. 'I don't know what got into me. I can usually take things on the chin. It's a shock to find out that you're everybody's business before you know it yourself. Besides I realised you didn't mean to say anything wrong. I think it was Mick, the auctioneer, that got under my skin.'

'Yes, he's a cunning one. You must look out for him. I hope we can meet again. Come along to my house, and we'll have a good chat,' said Eithne. 'I know how it is to be a newcomer on the island, before they accept you.' She gave Alyssa a light kiss on the cheek and was gone.

Alyssa slipped her dancing shoes into her bag and slipped on her flat easy casuals. Rory took her arm. Calling out friendly goodbyes, they disappeared together into the perfumed night.

CHAPTER SIXTEEN

Back at the cottage, Alyssa opened the door of her small unassuming home. Not many people locked their doors on Mora. She almost expected Rory to carry her over the threshold.

Was she completely mad?

'Come in, Rory,' she invited, suddenly nervous. 'I'm sure you've seen the inside of these cottages before.'

'Not for a long time. Remember I've only just come back to Mora to stay with Dad, and I don't make a point of taking the holidaymakers home!' His voice was teasing.

Alyssa laughed. It wasn't what she meant, but she was trying to make small talk, because she knew something momentous was ahead, and she wasn't sure she was ready for it. She knew if she allowed Rory to take her to bed, she would be hopelessly lost. There would be no turning back to her old life. She wasn't ready to make a commitment to settling down in this remote island, blinded by pure sexual attraction, and yet there was more. A lot more.

Rory seemed to understand her dilemma. He put his arm round her, drawing her towards the faded chintz sofa. 'It's not easy for me either, you know.' He stroked her arm soothingly as if gentling a frightened animal. 'I don't want to get involved with someone who's leaving next month or even sooner.'

Alyssa lay her head on his shoulder and relaxed against him. The room was so quiet, she could hear his steady breathing, in – out, in – out, almost more intimate than a kiss. They sat there comfortably for some time, until Alyssa began to feel an urgent longing for him to hold her tighter. She stirred restlessly turning her face up towards his. Her lips formed a kiss as she stretched upward to him, her arm slipping round his neck.

It was as if a dam burst. Two bodies that were holding themselves in check suddenly released their hold and let passion flare. He slipped on top of her, pressing her down on the narrow sofa. She revelled in the feeling of the rough, heavy kilt and the iron stiffness under it. Her legs spread wide in natural response.

She felt him raise himself off her. 'Come let's go in here. There must be more room.' He drew her into the small bedroom.

Alyssa stifled a giggle. There really wasn't much room on her bed, which completely filled the bedroom, although it was meant for two. Rory laughed too, and with arms round each other they collapsed on the bed.

'Is this all?' Rory surveyed the rather shabby room. 'There's more room in a shepherd's bothy!' He was laughing again as he pulled her down.

'Now you can undo my kilt straps,' he invited. 'I bet you've never done anything so exciting in your whole life as undressing a highlander.'

Alyssa was laughing too, but eagerly she struggled with the stiff straps of the kilt and the sporran, releasing them so that they fell in a heavy heap on the floor. She breathed in the exciting male scent of him, then helped him lift her dress over her head. The silky fabric slipped to the floor, and his cool, strong hands caressed her burning skin. She quivered as his lips teased her peaked nipples, sending currents of desire flooding through her.

He was touching her, kissing her in forbidden parts that had been too long starved of the pleasures of love. He slid his hand between their two bodies and massaged gently. Then he lifted himself above her, drawing closer until she gasped in sweet agony as he penetrated her. Skin on skin, they moved sensuously together in an age-old rhythm until the exquisite sensation exploded between them. Her body began to shudder as he took her with him to a haven of fulfilment.

The waning moon outside offered a weak glimmer through the gap in the faded curtains. Alyssa lay curled into the curve of Rory's long length. She fell into a dream world clasped in his arms in the ancient bed.

Chapter Seventeen

Sir Peter sat in the front room smoking one of his Havana cigars. The rich, greedy aroma seeped through the house vying with the fresh tang of the waves blowing up from the sea.

Grizelda was tidying up the remains of the breakfast in the kitchen, before going out to look at the animals. She sneezed and opened a window to let out the strong odour. Heavy cigar smoke was out of place in the Spartan lives of the hard-pressed islanders.

She was annoyed. Why couldn't Peter come outside and help on the farm, instead of wasting his time indoors? The window banged shut as the wind outside increased in strength. She tried to fasten the window securely as she peered outside at the mackerel-tinged sky.

The curtains fluttered and the dishes in the cupboard started rattling. She moved to stand close to the warmth of the kitchen range, but still she felt the licking fingers of the wind follow her as it crept through the nooks and crannies in the walls.

Really Peter should stir himself. There were a thousand tasks that needed to be done. But she was too proud to go and ask for his help. Besides she was no languid lily. She would manage because she was used to hard work from the moment she rose from her bed in the morning to after the last cow was milked in the evening. And that included helping Mrs McMorran to prepare meals for the menfolk.

But of course menfolk were always skiving off. Grizelda was used to their fly ways of dodging the work, because they knew that she would step in and take over the unfinished tasks. She was blessed to have been born so hardy and with good strong arms and legs to bear the heavy load of the daily work on the farm.

She pulled her warm woollen cardigan around her and took down her shabby old Harris tweed coat from the peg in the cloakroom. She'd put off buying a new one for ages because she never had time to travel the distance into Oban in search of clothes. Besides clothes didn't really interest her. The living, breathing farm was much more exciting. The dramas that occurred, the problems that had to be solved were her life's blood. She wasn't going to sit nodding in the inglenook with her knitting. She was far too physically active for that, even if it did take its toll on her clothes.

She found her rubber boots and pulled them on. After a sharp tussle with the backdoor, which seemed to have developed an angry will of its own, she shut it behind her. Outside a harsh chill lay like a pall over the farm steading. She began to walk up the hill towards the sheep, almost bent double against the buffeting of the wind.

The December gales were always treacherous. Once or twice every winter, the wind mounted to whining gale force, trying its damnedest to snatch away unwary sheep if they ventured too near the cliffs.

Grizelda called to the two sheepdogs to come with her, but they cowered, shivering beside the byre, and for once in their lives refused to obey her. She pressed on alone, the wind whipping her breath away, but the air was so fresh she felt exhilarated and this drove her on.

At the top of the cliff, the gale hit her with hard physical impact. She could almost feel her bones cracking, and it was difficult to navigate a path upwards. She dropped down and crawled on her hands and knees for she could just make out the frightened bleating of a sheep. Creeping forward she saw it had slipped over the edge and was entangled with a gorse bush. It was struggling feebly, and bits of white wool were snagged on the bush. If she didn't act quickly it would be lost for ever.

She'd have to clamber down and shove the frightened creature back upwards before it blew clean away into the water, dragged down and drowned by the solid weight of its wool. She lowered herself down the cliffside to the ledge where the sheep was caught.

Davy, the young shepherd, appeared from nowhere in his silent way. He carried his long shepherd's crook with its carved head. He forced his way through the storm and looked down at her as she clung to a gorse bush.

'Come on, Davy,' screamed Grizelda into the wind, the words beating back on her mouth. 'Help me push this ewe back up.' If the silly thing struggled too much it could easily loosen her precarious hold and topple them both down into the angry waves.

Together Davy and Grizelda fought to get the terrified sheep upward away from danger. 'Loop your crook round her leg,' urged Grizelda. 'And for God's sake don't let go.'

Panting, with perspiration running down her face in a highly unladylike fashion, she pushed and shoved, while Davy wielded his long crook and grasped the animal firmly. He hauled with all his strength, the veins standing out on his forehead, but the sheep lay paralysed with fear in a slumped mass refusing to help itself.

'One more time, and together we'll have her,' Grizelda encouraged Davy. 'Just one more time.'

Inspired, Davy gave an even greater pull of his crook and Grizelda, taking a deep breath, gave a huge heave from below. The animal scrambled to its feet and forced its way upward over the lip of the cliff, vanishing over the top. Grizelda was left clinging to the last remnants of the gorse bush and Davy lay flat on his back. She let out an unlady-like cheer and climbed back up the cliff to pull Davy to his feet.

She stood back from the edge, trying to catch her breath. 'Now, Davy, you must check all the other sheep. I'm going back to the steading to see that everything is in order there. This gale could easily lift the roof of the byre or even the barn.'

She fought her way back through the blusters of the wind and found her brothers in the steading looking up helplessly at the roof of the byre. It was trembling like a sheet of grey paper in the force of the gale. It boomed like a trapped beast in the powerful gusts as John stood scratching his head looking up at it.

'Oh, my God.' With a quick glance Grizelda sized up the situation immediately. 'You'll have to get a rope round that or the whole thing will lift off.'

She started giving orders. Both her brothers looked re-lieved that she'd come to take charge. 'Quick, John, run into the barn and get that long thick rope we use for the hay. And you, Willie, roll over some of these heavy boulders so we can tie it onto them and hold it down.'

Where was Peter? Hadn't he noticed that something was wrong? Hadn't he heard the men's shouts and the bustle and flurry outside. A slow burning anger built up in Grizelda's breast. But all the while she chivvied the men along and forced them to fling stout ropes across the roof. She and Davy secured the rope ends to the heavy boulders on the ground as well as to the solid beams of the other buildings.

Dark clouds billowed and threatened. A few remaining crows were blown across the sky like pieces of burnt black paper as they sought to reach the shelter of the pine trees behind the farm buildings.

The wind blustered around the yard like an army of menace. Grizelda tried not to lose heart as she kept rallying the farm workers from their frightened apathy. Horrified, she saw that the wind was now attacking the dairy roof and sucking at the nails holding it down. Some of the guttering tore loose and clattered to the ground.

'Have we any more rope?' she shouted. One of the farm workers ran back into the barn. Grizelda worked her way round to the outer side of the dairy where it was unprotected by the cluster of farm buildings.

'Hurry, hurry,' she urged. 'The roof's just about to go if we don't get a hold on it.'

The words were snatched from her mouth and with a whoop and a scurry the whole roof of the dairy lifted off and waltzed tantalisingly away down the field, bumping and thudding like an enormous flying carpet.

And in its wake, Grizelda felt herself lifted and transported by an immutable force as if some giant had put his arms around her and lifted her bodily into another dimension. Her hair whipped free from its scarf. She smelt the strong tang of the seaweed rising from the seashore. For a moment she floated calm and free through the air.

Then panic gripped her and she began flailing with her arms, calling out, her words snatched away from her as the wind gloated and played with her. If it didn't let her go she would be dumped out at sea to drown.

She heard shouts behind her but couldn't turn. All she could see was sheets of water whipped up from the sea in silver streaks. The wind lowered her a little from its grasp, and her feet just touched the bumpy grass. But now she felt herself being shadowed and chased from behind while the sea in front approached at violent speed.

Her coat was snatched, first by one hand then by two. Now she whimpered and moaned, her eyes tight shut. She felt an almighty tug from behind then she fell sprawling on the seashore, her face scraping across a rough rock, while the waves rippled in to revive her.

'Grizelda, Grizelda.' A voice cried in her wind-deafened ears. 'Grizelda, are you all right?'

Sitting up suddenly, she snapped 'No I'm not all right. I'm nearly dead, nearly drowned.' Then she softened and collapsed, weeping hysterically in Peter's arms.

'You saved my life,' she wept. 'What would I have done without you.'

Peter lay flat beside her. His arm was clinging fast to a rock, while the wind tipped and teased at them both as they lay there. But it failed to win back its hold. Peter was clad only in his velvet smoking jacket and light woollen trousers. His breath was coming in gasps.

The wind retreated in a furious shrieking. Grizelda crept closer to Peter. She pressed her lips on his. 'I love you Peter,' she whispered. 'You're fleeter than the wind.'

'Then you must trust me more, Grizelda,' he said.

*

There was a new equality between them. Grizelda deferred more to Peter without losing any of her natural authority. The farm buildings had to be repaired after the vicious onslaught of the gale.

'Look at this, Grizelda,' said Peter showing her several pages covered with neat figures. 'It's time to make some new investments in the buildings.'

'Maintenance costs so much,' said Grizelda. 'We're always so hard pressed to find the money.'

'False economy, my dear,' said Peter. 'The buildings need to be better maintained and even expanded.'

Peter spent a week walking round the cowshed and the dairy, measuring and making rough drawings, which became carefully drawn plans. These went far beyond just the repair of the cowshed. He planned several new buildings and a new way of working so that the dairy produce would be much increased. He talked enthusiastically to Grizelda about installing a milking machine and buying in several cows. Suddenly money wasn't a bone of contention between them. Grizelda no longer felt she had to prove that she could manage without Peter's financial help. She didn't even need to ask him. Things got done almost by themselves. Peter pressed John and Willie into working steadily and forced them to cut down their visits to the pub. He made sure they didn't leave the farm until after the work was finished for the day.

For many hours each day, Peter sat closeted with men who came across to the island. They were builders and masons who would start work on Peter's plans to develop the farm buildings. Grizelda was happy to leave these tasks to him and to go about the daily work, milking the cows and tending the sheep. She enjoyed discussing the plans with him in the evenings.

She loved when he suggested that they go to bed early, for then she knew the velvet nights would be long and loving between two equals. She gave herself completely to Peter's caresses. She even got the maid to light a fire in their bedroom every evening. She discovered in herself a new voluptuousness, a sensuousness, a burning need that had to be satisfied. She no longer felt she always had to be in control. In Peter's arms she could be wild, wanton and free instead of the Grizelda, that was always cool-headed and in charge.

She loved the feel of Peter's body against her own. His silken skin. The place where his sun-browned face met the white skin of his neck. He knew just how to touch her in her most secret, ecstatic places. He could drive her into a frenzy of wanting him, teasing and tantalizing, before he thrust himself inside her, moving smoothly and rhythmically in her wet desire, bringing her to the pinnacle of pleasure before granting her ease.

'Again, again,' she cried, pressing eager breasts against him, her nipples peaked, and her body open and waiting for him to plunge again into its dark creamy depths.

His lips sought hers, as she demanded him, ripe and needy. He kissed her deeply, his tongue penetrating her moist and trembling mouth. They were alone in the world sailing on the seas of sensuous pleasure.

Grizelda wished it would go on forever. Until now her life had been full of constraints and obligations. She'd struggled so long to keep her brothers' noses to the grindstone.

No wonder they tried to escape down to the pub for a short spell of freedom. She was the slave driver. She realised it now.

But sometimes when the cold light of morning filtered through the curtains and the embers of the fire no longer glowed, she was assailed by self doubt.

Did Peter love her as much as his first wife? Was she, Grizelda, as attractive or did he regard her as a simple farm girl screaming as she was serviced by the bull. Certainly she couldn't compete in the drawing rooms of London, but here she had a wide circle of friends and she tried hard to be a good neighbour. There was poor Mrs Cameron who she visited regularly who had been struck down by tuberculosis. The sick woman had to spend most of her time in bed while her six children ran riot and her husband was at his wit's end of how to take care of his family. Grizelda often brought floury bread wrapped in a snowy napkin and hearty soups in the hope of reviving the invalid a little, as well as providing nourishment for the children.

'You're awfy guid tae us, Miss Grizel,' wept Mrs Cameron. 'It fair puts ma man in a guid humour tae find yon loaves and guid Scots broth.'

Grizelda was worried. There seemed so little she could do to help the stricken family. Secretly she paid the local doctor to look in on Mrs Cameron and do what he could. She herself was so lucky to have iron health and strength.

In time the weather lightened and spring came, so that the cows could be let out of the cowshed and the sheep began to drop their tiny lambs. Each year Grizelda was struck by the beauty and independence of the little creatures in their white fleecy coats. Davy was always on hand to help a ewe if she got in difficulties with the birthing so that fewer lambs were lost than usual that spring.

Grizelda never really knew where Davy was. He was part man, part pixie, she thought. So often he materialised when she least expected it but always when he was needed. She knew that he lived in a cottage at the end of the village with his old mother, and although he was only fifteen years old he bore the full man's responsibility for the home.

'I'm making you my head shepherd,' she told him. 'You look after the sheep so well and the dogs don't dare to be disobedient with you.'

Davy's eyes shone green. 'Thank you ma'am,' he said in his soft highland tones. Grizelda knew that if his father hadn't died when Davy was a wee boy, he would have been sent to school on the mainland and perhaps even to the university. Now it was up to her to ensure he had employment.

Grizelda began to relax and enjoy her happiness. Peter talked of his plans that they should be the first farm on the island to install a milking machine, and he wanted to invest in a bigger herd of cattle so that they would be the largest herd for miles around. He knew how to run a farm on a large scale and he intended that Balvaig farm should become the leading one on the west coast of Scotland. Grizelda was ecstatic. She believed in Peter. Great ambitions powered by long experience were bound to succeed. The scheme couldn't fail.

'I think we should have a new milking parlour instead of the old dairy. Some calf pens and perhaps even a bull box,' Peter said. 'Balvaig farm with our new herd of pedigree, pampered Ayrshire cows, will become the chief milk supplier as far as Inverness.'

The new cow shed, so much finer than the old byre, began to take shape. The builders and masons worked long hours, and then the painters came. The solid roof was constructed to withstand a thousand gales, and even a flood would not stir the building. New drainage was put in the yard, so that the stinking puddles were whirled away and the floor of the yard dried swiftly even after heavy downpours.

In the spring, the arrival of the snow-fleeced newborn lambs reminded Grizelda that there was only one thing lacking in their happiness. A child of her own.

A few of the little lambs, which had lost their mothers and were too feeble to withstand the highland storms, were brought in for feeding in the kitchen. Grizelda often picked them up and held the small warm bodies close to her heart. Their frailty made her feel a great tenderness. She longed for a baby to set the seal on their union of passion. She knew Peter didn't have any children from his first marriage and she believed that this would secure her position as the preferred wife. But month after month, the hateful tell-tale red spots in her knickers destroyed the dream.

She could not rest. She threw herself even more strongly into her daily work. Out on the hill at dawn, she would help Davy with the birthing of a lamb. Sometimes this was very heavy work if the ewe had got herself in the wrong position and had to be turned over on her side.

Grizelda knew this wasn't very wise and that perhaps she should take things more easily when she was trying to conceive a child. But if she sat down or even reclined on the sofa for a short time, the black thoughts and un-certainties came flapping back so that she would have to jump up and do something active and busy to drive them away.

She didn't want to tell Peter of her longing for a baby. She felt that this would underline her failure and he never spoke of wishing to have a child. Even the loving nights in the bed began to be a marathon task for her. She must surely get pregnant this month, or perhaps the next one. But 'her visitor' as Mrs McMorran, the housekeeper, called it, appeared with unfailing regularity and each time her hopes were dashed.

CHAPTER EIGHTEEN

Alyssa stirred and whimpered. Her legs felt leaden as she tried to kick away a heavy rock that was impeding her. She felt strong arms holding her, and she writhed in fear, trying to break free.

A voice spoke in her ear: 'Alyssa, wake up! It's morning and I have to leave you!'

Alyssa pushed at the bedcovers and tried to hold on to the remnants of her dream: 'I'm just coming, Peter. Get Davy to bring in the cows,' she mumbled.

Stillness. '*Who* did you say?'

Alyssa opened her eyes and scrubbed the sleep out of them. She looked up at Rory, standing at the side of the bed.

'Who's Peter?' His face was grim as he dressed swiftly, pulling on his shirt and strapping on his kilt and sporran.

'It was just a dream I had,' Alyssa fumbled for words to explain away her lapse.

'You called me, Peter,' Rory insisted.

'I don't know any Peter particularly well,' Alyssa's face felt hot. 'It was just a stupid dream.'

Rory's gaze held suspicion, but he turned and pulled on his shoes, lacing them up firmly. He hesitated for a moment. Then he said: 'Meet me down at the pub after lunch.

I've found someone who might help with the claim to your inheritance.' Then he was gone, banging the door behind him.

*

Alyssa sat in the lounge bar of the pub, cocooned in a red plush chair as she waited for Rory. An odour of ancient beer-spills rose from the patterned carpet. She toyed with some plain fizzy water with a twist of lemon, and munched on the crisps and olives thoughtfully provided by yet another blue-eyed highlander with dark wavy hair. Although the barman here was about ten years older than Rory, it seemed to Alyssa that there were a lot of clones of the same person on the island. First Rory, then Neil the ferryman, and now the proprietor of the pub. Either they were clones, or someone had been exercising his droit de seigneur on overtime.

Thoughts of Great Aunt Grizelda, Rory, Mick and Miss Brodie tumbled around in her brain. But she pushed the thought of William Finlay aside. It was only a scribbled family tree on a piece of paper after all. Within a few days she had emerged into a completely new existence. A month ago she hadn't known any of these people and now they were at the centre of her life.

The door to the lounge flew open and three men stumped in. They went over to sit in a far corner of the room. The sound of a familiar raucous laugh disturbed Alyssa's peace. She looked up to see Mick, clad as usual in a loud check jacket. This latest one was even more nauseous than usual with strong orange and green checks vying with each other.

Was there no getting away from this man? Was he born to plague her? She watched him cross to the bar and order three foaming lagers. His eyes bore down on her like a laser beam as he honed in on her.

'Hello, Aleesie.' His voice caused her to shudder. His fat arm encircled her like a band of iron and he planted a smacking kiss on her cheek just missing her mouth as she turned her head sharply away with an instinct of self-preservation. 'Come and take a drink with us.'

Alyssa recoiled. She looked over to the table where the two other men were sprawling, their legs stuck out in front of them, each taking up maximum space. Beefy types both of them, just like Mick.

Like the cut of a sword, she said 'I'd rather go to hell and back than sit down with you and your cronies, Mick. You're dishonest, underhand and sneaky. You tricked a defenceless old woman into changing her will when you knew the last thing she wanted was to have anything to do with you.'

Rage at Lady Grizelda's suffering almost choked her, and she threw the last vestiges of good sense to the winds. 'By the way how did you get Miss Brodie to run your errands? She doesn't seem like your type of person?'

Mick's blubber-mouth was working soundlessly. It was not a pretty sight. He drew out a chair from the table and lowered himself onto it close to Alyssa, his big knee banging into hers. He pushed his face up to hers, imprisoning her by his breath. Her nerve endings stretched like taut violin strings.

Mick found his voice. 'Do you know what you're saying, Aleesie? It's very dangerous to tell lies and to make up stories. Didn't your fine English mother tell you that? I can clap an injunction on you, as soon as look at you. Nobody'll believe that garbage you're spouting. Who's this Miss Brodie woman anyway?'

Alyssa rallied. It was so obviously a lie. Of course he knew Miss Brodie.

'You forced my aunt into changing her will,' she repeated. 'That's coercion for the first. You went to a frail old woman and frightened her, terrified her. It's a wonder she didn't die on the spot.'

She had to stop because a mist was swirling down over her. She put her hands up to her face and tried to clear her dry throat. Her breath came in gasps. Another swirl of the mist, and soft words seemed to whisper through the air. The words reverberated and grew louder and louder, blotting out the clink of the glasses, the general murmur of conversation and all the normal sounds of the pub.

'I hated Fordyce with all my heart. I would never ever have given anything to his son,' murmured a voice in Alyssa's ear as a cold shiver slipped down her spine. She looked round to see who was whispering in her ear, but there was no one to be seen.

White gauze shimmered and wavered in front of Alyssa's vision. She found herself breathing slowly and deeply. Her eyes flickered, and an indistinct tableau of two or three menacing figures bending over an old lady took shape in front of her eyes. The old lady lay in a narrow white bed. Her eyes were blazing with ice blue luminosity, which seemed to hold the threatening figures in check even as she shrank back against the pillows. Alyssa tried to speak, to reach out to the figures in the group. 'Stop, leave her alone. Don't harm her.' She forced the words out from her dry throat, but she couldn't move. The mist swirled again and the picture faded. Alyssa peered into the white depths of the mist as a new picture formed. Alyssa tried to call out but she was falling, falling... into a soft goosedown bed and her eyelids shut.

*

Grizelda threw off the crushed sheet, and untangled her feet from the blankets. She staggered over to the window. At least her head had stopped whirling. She felt her forehead gingerly but it seemed quite cool. She spread her arms, stretching luxuriously. The bout of influenza was nearly over, but it had left her weak.

She looked down at her crumpled white nightgown and in one fluid movement she pulled it off. Rummaging around in the depths of the heavy oak wardrobe she found her warmest woollen skirt and a heavy dark green jumper.

She pulled on her vest and liberty bodice. With her knickers and thickest lisle stockings, she was ready to go out and take up her duties on the farm again. She poured some water from the ewer with the pink roses, and shivered as she gave a quick dab to her face and hands. The water had chilled because she had waited too long since Mrs McMorran had brought it up fresh and warm.

Pulling open the bedroom door she ran downstairs. At the bottom she met Mrs McMorran.

'Miss Grizel, whatever are you doing out of bed?' cried the housekeeper. 'You'll catch your death and be back under the blankets before the hour.'

'I have to look to the cows, Mrs McMorran. And soon the calves will be coming so I must be there. Davy can't do everything.' Grizelda pulled out her waterproof coat from the hall cupboard. 'I can't loll about in bed all day. The animals need to be looked after.'

'Where's your man, then?' said Mrs McMorran. 'Can he no' go instead?'

'Sir Peter knows little about calving.' Grizelda's cheeks grew hot with annoyance whether at Peter or Mrs McMorran she wasn't sure. 'He spends his time drawing up plans or writing about exotic orchids. And if there's any time left over he sits totting up the accounts for buying the new milking machine. He's not an outdoor man.'

Then she felt guilty at accusing Peter in that way. He'd certainly made a difference to the farm. She was so proud of the new milking parlour and the fifty new cows that stood there every day, placidly chewing the cud while the machine relieved them of their precious burden of milk. She was so proud that Balvaig was the first farm to install a milking machine, and the milk sales from the farm had tripled.

She was lucky that Peter had taken over most of the paperwork, and made the plans for their future and the farm's prosperity. Just because she would rather avoid keeping the accounts, it didn't mean they could be left and forgotten. But she did wish he would come outside more, instead of putting his plans on paper without ever studying the farm buildings. She pulled on her waterproofs and her boots and went outside in the chill wind.

What price the sophisticated Lady Lovat! It was a wonder that Sir Peter had wanted to marry her, and it seemed she couldn't even bear him a child.

Behind her, the back door was torn open and Peter appeared. 'Grizelda, go back to bed at once, you'll catch pneumonia,' he ordered, pointing upstairs. He marched over and seized her arm, pulling her indoors again.

That was enough. Grizelda felt the tension and frustration she had been holding back inside her burst forth like a torrent of water breaching the dam.

'Damn you, Peter!' she screamed. 'This is my house and my farm. I haven't seen you doing so much around here. You told me you were an expert on cattle. Was it two hundred beasts you had out in Jamaica, or was it all a great story just to impress me?'

Peter was overwhelmed by a huge sneeze. His head was turned away from Grizelda, but all the well-polished crystal glasses tinkled in the glass cabinet. He sneezed again, then pulled out his handkerchief and blew his nose loudly.

'Now you've got influenza too.' Quick sympathy rose in Grizelda's breast. 'You go upstairs and get Mrs McMorran to bring you a hot toddy. Two spoonfuls of honey in a glass of whisky will make you feel better. Now I must go to the animals.'

'Not so fast!' Peter held her back. 'You're still too fragile. Go back to bed. Leave me to go and help Davy.'

Once Grizelda was safely back in bed Peter pulled on an old Macintosh and stepped out into the yard. Young Davy came running toward him.

'Sir Peter,' he called 'You'll have to help me with Daisy, the cow. Somehow she's got over to Eilean Beag, the wee island, and got herself stuck in the bog there. She's due to calve this week. So we'll have to get her back.'

Peter thought longingly of the warm house he had just left. The last place he wanted to go to was an uninhabited island open only to the birds, and with a treacherous bog. Worse, the island was only accessible at low tide unless he took the rowing boat. But Grizelda must be protected. He hoped she was now be lying comfortably in bed in a nest of warm blankets. She'd have to stay there or she'd have a relapse. He certainly wasn't going to tell her what was going on, although he was feeling pretty peculiar himself. But no matter, he was here to do a job.

'Is the boat bailed out and ready?' he asked Davy. 'We'll row over and try and get the cow out. Have you got the ropes?'

The rain was now sheeting down in sharp needles, piercing his face. He pulled his black sou'wester down over his ears and turned up the collar of his oilskin, but the moisture still found ways to seep down his neck.

They got into the small rowing boat and Peter took the oars. He couldn't let a small chap like Davy fight against the boiling sea, even though the strait between the two islands was very short. Davy, obedient to his master, sat in the stern of the boat clutching a great hank of rope. He didn't seem to have much protection apart from his ancient Mackintosh and rubber boots. His head was bared to the elements and rivulets of water coursed down from his sodden black hair.

Peter was shivering with cold, but he struggled to pull on the oars and make slow headway across the frothing sea. But the boat hardly seemed to move. The sea held them in its hungry hand. Warm, debilitating sweat ran from his underarms to add to the icy trickles of rain sluicing down his back. He'd have to bathe before he went in to see Grizelda when they got home, he thought irrelevantly. He must smell like a horse.

'Look out,' cried Davy, 'you almost hit the skerries. Bear to starboard.'

Peter snapped out of the haze he had slipped into, and turned round to see where they were headed. Which side was starboard? Of course he knew. Why was his mind so cloudy? He pulled hard on his right oar and dimly heard

178

Davy's voice, '*Chust* a little farther and we're there. The beach's right there.'

Peter's arms were now aching at the unaccustomed exertion, and he could feel a blister starting on his hand. *Like a bloody woman. I must get out more. I have no strength. Grizelda's right to challenge me. I sit too much over my books.* His foggy mind became crystal clear. He heard Davy shouting. 'Stop rowing now, Sir Peter, we're on the shale. No need to row any more.'

Indeed the boat was stuck like a stubborn donkey, and Peter's arms were flailing uselessly against the heavy shale. Davy jumped out, his boots crunching on the sharp shells and stones. He came round to the side to help Sir Peter out. He pulled the boat further up the short beach for safety, and carrying the ropes he led the way inland up the path till they reached patches of bright green moss where the stricken cow lay. Sir Peter heard her bellowing frantically as if she were trying to show them the way.

She lay there on her side, her eyes opaque and pleading. Spasms of fear ran through her as she tried to drag her ponderous shape out of the bog. A nasty sucking noise rose from under her as the greedy fingers of the bog dragged her down.

Davy uncoiled the rope from his shoulder and gave it to Sir Peter. 'I'll go up close to her and try to calm her. You must tie the rope into a big loop and throw it over her neck. Then pull, for you'll be standing on the firm ground.'

Throw it over her neck! Peter kept his mouth shut. He knew he wasn't capable of such a thing. He'd spent his life in pampered luxury, hiring in others to work for him. Now he was faced with a great test of physical endurance. Could he manage it?

He gritted his teeth, reminding himself that he was a fighter. He knew how much the cows meant to Grizelda. She'd never let one of her cherished herd perish without putting up a good fight for its life.

The cow lay very still, softly moaning, an almost human sound. The only movement was slight rise and fall of her swollen right flank. Peter tossed the rope trying to get it round her head, but only succeeded in catching one of her horns. Davy stepped in closer on the treacherous green bog, and managed to drag the loop free again.

Three times Peter cast the loop. Almost like trying to catch a big fish, he thought, laughing to himself and then found he was laughing out loud. He saw Davy looking at him strangely, and clamped his mouth shut. His cotton wool legs buckled under him.

With a superhuman effort he cast the loop once more and this time it dropped neatly over the cow's head avoiding her horns. It slipped down over her neck, and Peter pulled it tight. The rain had stopped and it was easier to see. Davy sprang back from the shivering bog, and stepped behind Sir Peter. Together they pulled strongly on the rope. Nothing happened. The cow continued to recline in her uncomfortable position. If they weren't quick the bog would win the tussle as the helpless cow slipped down even farther.

But the fresh air was reviving and a gentle warm breeze had got up. 'Come on, Sir Peter,' cried Davy. 'Just once more and we'll have her.'

Peter's arms were weak as cloth, but he summoned up his strength, taking great gulps of the fresh air.

'Pull!' Davy shouted. 'Come away, pull!'

Suddenly the cow plunged in an alarming way, and the bog made a loud, liquid sucking noise. Her hind legs were free. With another great plunge, she scrambled up onto the high ground where she stood bemused, shaking her head.

With the rope around her neck, Davy led her carefully down to the rocks above the beach. Sir Peter could hear him whispering soothing words into her ear.

Sir Peter marvelled at how close animals were to the people of the islands. Their lives were so valuable, and not just in monetary terms. He would try to better understand Grizelda's obsession with her land and her animals. To him she was like a shy violet unfurling her petals ready to give him her heart and her trust. Then by some clumsy remark, he'd make her retreat into herself again, putting up the barriers between them.

He swept his arm across his hot forehead. He found it hard to focus, but Davy was speaking to him again. 'We'll have to sit here for a couple of hours, so when the tide goes down, we can just lead Daisy home across the causeway.'

Sir Peter nodded. Fatigue engulfed him and his whole body ached. He was still very warm. A spasm of coughing shook him. He slumped down against the rock and closed his eyes. He thought he saw Grizelda floating towards him, clutching a white bundle and weeping. He tried to rise. But then there was nobody there.

*

Some hours later Grizelda bent over Peter as he lay in their marriage bed, white and still. His forehead was burning hot and Grizelda's fear rose in her throat almost choking her.

Dr Anderson, who'd come across from the mainland, fussed around, before packing his instruments away in his black bag. 'Your man's verra sick. I doubt he'll see the

181

morn's light.' His rough lowland tones jarred on Grizelda's ears like stones dropping in a freezing pool.

'I'll send the district nurse round,' the doctor said. 'I'll be back later to see him after my other calls. But send somebody for me, if you must.'

Grizelda sat on the bed. Her tears flowed as she cradled Peter's head in her lap. Mrs McMorran came bustling upstairs with offers of tea for Grizelda, or gruel for the patient.

'Bring hot water bottles for his feet and his back,' Grizelda said. 'It's all we can do at the moment. And bring some light orange squash and I'll try to get him to drink something.'

The small hours of the night dragged. The district nurse came and went, her face serious and sad. Mrs McMorran puffed up the stairs, carrying hot bottles, and orange drinks that Peter wouldn't or couldn't touch.

Grizelda alternately wept and prayed. She was full of guilt because she felt she should have insisted on going out to rescue the cow herself. She shouldn't have let Peter persuade her to stay at home. She wept because she believed she hadn't loved Peter enough. She wept for her own loneliness. She wept for her fear of letting people come too close to her.

She sat hunched over him in her nocturnal vigil. The night slipped by on silent wings, broken only by Peter's sonorous breathing. Grizelda began whispering words of love in his ear. Words that should have been said long ago.

'Dearest Peter, you gave me a new life and standing in the community. We shared laughter and great passionate love. You are my perfect mate. How could I not have seen that before? I was headstrong and too independent, yet too unsure of myself to let go and surrender to you. I was frightened of being second best to your first wife. Oh, couldn't I just have trusted you instead of playing the aloof, untouchable Miss Grizel!' Her warm tears dripped on Peter's face.

His eyes opened. 'But, Grizelda, you have always been my perfect mate. The incomparable Lady Grizelda. The brave, shining bright, Lady Grizelda, who lit up my life and showed me the value of the world around us. That it couldn't be measured in pounds and shillings.'

'Don't leave me, Peter,' pleaded Grizelda. 'Get better, get stronger. I can't manage without you.'

Peter's breathing was becoming more laboured, his eyes clouding. Grizelda held him tighter, her tears streaming and unstoppable.

'I shall always be with you, Grizelda, for you lie on my heart.' His voice was clear and strong. 'How I have loved you. No wife has ever been so adored.' He sank back on his pillows, and with a last puff of breath he slipped beyond Grizelda's reach. She was left embracing an emptiness without a soul. Her sobs tore her apart. Then quietening, she kissed his relaxed pale face and lay down beside him, cradling him for the last precious hours they would have together until the first streaks of dawn crept over the hills.

Rousing herself, she gave his still, white face one last kiss, and stroked his cold cheeks. Then gathering all her strength, she rose from the bed. She went over to the window and pulled back the curtain. A circle of pale bluish light moved slowly away from the house and along the road, an uncanny sight, touching and illuminating the trees. Grizelda caught her breath and shivered, her eyes following the progress of the unearthly radiance. 'The death candle,' she gasped, clutching at her breast. 'I'd hoped never to see it. Oh, my dearest Peter, you've truly been taken from me.'

She could bear it alone no longer, and with a last glance at Peter's quiet form lying on the bed, she walked over to the door and opened it, 'Mrs McMorran,' she called.

*

The picture faded. Tears were pouring down Alyssa's cheeks. There was a persistent humming in her ears. Her heart pounded as if trying to leap out of her breast.

Mick's rough voice assailed her. 'Aleesie? Damn the woman, what's wrong with her?' He shook her arm.

Alyssa rubbed her cheeks with the back of her hand, and surfaced back into the here and now. She looked hazily round the pub, trying to remember where she was. Fighting her dizziness she pulled herself to her feet and forced herself to look straight at Mick, ready to define the battle lines.

'Mick, just watch out. I'll show you up.' Her voice was hoarse and strained. She coughed to clear her throat. 'You've taken something that wasn't ever meant for you. I'll find the proof that Great Aunt Grizelda really wanted to pass her house on to me. To me, not you! One day you'll get what you deserve!' She gripped the table to stop swaying and keep herself upright.

Mick's face reddened like the swollen wattle of a turkey cock. 'Interfering bitch!' he flung at her. 'And a Sassenach too.' His arm swiped Alyssa's half-empty glass to the floor. There was a crash of splintering glass as he turned away and barged back to his cronies.

Alyssa slumped back in her chair and avoided the eyes of the three men sitting with Mick. The door of the pub opened with a blast of fresh air and Rory walked in. He caught sight of her immediately and came over to her. She gazed at him wondering how she ever could have compared the proprietor of the pub to vibrant, vital Rory. Only their colouring was similar. No one had a smile like Rory's, no one else had that quirky way of raising his left eyebrow. Nor that keen, intelligent gaze that took in a situation at the blink of an eyelid.

He gave her a quick kiss, reminding her of the secret world they had shared last night. Behind him she saw a burly man of about fifty, with tufts of white hair sprouting up on either side of his head like benevolent horns.

Rory drew him forward. 'I've got someone you'll really want to meet, Alyssa. This is Dougal Campbell. He's a porter at the hospital. I know you'll be interested to hear his story.'

'Hello, Miss Alyssa,' said Dougal formally, a pronounced highland lilt in his voice. 'Mr MacDonald here saved the life of my bitch and her five puppies. I don't know how to thank him.' He took Rory's hand and shook it hard, swallowing as if to hide his emotion.

'I'm so glad I could help the mother, for these puppies of hers were very large and it was a hard delivery for her. Let me buy you a drink to celebrate their safe arrival.' Rory walked over to the bar.

'So you're Lady Grizelda's niece,' said Dougal, looking at Alyssa with approval as Rory strode over to the bar.

'Tell me your story, Dougal,' said Alyssa softly. She fixed her eyes on his. 'Did you know my great aunt well?'

'No, in fact I only saw her the once, and no' under happy circumstances, you might say. That's the strange part.' Dougal looked up as Rory put two glasses of lager on the table.

'And here's some white wine for you, Alyssa,' Rory said. 'Go on, Dougal, you're keeping us on tenterhooks.'

Dougal cleared his throat and shuffled his feet. 'You see it was a Saturday morning. I was outside the hospital in the garden having a quiet smoke. Then this lawyer chappie appeared from nowhere followed by Mick McDermott. It was awfy strange for thon Mick'd never given me the time of day before. Here he was now, brandishing a twenty pound note like a fawning dog and asking me to come to the old lady's bedside. A wee matter of witnessing a document that was to be signed, he told me.'

Alyssa sat riveted at Dougal's story. She dug her nails tensely into the palms of her hands.

'Weel, I was short of cash, what with my wife at home and three bairns with hungry mouths, so I said aye, I'd do it.' Dougal paused to take a pull at his beer.

Out of the corner of her eye, Alyssa saw Mick and his two drinking cronies move towards the door of the pub. Mick's eyes flicked over Dougal, then he and his cronies left like three slinking rats. She sat back in her chair, glad that the three drinkers were gone. The last thing she wanted was for Mick to blunder over to their table and start asking questions.

Rory winked at Alyssa and she knew he was reading her mind. 'Come on, Dougal,' she said trying to contain her impatience. 'You have to tell us the whole story.'

'What was it McDermott wanted you to do?' Rory leaned forward.

'He wanted me to sign some something,' said Dougal.

'You mean McDermott bribed you to sign as a witness, and to what? Was it Lady Grizelda's will?' prompted Rory.

'Oh, aye,' said Dougal, 'It must've been her will, but I never got a keek at it, mind. They kept the papers covered up, except where it said 'Witness'. They held their cards right close to their chests.'

'How was Lady Grizelda when they took you in to her?' Rory's question was incisive.

'She wasnae guid,' said Dougal. 'She lay tipped over in the bed wi' her mouth wide open, snoring. She was no' in this world. She didnae ken what was happening.'

'Who else was there?' Rory was now taking notes in a battered black book.

'Weel, thon Mick, o' course, and thon daft wumman all dressed up in a muckle great cape and heavy trousers and a deerstalker. I couldnae believe my ears when they called her Miss Brodie. I thocht first 'he' was a man. She was taller than myself with great broad shoulders – what kind of a wumman is that?' Dougal wiped his mouth with the back of his hand. He looked at the bottom of his glass and then he looked at Rory.

Rory signalled to the barman to bring over another pint of lager for Dougal. 'Was that Miss Brodie from Luan?'

Dougal took a refreshing draught. 'Oh, aye. Thon Brodie wumman was gey careful not to sign anything herself. And then there was that smart alick lawyer from Edinburgh, with his skeery eyes flitting round in his head and thon physio-wumman that came in three days a week. The wee Edinburgh lawyer was fair sweating, I can tell you. He wasnae happy at all. Mick McDermott was the one bossing us all around.'

Alyssa could hardly contain her excitement. 'So you were really there when they forced my great aunt to sign a new will, Dougal. It sounds like they were treating her very badly.'

'Aye,' he nodded. 'The physio woman made a wee protest. She said she didnae ken Lady Grizelda. She hadn't treated her ever. But McDermott soon put a stop to that, saying it was something to do with the old lady's pension and if the poor old soul didnae sign, she wouldnae be getting any money. So the physio woman backed down.'

Alyssa was shocked. 'But that wasn't true was it? It was just a trick.'

'Weel, I dinnae ken, I was afeared too that we'd be hurting the old lady and doing her out of her pension if we didn't sign. You see at the time I wasnae sure it was her will.' He sighed. 'Then there was a wee problem because they couldnae wake the old lady. She'd slipped down in the bed and was breathing right heavily. The Brodie woman stepped in just like a sergeant major. She shook poor Lady Grizelda and got her to open her eyes. Then she pulled her back up against the pillows, supporting her while the wee shilpit lawyer put a pen in her hand. It was Miss Brodie who helped the old lady to form the letters of her name, for Lady Grizelda's hand was trembling like a wee leaf so it near slipped right off the paper.'

'How could they be so cruel to a frail old lady,' Alyssa's face was full of concern.

'McDermott was gey relieved when she'd signed it. Then he pushed me and that physio woman forward to sign as witnesses. He watched us like a hawk until we'd signed. Then he couldnae wait to get rid of us after that. Nearly pushed us out of the door in his haste to get rid of us.' Dougal sat back looking at them both. Then he said: 'I'm gey glad to get that off my chest, Mr Rory. It's been troubling me many a night. I didnae mean to do the old lady any harm.'

188

'Well, Dougal, you may have to testify to a court of law to help Miss Alyssa,' said Rory. 'Would you do that?'

'Would I do that, after all you've done for ma poor bitch and her puppies?' Dougal slapped Rory on the back. 'Of course I will.'

CHAPTER NINETEEN

In the balm of the evening, Alyssa and Rory walked together along the beach. The waves lapped gently at the shore. Alyssa wore shorts and a light halter neck top. She revelled in the scrunchy feeling of the white sands under her bare feet and the warm caress of the sun on the nape of her neck. She was taking time out. She'd reached a watershed in her life. Soon she must decide whether to stay on this island, with or without inheriting the old house. Or maybe she should just go back to London, her tail between her legs, mission unaccomplished.

She looked at Rory, tall and strong walking sturdily beside her, the dogs as usual swirling round his feet. Her heart lurched and a wave of desire swept over her, so strong she almost stumbled. Could she really return to London if things didn't work out? Could she leave Rory and this paradise?

Her resolve hardened. She'd come several steps on the way this afternoon, thanks to Dougal. She would shake out the truth and she was ready to fight tooth and claw to hold on to her inheritance. Her vehemence surprised her.

'Look out!' Rory put out a hand to hold her back as they reached the rocks. There were five pairs of eyes staring at them inquisitively. Five grey seals lay basking in the sun, plump and placid. They were well camouflaged by the rocks they were lying on. As Rory and Alyssa stood watching them, they lazily slapped their flippers against their sides and eased themselves into more comfortable positions, like old men dreaming.

'Beware the selkies!' Rory looked mock-sternly at Alyssa. 'You don't want to become one of them.'

'The selkies? What are they?'

'Here on the island the old belief is that seals are really human,' said Rory. 'They live in an underwater world or out on the skerries. They're humans. Just look at their eyes, and listen to their cries! But they are tied to the sea. Don't you know about the selkie women who marry human men? But they keep their seal skins secretly hidden in a cupboard, so they can put it on and return to the sea.'

Alyssa looked at the seals. 'These ones don't look so glamorous. They look more like a councillors' meeting!'

'You're too rational. That's not how we live up here. Just don't open your door to a man or woman with the sea running off their backs. You must look if their fingers are webbed. For you could be inviting a selkie in to live in your house, and maybe they would want to marry you.' He smiled teasingly.

It was an enchanting legend. Alyssa looked at the seals and they gazed back at her with their soft dark eyes. She felt the city asphalt flowing out of her veins as the tranquillity of the place enfolded her. Could she ever be a town dweller again?

'People from London think we islanders wander around in faraway dreams,' said Rory looking at her quizzically. 'When you go back to London, will you regard us just as a pleasant interlude? Will it be a relief for you to get back to hot running water, no dangerous dogs and no mice in the wainscotting?'

Alyssa moved her head slowly from side to side. He couldn't be more wrong. The island had cast its spell over her. Rory too had cast his spell on her if only he knew it. Her eyes fastened on where the tide had washed up a pile of seaweed and some driftwood leaving it at the edge of the wet ridged sand. But the blinding afternoon sun and the shimmer of the waves were making her dizzy and uneasy.

She was drawn back to the present moment as Rory took her hand in his warm one and swung it freely, pulling her over the rocks and away from the unhurried waves that lapped against the shore.

He was frowning. 'Do you know your lips are moving and you're murmuring to yourself. What are you on about?'

'Ebb and flow. That's how I feel my life is at the moment,' she answered. 'Why do you force me back to London, without even giving me a chance to prove myself?'

Rory looked at her and considered. 'Could you stand it here? What about the winter? Won't that be too much for a gently reared London girl like you?'

'Not so gently reared,' said Alyssa. 'I told you I can milk a cow, churn butter and muck out a byre.'

Rory laughed scornfully. 'Well that won't help you much. Except for the mucking out, everything else is done mechanically. But it's quite an impressive track record. Maybe there's hope for you yet.'

Why did he always seem to push her away, rather than welcoming her to the island? Did last night mean so little to him? Was it just a one-night stand, when for her it had been life-changing? How stupid of her to go against her instincts and allow herself to be swept away by an attractive highlander when really she was only here to sort out her inheritance. The beauty and peace of the island had surrounded and seduced her. But most of all it was Rory who bound her to him however hard she resisted.

She watched the herring gulls, gannets and terns skim across the blue water. She was proud that she could now distinguish them from each other. She looked at the blue jellyfish that lay stranded at the high water mark. A moon jelly, magical and strange like so many other things on the island.

Her eyes met Rory's unflinchingly. 'Don't underestimate me, I can adapt. Remember the island blood's in me too.'

'And how will you adapt?' he challenged. 'Remember life's hard here, especially in the winter. It's quite different from the London rat race.'

His words jarred on her. 'Will you never accept me?' she shouted. 'You look on me as a flighty incomer from London. Why do you support me the one day and knock me down the next?' She pushed her clenched fist against his solid shoulder. 'Tell me, you owe me that!'

Rory's face was white, and his eyes black. Alyssa pushed closer to him, her face turned up to his. His hands came round her waist and he gathered her firmly to him. 'I can't resist you,' he said. 'Even though I know you'll leave tomorrow or next week.'

His hands were behind her head holding her so that she couldn't move away. He kissed her thoroughly, open-mouthed using his tongue, probing and delicate until she felt her legs giving way and she slipped down on the sand drawing him with her. His breath was coming in rough gasps and she could feel him pressing hard against her. His hand stroked her breasts and he gently lifted off her halter-top pressing her softness to his sunburnt chest. Delicious tremors shot through Alyssa, as she felt the weight of his hard body pressing her against the sand. He tugged at her shorts easing them quickly down over her legs. She fumbled at the stiff buttons of his jeans and he brought his strong hands down to help her.

She felt him heavy and hot against her thighs as he whisked off her panties, tossing them casually onto the rocks. She laughed with him, feeling abandoned and free.

Naked, they lay on the warm white sand as it curved to accept them. Rory gently slipped his hands under her hips and lifted her onto him. He entered her slowly, pushing with determined ardour, his hands under her body, cushioning her. Raising himself, he pushed back her tumbling hair, and kissed her some more, savouring her mouth and fuelling her excitement. The rhythm built up between them, slow at first and then getting faster and faster.

At last she peaked and cried out as waves of ecstasy throbbed through her. She felt Rory spilling inside her, as he held her tightly to him, their sweat and moisture mingling. There was no sound on the beach except the gentle insistence of the waves and the murmured exchanges between Alyssa and Rory. Forever, forever, forever said the sea to Alyssa as she lay cradled in Rory's arms.

She was enchanted by this man, and by this island. Her mouth was bruised and swollen by his kisses. She felt cared for and fulfilled. They lay clasped together, satiated and at ease with arms and legs relaxed around each other, but the sun was sinking and the temperature was cooling.

She silently admitted that she was caught up in an enchantment so binding and so deep that she'd never be able to break the spell. But what did Rory feel about her, apart from the obvious sexual attraction?

CHAPTER TWENTY

Grizelda came to Alyssa in the night. Young, in white bridal clothes, she slipped in through the half-open curtains and perched on Alyssa's bed watching her as she slept. She peered curiously at the young woman, with her rippling auburn hair so similar to her own.

She studied Alyssa's sleeping form, willing her to think kindly of her, to understand what she had been through. There were faint lines of pain etched round Alyssa's sensitive mouth, a reminder that she too had suffered shock and distress.

If only Alyssa could avoid plumbing the depths of sorrow that Grizelda had suffered. She intended to guide Alyssa as she tried to sort out her life and reject Mick's bogus claims. Grizelda rejoiced that Alyssa was drawing closer to Rory, son of her very dear friend, Robert MacDonald. She floated lightly on a wispy ribbon of gauze and took up position at the head of Alyssa's bed.

Grizelda sighed as she thought of how her life had been turned upside down when Fordyce abducted her and Peter on their wedding day. That was the start of how everything had been thrown out of kilter. Somehow she had never been able to put it completely right. It had only got worse after Peter's death. She'd become mistrustful, ungrateful, bossy and angry at life. She realised that now.

Her sigh was like the sound of leaves falling in the breeze. Memories flooded over her, causing her to weep at the loss of her happiness. Why had she failed to appreciate Peter fully? She was ashamed of the times she'd ruthlessly trodden over him as if with heavy hurtful boots. She'd been too much taken up with running the farm and less with the people around her. How could she have overlooked Peter's great love for her? And even worse her great love for him. She had kept it tamped down, fearing to show it. Only seldom had she allowed it to show like bursts of sunlight through the clouds. But at least they had understood their great love for each other in the end. She tried to hold on to that. Now she was left to wander alone in the dimension between the worlds of the living and the dead, searching for her lost happiness and trying to atone for her mistakes. Tears glistened on her cheeks. She had to find Peter again. Had she really lost him? Her soul mate and lover throughout time. She would search unceasingly for him, but she was in desperate need of Alyssa's help if she was to achieve that and be cleansed and free. She shimmered lightly through the room.

'Alyssa,' she whispered in a voice like far-off church bells. 'Alyssa, can you hear me?'

Alyssa stirred and her eyes opened briefly before she squeezed them shut again.

With a billow of silk, Grizelda sat down on the flowery eiderdown, light as a piece of thistledown. Time was running out. Soon the sun would be up and she could no longer hide in the mists of the night, but she had a message to give before dawn crept over the sea and sky.

Her hand moved over Alyssa's face, stroking it gently. The scent of faded roses wafted through the room and once more Alyssa stirred.

197

She sat up abruptly, pushing her heavy hair out of her eyes. 'Grizelda, is it really you? I've longed to meet you. There are so many questions to ask. Did you really leave your house to me? Was that your intention or did you change your mind at the end?'

'I left the house to you,' said Grizelda. 'I didn't know what kind of person you were or even if you would ever come up here to this far off island.' Her voice was breathy and indistinct, rising and falling like soft puffs of wind so that Alyssa had to strain to hear her words.

Grizelda went on. 'My mind was changed for me, when I had no mind. Do you think I would leave anything to Fordyce's spawn? Fordyce McDermott despoiled our wedding day. His son, Mick, tricked me and so did Moira Brodie whom I trusted for so long.' She moved restlessly, with a stirring of silk.

'What shall I do to put things right then?' Alyssa wrinkled her brow. 'Is that what you want of me?'

'Talk to Moira Brodie. Get her to speak and tell the truth.' Grizelda's voice was clearer. 'I cannot leave to join my beloved Peter until my house is in the right hands. You must do this for me, Alyssa. Love Rory, give him your heart. It's the right thing to do. Do this… do this… do this for me…' The words drifted through the soft air as the pink fingers of dawn crept over the landscape.

The echo faded slowly and Grizelda was gone. Alyssa threw off the bedclothes and ran to the window. There was no sign of her ethereal visitor. Had she been dreaming? Or had Grizelda really been there? She felt relaxed and warm as if she had been chatting to a close friend. She pulled back the curtains fully to greet the new day.

First things first. Alyssa hurried from the cottage to catch Rory before he finished his surgery, and before he could leave on his rounds to an outlying farm. She kept her conversation with Grizelda secret. She wasn't sure Rory'd believe her. In the clear light of day she was doubtful herself. Whoever had a visit from their long dead great aunt in the middle of the night? He'd just laugh at her. But the thought didn't deter her from her intention to visit Miss Brodie again to try and uncover some more of the truth, just as Grizelda wished.

Why on earth should Miss Brodie take up with Mick? They seemed a very unlikely pair. If Miss Brodie had been a good friend to Grizelda, why would she set out to change the will? There was no personal gain for her, was there? Of course Mick could have bribed her or paid her in some way, but Alyssa didn't think that the direct and brusque Miss Brodie was one to be bribed. She seemed quite happy with her life. But Mick could have bribed her with offering to pay for inlaid water pipes for example. But it seemed to Alyssa that the brusque and straightforward Miss Brodie would have too much integrity to profit from her friend Grizelda's suffering and illness. No, there was some mystery there. Some other explanation.

The door of the surgery opened and Rory came out together with an old man carrying a striped cat. The cat's tail hung down lifelessly and it seemed to be in a very deep sleep. Rory spoke a few words to the man, and patted him on the shoulder. Then he caught sight of Alyssa and came over to her. He put his hands out and held her by the shoulders looking at her intently.

'I need you as a witness,' said Alyssa.

He looked startled. 'Witness to what?'

Alyssa knew it was truth-telling time for her. She'd have to admit to her heinous crime of taking the letter from Miss Brodie, but she wanted Rory to see the false signatures too, so that it was not only *her* word that would be called into question.

'I've done something so awful, that I hardly dare tell you.' She kept her eyes down.

'What, committed a murder?' Rory smiled and tipped up her chin with one finger. He gave her a quick kiss. 'Out with it then, it can't be so bad.'

Heartened by his action, Alyssa told him about her previous visit to Miss Brodie. 'I've got to put things right,' she said. 'Will you come with me so that you can examine the letter and also see how my great aunt's signature was falsified? I need an independent witness as well as what Dougal has to tell to help prove that other people were involved in the signing of the second will.'

'Meet me down at the ferry at six o'clock this evening, and you can tell me more about it,' said Rory, pulling himself up into the Land Rover and driving off with a quick wave.

*

Rory and Alyssa walked down to the ferry, which would take them over to Miss Brodie's island of Luan. They stood together as Neil, the ferryman, manoeuvred the small craft alongside the jetty. He put out a hand to help Alyssa aboard, while Rory leapt down easily.

'Goodness you're as alike as two drops of water!' Alyssa was struck anew by the similarity between the two men.

'Neil's my second cousin once removed,' Rory said laughing. Alyssa had forgotten the highlanders' complacency of keeping track of family relationships. 'We're all related up here, you know. Maybe we could do with some fresh English blood to strengthen the genes!'

Alyssa turned her face away. Maybe she wasn't English after all, if William Finlay was her father. But she couldn't face searching to find out if he was her true father yet. She pushed aside the thought and let the breeze lift her spirits.

The little motor boat ploughed its way across making the now familiar dip and lurch through the waves. 'Watch out for old Thor.' Rory and Neil spoke in unison, both studying Alyssa's face to see her reaction. But she just laughed and turned her head toward the island.

Although it was still broad daylight, a lantern beamed out a strong light from its high up position on the rocky promontory. Alyssa could see a figure lifting and turning it so that it beamed even farther out over the sea. Was the person there Miss Brodie? Alyssa felt uncomfortable, and her heart pounded with guilt. What was she going to say when they came face to face? She still hadn't dared tell Rory the whole story about the last time she visited Miss Brodie. He didn't know that Grizelda had been there at her elbow, egging her on to take the letter. She was afraid that he would look at her strangely if she told him that she was seeing ghosts.

Safely on the other side of the narrow strait, Alyssa and Rory left Neil and the ferry. Alyssa waved to Neil as he cut a long swathe through the waves on his way back to the other side.

An angry rumbling of voices greeted Alyssa's and Rory's approach as they toiled up the rough path to Miss

Brodie's cottage. Alyssa recognized Mick's voice rising out of the jumble of sound. 'Daft old wumman! What have you told thon English lassie? She's sticking her nose in everywhere.'

Rory put his hand on Alyssa's arm and they stopped short. She felt a sweet languor sweep over her, and suddenly she didn't care what these people were quarrelling about or anything about her surroundings. She leaned against Rory's tall body, relaxing for a moment, but then he moved on with long purposeful strides, pulling her after him.

The voices started up again, and Alyssa recognised Miss Brodie's deep mannish tones. 'Mind your own business, Mick. The girl is Grizelda's great niece. I had to speak to her, and besides she's the looking glass image of Grizelda herself. I felt quite weak when I saw her. There's no doubt she is who she says she is.'

Rory smiled down at Alyssa. 'I don't think Miss Brodie's so bad,' he murmured in her ear.

Miss Brodie's voice sounded again. 'You played a trick on me, Mick. You said Grizelda had no living relatives. That's why I went along with you. I wanted to help Barbara for one thing. And I thought Grizelda would be pleased to find she had a long lost nephew. But you made me cheat the law, and cheat her niece as well. I feel sick about it. How could I betray Grizelda like that? You made me do cruel things. You're a dirty pig, Mick!' The childish expression sounded all the more shocking in Miss Brodie's deep mannish voice.

Alyssa and Rory rounded the last bend of the path. Now they could see the old woman and Mick standing facing each other, like two cockerels spoiling for a fight. Even though the air was warm and balmy, Miss Brodie wore a black sou'wester on her head, her grey hair straggling down on either side of her cheeks. Alyssa thought she looked like a sturdy witch although witches were usually skinny old crones. The old woman swung a large, heavy storm lantern in her hand, while Mick shouted accusations at her. He was no taller than Miss Brodie, but broader and angrier. Miss Brodie's right hand lay across her chest like a protective breastplate warding him off as she cringed away. As Alyssa and Rory watched, Mick took a step closer to the old woman and raised his arm.

'What's going on here?' Rory dropped Alyssa's hand and marched forward. Alyssa's sympathies were with the old woman. She might be as large as an average-sized man, but she was well over seventy. Alyssa sprang up the steps and joined Rory. The seagulls whirled and screamed abuse above their heads, reflecting the mood of the people on the ground.

Miss Brodie seemed relieved to see them. She stepped towards them a half smile on her face. 'Here's Grizelda's niece,' she cried. 'I'm going to tell her the whole story, and you won't stop me, Mick McDermott!'

Mick spun round and saw Alyssa and Rory. His face flushed. 'Here come the reinforcements. Well, you can just turn round and go back to where you've come from. We dinnae need nosey-parkers here.' His voice coarsened and his rough accent was pronounced. 'I hear you've been har-assing this poor old woman,' he accused Alyssa. A fleck of spittle flew out of his mouth and landed on the lapel of his jacket. To Rory, he shouted, 'Get back to your dogs and your sheep and dinnae poke your nose into ma business!'

'What is your business?' Rory said smoothly, folding his arms. 'Doesn't bear looking into too closely, does it?'

Mick barrelled up to Rory pushing his stout chest forward. Rory remained calm. He simply placed one palm on Mick's chest and thrust him away, so that Mick stumbled backwards, tripping over a loose stone. His eyes were bloodshot, probably from knocking back too many whiskies. He was all bluster, no bludgeon like a turkey-cock.

'Well, Mick, if anyone's doing any harassing it's you.' Rory towered above him. 'You can't raise your hand to a woman forty years older than you. You'll be had up for assault.'

Mick's anger made him swell up. Rivulets of sweat snaked down his red face. He turned viciously on Alyssa. 'You're a wee thief,' he accused her once again. 'You stole something from this cottage.'

Alyssa struggled for calm for his anger was contagious. 'What do you mean?' She wasn't going to let herself blurt out anything to Mick, the twister and two-timer. She'd make her peace with Miss Brodie then she and Rory could leave. 'I didn't expect to see you here, Mick. Do you make a habit of visiting old ladies?' She caught Rory's eye and he winked at her. *A strike for you, Great Aunt Grizelda!*

Aloud she said, 'Why did you keep visiting my great aunt in hospital? She didn't know you and by all accounts she didn't want to know you.'

Mick stared at her without answering.

'The lawyer said that she hadn't recognised people for ages and yet you started visiting her regularly. You were only a very distant relative. Only a third cousin twice removed if we're to get it right.' She was affected by the highland need for accuracy on relationships.

'You were never there at all, miss,' said Mick. 'Where were you when your wonderful great aunt was dying?

Dancing about in London night clubs, I suppose.' He laughed sneeringly, his face purple.

'And here's your fine boyfriend, the vet,' he spat out. 'What are you doing here? Haven't you got some cows calving?'

'Just cool it.' Rory took command. 'You're a complete bastard, Mick. It seems you like to lie and cheat poor defenceless women, young or old. We don't need your sort on these islands.'

Miss Brodie had now caught her breath. She turned her back on the group as if disowning it and plodded over to the rocky promontory above the half-cavern of the boiling sea. The waters rose and fell in angry bursts of foam. Above the gurgling hole there was a large rock, painted white, and beside it stood a paint pot and brush. Alyssa watched as Miss Brodie, agile for such a heavy woman, scrambled up to the large post. The old woman stood on the white rocks, and reached up as high as she could to lift down the storm lantern.

'That's for passing yachtsmen,' Rory told her as he came up behind her. He pointed at the lantern. 'It can be seen for miles around and warns unwary skippers that they mustn't tack this way or they'll be taken by the undertow. Miss Brodie keeps it painted.' He smiled reassuringly at the old woman.

Alyssa, busy with her thoughts, moved away from him. She had to speak to Miss Brodie privately. She certainly wasn't going to return the letter to Miss Brodie in front of Mick, but she was bound by Grizelda's entreaties to find out why Mick and Miss Brodie were in cahoots. How on earth had he got this elderly lady to compel her dying friend to make a new will leaving everything to a stranger? Alyssa was a complete stranger too, but she was of the same flesh and blood. Great Aunt Grizelda had been clear headed and decisive when she drew up the original will five years back. And Alyssa was her closest living relative.

Rory moved over to Miss Brodie and spoke to her in low tones as if gentling a horse. 'Perhaps you would like to tell us what really happened. What did Mick make you do? You were Lady Grizelda's friend. Did Mick force you to do something you didn't want to?'

Before the old woman could reply, the cottage door opened and a dark-haired young woman emerged from the gloom of the crumbling cottage. It was Barbara and she looked like an exquisitely-coiffed, young Joan Collins.

How does she do it? Alyssa felt tousled and windblown from the ferry crossing. Barbara must have sailed in the same small windy boat to reach the island, but it'd left no traces on her. It was unlikely that Miss Brodie had anything as modern as a hairdryer in her primitive cottage for Barbara to touch up her curls. Anyway what on earth was Barbara doing here?

Mick blustered in, his sharp elbow connecting with Rory's chest, but Rory didn't flinch. Alyssa saw Mick almost choke with rage. 'You dirty bastard,' he swore at Rory. 'I only brought flowers to a poor lonely old lady, forgotten by her relations.' He stared accusingly at Alyssa.

Miss Brodie came up from behind and gave Mick a sturdy shove. The lantern lay forgotten on its side beside the white painted stone.

'What the devil,' Mick roared, reeling back.

Alyssa stood on the outside of the ring and watched. She was glad she wasn't part of it. They looked like a herd of young bullocks butting each other and testing their strength. Rory stood calmly, unfazed in the middle of the skirmish.

He moved away from them and smiled pleasantly at Barbara. 'We came to talk to Miss Brodie. We didn't expect to find her with so many visitors.' He patted Barbara's arm, and Alyssa felt a pang of jealousy. What really was the relationship between the two? Did Rory really like playing the field, although admittedly it was not a very large one on the island.

'Mick's a good man,' said Barbara, casting a hostile look at Alyssa. 'Why are you trying to make trouble along with this English person? We islanders must stick together, Rory, darling.'

Alyssa watched Rory carefully. She tried to suppress the twinges of jealousy running through her. He didn't react at all to Barbara's endearment. Were they such close friends? How much did he care for Barbara? It was hard to tell. Alyssa swallowed the bitter taste of self-doubt.

'Come on, Mick. Out with the facts! Why did you tow in an outside lawyer to harass Lady Grizelda when she was lying weak and helpless in her bed?' Rory moved closer to Mick. 'Let's get everything straight. Alyssa and I aren't leaving until you tell us.'

'No' me,' said Mick. 'I'm damned well no' clacking wi' you lot.' He set off at a fast pace, his boots clinking against the stones of the path. Suddenly he pitched forward cursing viciously. Miss Brodie's fat grey tabby cat sprang out from under his prone figure, yowling furiously. It recovered itself quickly and, raising its tail like a flagstaff, stalked away.

Mick's arms and legs were flailing. It was hard for him to raise his stout well-fed body. Alyssa began to laugh partly from nerves and partly because of the farce-like situation.

Rory turned swiftly away from the door of the cottage and ran lightly down the path to Mick as he seemed unable to get off his knees. Rory hauled him up to his feet like a flaccid sack of potatoes. Mick stood there for a moment, swaying like a beleaguered ship. Then at the sound of the ferry's horn he jerked his arm from Rory's grasp and plunged back down the path.

Alyssa watched his progress down to the jetty and saw him scramble onboard the small craft, rocking it alarmingly. Then it backed out again and Mick was transported away.

The evening sky was darkening, and the sun was covered by black shrouds of clouds. Soon heavy raindrops began falling like hissing gobs of acid.

Rory walked up to the little group, left standing after Mick's departure. 'Perhaps we could all go inside and discuss what really happened to Lady Grizelda,' he said, taking command. He ushered Miss Brodie in front of him and stood waiting at the door for Alyssa and Barbara to go inside as well.

Alyssa hung back. She didn't know if she could stand the stifling air of the cottage, but Rory urged her forward.

Inside, Barbara snuggled up close to Rory on the green sofa. He didn't reject her closeness. A fire was burning in the grate despite the earlier heat of the day. Alyssa felt trapped as the light faded inside the cottage. She knew she would have to confess to Miss Brodie her crime of purloining the letter, but she was not going to do so under Barbara's supercilious gaze.

Rory stretched out his arms along the back of the sofa, spreading a confident benevolence over the room.

Miss Brodie had taken off her sou'wester and hung it on a hook by the door. Her grey hair sprang up in a bushy halo, making her appear more friendly, less threatening.

'Could I make some tea,' Alyssa was unable to sit still. Then she wondered if she'd done the right thing. She didn't know Miss Brodie well enough to start poking about in her kitchen and serving cups of tea to the assembled party.

Miss Brodie sat slumped down on her rocking chair, which began to rock violently under her weight. She lifted her head, a relieved look on her face. 'Please do, dear. The kettle's filled and ready to boil.' She looked flushed and exhausted, reminding Alyssa that this was an elderly woman despite her size and strength.

Out in the kitchen Alyssa began opening and shutting the cupboards to find cups and saucers. Miss Brodie had some surprisingly beautiful china, she noticed. Wedgwood, and some lovely Royal Doulton with blue and purple thistles on a delicate white background.

She was picking some shiny silver teaspoons out of the drawer of the old kitchen dresser to place on the saucers when a dark shadow loomed in the doorway. It was Miss Brodie. She looked flustered and hot, and cleared her throat with a mannish harrumph.

'I have something to confess to you.' She pushed the kitchen door shut, so that Alyssa was trapped alone with her. 'I can see you're a very decent girl,' she continued.

Alyssa felt herself flush. Her feeling of guilt increased. She put down the cup and saucer she was holding.

'That's just it,' said Miss Brodie. 'These cups and saucers…'

A voice from nowhere whispered in Alyssa's ear. '…*are mine.*'

The now familiar white mist began slipping over Alyssa, and she fought to resist it. Great Aunt Grizelda was trying to take over again. Alyssa refused to let herself be overwhelmed. She pushed away from the kitchen dresser and turned to Miss Brodie.

'What are you trying to tell me?' she asked, shaking her head and trying to block out the echo of the voice repeating '*...are mine ...are mine.*'

Miss Brodie stepped closer and looked Alyssa squarely in the face. 'These cups and saucers are really yours. And so is the silver. Mick said I should take it all. And I thought that since my sister's child is getting married, she would like to have the tea-set. There was no one left in Grizel's family. At least that's what I believed. I'm sorry.' She swallowed and seemed to be struggling to say more.

Alyssa waited. She didn't feel too happy herself.

'I took them because I thought my niece would care for them and appreciate them. Grizelda was my dear friend and I was very fond of her. She didn't need the china any more,' said Miss Brodie. 'She'd retreated into her own world and she didn't know what was going on around her. She'd no idea she was signing a will. She'd no idea whether it was morning or midnight. Poor lonely soul.'

Alyssa put her hand on Miss Brodie's arm. She looked into the tired, sad eyes of the older woman.

'I believe you,' she said. 'You thought my great aunt was alone in the world. And in a way she had left this world even before she died.'

'Yes, yes,' Miss Brodie nodded vigorously, grey strands of hair obscuring her face. 'That's why I was so happy when Mick McDermott appeared. I thought that here at last is a blood relative to care for her. Though I don't think she ever understood who he was. He was just someone that appeared and was forgotten as soon as he left. I should never have meddled and gone along with Mick's plan.' Her eyes were shining as she fought to repress her tears. She looked so guilty that Alyssa couldn't bear any more and rushed to stop her.

'Of course, I understand,' she soothed. 'I'm glad some- one bothered about her in the end, for I know she was very lonely.' Her guilt at taking the letter made it hard for her to meet Miss Brodie's eyes. With an unsteady laugh she said: 'And I have something to tell you. I took a letter from you... I needed it for proof. I'm so ashamed.' And the story all came tumbling out. By the end of it, both Alyssa and Miss Brodie were weeping and apologising to each other.

A tip-tupping of sharp heels crossed the stone floor outside the kitchen door. Barbara pulled it open, her eyes scanning Miss Brodie and Alyssa accusingly.

'Come on, Aunt Moira. We're still waiting for the tea,' she said in a condescending tone as if they were her serv- ants. 'You haven't even put the kettle on.'

'Barbara's your niece?' Alyssa was stunned.

'Yes, indeed,' Miss Brodie smiled at Barbara and turned to put more plates on the tea tray.

Rory appeared behind her. 'We'd better get back be- cause it's blowing up a storm. Neil may have to moor the ferry for a time and then we'll be stuck here unless you want to swim.'

Stuck on this island with Miss Brodie and Barbara, aunt and niece, even though Rory would be there too. No thanks! Forgetting the tea, Alyssa almost babbled her fare- wells. Stopping only to give Miss Brodie a quick hug, she ran down the path to the ferry. Old Thor or no, she was getting back to the main island.

Chapter Twenty-One

Alyssa stood at the large picture window in her sitting room at the cottage. Outside the landscape was grey and weeping. Sea and sky met, dissolving into colourless eternity.

The landscape reflected her sombre mood, but she decided it would be a good day to clean and tidy the cottage. She got out the small vacuum cleaner and started pushing it around the sitting room as thoughts of Grizelda still buzzed around in her head. She didn't know how she was going to break free from Grizelda and her insistent demands. She wished she would leave her alone.

After washing the wooden floor in the kitchen, Alyssa decided it was time to speak to Graham Shaw, in Oban. She was dying to tell him what progress she had made both with Dougal, the porter, and with Miss Brodie. Rory had been a big help there. She smiled as she remembered how he'd tackled Mick, but she mustn't allow her strong feelings for him to knock her off balance.

The rain was still sheeting down outside as she fumbled in the cupboard looking for some rubber Wellingtons. After scrabbling around for some time she found she was out of luck. That meant she'd just have to make do with her heaviest shoes. She didn't even have a proper waterproof so she pulled on her light cotton raincoat as her only protection.

She felt in her pocket to make sure she had enough small change for her call to Graham Shaw on the public telephone. As usual her mobile phone showed the frustrating message that her phone was 'out of range'.

The weeping skies didn't steal away her determination that after she had spoken to the lawyer, she would return to *her* house and stake her claim to her territory once more.

She heard the light toot of a horn outside the cottage and ran to the door. As if in answer to her thoughts, Rory got out of the Land Rover and strode up the path. He carried some oilskins and a pair of rubber boots as well as a black sou'wester.

Alyssa's heart turned over. He looked so good. So much for her control over herself in regard to him. He followed her into the house.

'I thought you'd need these if you're going out today.' He gave her a quick kiss on the cheek. 'I don't suppose you've anything like these in your London wardrobe!'

Alyssa smiled at him, feeling her spirits lift at his thoughtfulness. 'Well I really am going native. I'll look exactly like Miss Brodie if I pull the sou'wester down far enough.' She perched it on her curls and twirled in front of the mirror in the small entrance hall.

Rory laughed. 'You'll have to put on at least thirty pounds before you reach her size!'

'I'm going up to *my* house today, to stake *my* claim.' She shrugged herself into the oilskin jacket. 'So thanks for the loan. These'll really keep me dry. I like the exclusive scent too.' She wrinkled her nose as she sniffed at the jacket.

'Good country scents, probably from the last lambing.' Rory smiled at her. 'Well, there's two cows due to calve any minute up on the other side of the island, so I must get

213

off. So you know I'm making a sacrifice by lending you these!'

'I'll have to get my own soon so you can get all these back. That is if I decide to stay here.' She bit her lip. Now she was wavering again. It was so hard to make a decision. She couldn't stay here indefinitely without a job, however comfortable and at ease she felt among her new friends on the island.

'I should have come with you up to Balvaig House, because of old Alastair,' said Rory. 'But as I drove past I saw the caravan had gone from behind the house. Presumably old Alastair and his dog have gone too.'

'Who is old Alastair? What right had he to set his dog on me?' Alyssa found herself shaking with fury.

'Mick has been extorting money from him for a grazing lease on the land. He keeps a few sheep there,' Rory explained. 'He seems to think it gives him the right to chase people off his territory.'

'Well, thank God he's not there at the moment. I hope he stays away for good.'

Rory walked out of the door and drove off waving his hand.

Alyssa looked out of the window, her eyes following the Land Rover as it wound its way up the hill. She tried her mobile phone for the umpteenth time, but once again got the depressing message that it was out of range.

Pulling on the oilskin jacket and trousers, she studied her all-black reflection in the mirror, and laughed. Banging the cottage door behind her she set out to walk up to the red telephone box outside the grocery store. The wet green leaves of the trees alongside the road hung low and heavy in the downpour, but the air smelt citrus-fresh and sharp.

214

In the old telephone box, Alyssa put in her money and dialled Graham Shaw's number. As she waited to be put through to him she pictured him sitting behind his huge desk, sharply dressed, just like the men in her old life in London. Although she thought he was a little tweedier than the men in her fast-paced London circle.

'I've found some people who are prepared to testify about my Great Aunt's state of mind at the time of her death.' Alyssa didn't beat about the bush. 'I'm not letting Mick McDermott get away with it. I'm convinced Great Aunt Grizelda wouldn't want that. How could she? Mick's father completely ruined her wedding by snatching her away in the middle of it all.'

'I quite agree,' Graham's warm tones came over the telephone line. 'I've some news for you too. I took a trip up to the hospital and confronted the doctor who attended Lady Grizelda during her last months. I pressed him to explain how much she understood of what was going on around her. Was she capable of signing a new will? I said to him that it appeared the hospital had been negligent in allowing a strange lawyer into the ward without the consent of the proper nursing staff. As I expected, he cracked under pressure and went back on his statement.'

'What great news! You must have pressed him hard,' said Alyssa, excitement rising in her.

'Well, the truth is he couldn't be bothered to argue any more,' said Graham. 'Not after I talked to one of the nurses as well. She told me she knew your great aunt well and insisted that Lady Grizelda was confused most of the time. Now the doctor's retracted his former statement and he admits that your great aunt only had occasional lucid spells.'

Alyssa felt some of the tension slipping from her shoulders. Perhaps things would begin to turn her way and Great Aunt Grizelda's wishes could be fulfilled.

'Things are coming together,' said Graham. 'After what you told me, I should be able to get statements from the nurses, Dougal, the porter, and from the doctor himself saying that Lady Grizelda was in an unfit state to sign a new will. I believe McDermott's case will crumble. We won't even have to take him to court.'

'So the house will be mine? That'll be the next dilemma. Whether I should stay here in the highlands or return to London.' Alyssa sighed.

'The choice is easy,' Graham said. 'What would you want to go back to London for?'

'Good question. Anyway I thought I'd walk up to the house now,' Alyssa said, 'I've hardly had a chance to look around. There are all sorts of things to be decided. Should I stay and fight? That means looking at the holes in the roof, or should I go back to London? I have to get a feel of the future. It's all so up in the air.'

Graham laughed. 'Well it's just the right sort of day for testing the holes in the roof. Good luck!'

It was perhaps not the best day to visit Balvaig House. Her Balvaig House! Alyssa felt a surge of exhilaration as she trudged along in her borrowed boots through the sluicing rain looking at the wild flowers which had bravely opened their brightly-coloured faces to the life-giving water.

With a slight shiver, she trudged up to the ramshackle gate which no one had bothered to pick up. She hoped the black dog had truly gone, and wasn't hiding, lying in wait for her. Perhaps she was foolhardy to come, but she had to face up to her fears.

She looked cautiously around her. There was no sign of the battered, red caravan. At the front door of the house she took the big key ring out of her pocket, ready to nip inside should old Alastair and his companion appear from nowhere. But all was quiet.

She struggled with the key for a moment or two as it refused to turn under her fingers. Suddenly the door swung open, and banged against the wall, although the key hadn't budged. Alyssa pitched clumsily over the threshold. Funny! Could she have forgotten to lock it last time she was here?

The interior of the house was dim, and Alyssa stretched out her hand, automatically searching for an electric light switch. How stupid, of course there were none. That was another big expense to add to her list of calculations, water, electricity and, of course, a telephone if she were to get connected to the outside world.

She strained her ears, just catching a sliver of sound upstairs. Was it only her imagination? Or mice? She shuddered at the thought.

Steeling herself, she started towards the staircase. The house was silent as if holding its breath. The hush fell around her like cobwebs and held her still so that her feet refused to move towards the stairs.

Is Grizelda up to her tricks again? Is that why I feel rooted to the spot? I must manage on my own. I must stop her taking possession of me, or I'll never get my life back again. Alyssa gritted her teeth. She made a great effort to block Grizelda out.

Something seemed to slip away into a corner. An unexpected scent of roses wafted toward her and became so strong it almost choked her. But the chill that had immobilised her shifted suddenly, and the unseen chains that bound her released their hold.

She whipped the black sou'wester off her hair and let it drop to the ground. She ran up the stairs before her fears took hold. She'd open the windows, even if she had to knock down some of the boards. She'd let out the past. Wasn't that what one was supposed to do when a person died? She would release Grizelda's spirit to let it move on to a better life. She wouldn't let the sheeting rain stop her.

Then she froze. There was a rustle of paper. Then a deep cough. She heard somebody opening and shutting drawers in the bedroom. The lingering scent of roses was gone, smothered by the smell of burnt coal, mingled with a faint whiff of moth balls and musty papers. The odour of an unloved house. The acrid smell of cigarette smoke crept into her nostrils. Slightly sickened, she crept close to the wall, her rubber boots making no sound. Her heart skipped a beat as a loose floorboard creaked under her foot. Her ribs seemed to grow tight and constrict her breathing. Friendliness had slipped out of the house. Even the misty presence of Grizelda was no longer in the background. Now Alyssa regretted chasing her away.

The house leaned forward and listened with Alyssa. She took a deep breath and tip-toed onwards. A chair scraped across the floor in the bedroom, and the scrabbling sound came again.

The rain outside streamed down relentlessly, darkening the one unboarded window, the raindrops making slipping shadows on the dusty pane. Through the broken boards of the upper window she could hear water splashing down a broken drainpipe.

Now the stench of cigarette was unmistakable. She fingered the key in her pocket. No one else had a key, did they? Graham Shaw had been adamant about that. Hadn't he told her that he'd refused to give the keys to anyone but her?

A man coughed, and she fell back, the blood pounding until it hurt in her ears. An intruder in her house! On a rush of adrenaline she burst into the master bedroom.

Someone had dragged out an old chest from under the bed. The heavy lid was thrown back and a stack of old letters lay strewn in a heap round his feet, some of them marked by his careless footprints. The musty smell in the room made Alyssa choke.

'Mick!' She exhaled in relief that it was someone she knew, even though he was her least favourite person. 'How did you get in here? Have you got a key?'

He turned slowly towards her, his face dark and unreadable.

'What are you doing here?' she demanded again. 'This is my house, my property and, not least, my wooden chest. What are you looking for anyway?'

She stepped forward. At the bottom of the chest lay a bedraggled wedding wreath of white artificial flowers. Under the wreath, half concealed by its wrapping of yellowed tissue paper was an elaborate wedding dress which must at one time been white. Scattered over the dress lay some fuzzy black and white photographs which Mick's clumsy hands had allowed to fall out of an old, yellow Kodak folder.

Mick maintained a strange calm, his eyes slithering avidly over Alyssa. 'Well, if it's no' ma wee cousin, Aleesie! I didnae expect you out in this weather. A nice English girl like you, doesnae want to get her feet wet. But since you're here we can have a wee chat.'

'Chat!' exclaimed Alyssa. 'You can chat to the lawyer and tell him how you tricked a poor helpless old woman. And while we're at it: what gives you the right to allow that vicious old Alastair to stay on my land – and extort money from him?'

Mick didn't seem to react to her accusations except for a livid flush that rose slowly up his neck. He strode over to Alyssa putting his body close to hers. She was forced to step back until she found herself pinned against the wall.

'Ma wee cousin,' he repeated, putting his hands on either side of her head against the wall, caging her like a bird. His breathing was getting faster.

Alyssa turned her head away helplessly. His sour breath and the heat of his body made her want to retch. Why had she come here alone? What was she trying to prove? She felt trapped and helpless, sure that nobody could see what was wrong from the outside. Even the MacDonalds next door were too far away to hear her scream. No electricity in this old house meant no telltale lights could be switched on as a beacon. She hadn't even seen Mick's car parked outside. There were no signs to show that anyone was here at all.

'Rory, Rory, help me!' she called silently, willing him to hear her.

Mick backed off for a moment, laughing in a silent fashion. 'You weren't scared, were you, Aleesie?' he jeered. 'No' of your big cousin, Mick?'

Alyssa swallowed as her throat had gone dry. She tried to peer past Mick to see how far it was to the doorway.

'Oh, we're no' done yet.' Mick closed in on her again, his broad body cutting off her escape. 'We could play some nice games, just you and me and nobody any the wiser.'

Was Mick waiting for her to make a run for it? Did he see himself as the cruel predator and her, the rabbit. She tried to stop breathing and make herself as small as possible. The only sound in the room was Mick's own excited breathing, and the dismal swishing of the rain outside.

If she stayed silent and still, perhaps Mick wouldn't be stirred into action. She mustn't give him proof of her fear. That might fuel his excitement even more. His eyes continued to flick over her, and the red tip of his tongue slipped out to lick his lips.

She waited, Mick waited and the old house waited. Time lagged, but Alyssa's thoughts were racing. How long could she stand this situation before he made a move? Could she be sure she was handling him right?

Anger spurted in her, but she tamped it down, trying to keep her thoughts clear. In truth Mick had raped her all along. Even if he hadn't actually carried out the physical act, he intended to rape her of her inheritance. His father had raped Grizelda of her wedding and now Mick was preparing to assault Alyssa herself. She had to hold him back or Mick's most triumphant act would be to rape her physically.

'Grizelda,' she called soundlessly in her mind. 'I've tried to put things right for you, now it's your turn to help me. Come back, I'm sorry I tried to push you away.' Her attempts to release herself from the bonds between her and Grizelda hadn't been such a good idea after all.

A blanket of hush fell over the room. Mick's hands smoothed up and down his body, as he clenched and unclenched his fists. He was as aroused as an enraged bull, penned too long, unpredictable and violent.

Alyssa moved slowly sideways. She and Mick began to circle each other in a travesty of a mating dance.

'Grizelda, Rory!' she cried out loud, desperately. 'Come and help me now or it'll be too late.'

Just beyond her vision she sensed something move, but Mick's clammy hand was heavy on her arm. He pressed her forcibly against the wall with his body, while his other hand fumbled with her flimsy blouse and ripped it open, scattering the buttons.

She ducked and wrenched herself free, flinging herself out of the room and down the stairs. As Mick stumbled and cursed behind her, her foot caught on the last stair tread and she pitched hard forward at the bottom.

'Grizelda,' she screamed as she fell. 'Where are you?' Black mothlike shadows fluttered nearer as Mick's heavy boots clumped down beside her. His hands reached out to grab her.

The front door burst open with a spatter of rain. The tall figure of Rory stood there. He took one look at Alyssa lying spread-eagled on the ground, with Mick hunched over her. In two strides Rory was on him, pulling Mick's heavy body away from Alyssa.

He grasped Mick's arms from behind and frog-marched him like a sprawling doll out of the house.

Trembling and shaking, Alyssa hauled herself up onto the lowest step of the stairs and sank down, her head between her knees for a moment. Then raising her head again she saw through the wide-open door that Mick had torn himself free from Rory's hold, and landed a vicious punch in Rory's face. Then he rushed out of the gate. A string of curses poured from his lips as he ran.

Rory came back into the house, rubbing the side of his face, which was already beginning to swell. 'Are you hurt, Alyssa?' His arms clasped her strongly. She shook her head as the house swirled around her and she concentrated hard on not being sick.

Gradually she gathered strength from Rory's nearness and warmth. A shudder passed through her as she thought of what could've happened. Another wave of nausea swept over her and she began to shiver.

'Are you hurt?' Rory persisted.

'No, no I'm fine.' Alyssa forced the words out between tight lips. 'But if you hadn't come along just at this minute, I don't know what would've happened. He was trying to rape me. Oh God!'

Rory's arms pressed her closely to his chest and his hand smoothed her tumbled hair. He pressed feather kisses down her cheek.

Alyssa stopped him for a minute before he completely overwhelmed her. Holding his gaze she asked, 'How did you know to come and rescue me just in time? Did you hear something from your house?'

Rory pulled her against him again, clasping her hand closely in his. 'No, I didn't. But it's all very strange.' He looked deep into her eyes, and hesitated. 'I don't know if you'll believe it, but when I got back home from the farm, the phone rang in an odd dissonant way. At first I thought it was the heavy rain that'd affected the lines, but when I answered the call, a faint voice kept calling your name. *Alyssa, Alyssa.* Then it got stronger and quite clearly it said: *Alyssa needs you.*'

'How strange.' Alyssa wrinkled her forehead. 'Could it have been Grizelda?' She stopped short, nearly biting off her tongue because she hadn't meant to tell Rory about her visions of Grizelda. She was so afraid he'd think she was crazy.

Rory gathered her closer in his arms. He appeared to be considering his words. 'Was it a man or a woman?' Alyssa questioned, trying to cover up her slip.

'It was a kind of techno-voice like when you've dialled a non-existent number.' Rory spoke slowly. 'Like an electronic voice repeating a message. I knew something was very wrong. Something inside me told me that I should rush up to this house and see what was happening.' He squeezed her hand tightly. 'I'd never have forgiven myself if something had happened to you.' His voice was so low that Alyssa had to strain to hear him.

Her heartbeat speeded up at the full implication of his words. She paused and then in a rush of emotion she determined to trust him. How could she conceal anything from him when he had saved her from Mick. 'It must have been Grizelda,' she said.

Rory looked at her in amazement. 'Grizelda, your great aunt? But she's been dead for months. How could she have phoned?'

Alyssa looked at him and snuggled closer. 'Can you believe me, Rory? Grizelda is very close to me, and she's been appearing to me over the past weeks. She's told me a lot about what happened in the past. It's as if she can't rest until she's told her story.'

Alyssa waited. She gazed at Rory, trying to read his expression. She willed him to believe her. Gently he stroked her hair and pulled her into his lap. 'We who live on this island have always believed in the links between the living and the dead,' he said slowly. 'And in other links too. Sometimes I feel a close bond between me and the animals I treat, almost as if they try to tell me what's wrong with them. Or where it hurts.'

Alyssa clutched his knee as she sagged with relief. He understood her. He didn't think she was mad. Yet there had been moments when she'd doubted her own sanity.

Rory looked at her again. 'It's okay. Most of us on the island do believe in the supernatural. Some of us have the second sight. It's all part of our everyday life. I just didn't expect it of you, straight from the London rat race.'

Not again! Alyssa pulled away from him, her nerves raw. How could he say that? It meant that he still branded her as a townie. Would he never accept her? Her family like his, came from the Island of Mora for generations back. Twice over, if she was to accept that William Finlay, the younger, was her father. Blinking back hot tears of anger, she turned away from him and pulled the heavy key-ring out of her pocket. This time she'd make sure the door was locked. Now all she wanted to do was to get back to her little cottage, crawl into bed and forget the whole affair. Rory could go and hang!

A gamut of confused emotions rushed through her. Perhaps she was over-reacting but his words accusing her of being an outsider wounded her to the quick. She was behaving childishly, but her common sense had flown out of the window as a result of her extreme fright.

Rory seized her arm. But she pushed him from her. 'Leave me alone!' She wriggled free of him. 'I need to get back to the cottage.'

'I'll take you back. You can't walk down the road alone.'

'No, no.' She knew what would happen. She wouldn't be able to resist tumbling into Rory's arms. She longed to seek oblivion there, but she'd made such a fool of herself. A ringing silence stretched between them.

She pushed him away and started down the garden path, stumbling unsteadily as if she were drunk.

Rory stood watching her as she placed her feet like an automaton, one in front of the other. Blind determination kept her moving along. After some minutes of walking she began to inhale the soft clean air. The breeze against her cheek calmed and soothed her. Even though her legs were still shaky, she pressed on. She was just walking down the last slope of the road when she found she had company. The ginger collie was tracking her footsteps. As she turned, he ran up to her and put his nose in her hand. He wagged his tail and gazed at her with adoring brown eyes.

She bent down to hug him. 'You, at least, understand that I belong here,' she told him. London seemed so far away. Now she knew she'd never be able to fit in there again. It would be so hard to put on tights and high-heeled shoes when she had been living in shorts and jeans and wellington boots for so long. She loved the feel of the fresh damp air on her face, more effective than any moisturiser.

She couldn't face the thought of sitting stifled at dinner parties, searching for quick repartee and trying to pretend she was enjoying herself. Discussions of other people's divorces and how some people seemed to relish other people's misfortunes seemed pointless and cruel. She was glad she no longer needed to be involved with any of that. Glad that she wouldn't need to fight to get onto the London underground, or be caught in lengthy traffic snarls.

How could she have thought that two-timing Jeff was her soul mate? Thank God she'd sussed him out in time, and broken away from him. Never again would she spend hours in over-heated premises with a group of stressed-out business people, inhaling recycled air which would give her a headache.

Maybe she'd enjoyed going to the theatre and some of the West End shows, but she'd rather take part in a wild highland ceilidh any day.

Tomorrow she'd show Rory, just show him! She was a real highlander capable of facing up to anything. It seemed that she truly was William Finlay's daughter. But what a fool she'd been, to be so touchy, when Rory had rescued her from Mick's clutches. She lifted her hands to her face and groaned. If only she hadn't driven Rory off. She lifted the latch of the cottage gate and Ginger pushed through in front of her. He bounded up to the door, and stood wagging his tale waiting for her to open it.

Tomorrow, Alyssa promised herself, she'd make her peace with Rory. Tomorrow she'd make a fresh start.

CHAPTER TWENTY-TWO

Alyssa tossed and turned all night, thinking of Rory, the unresolved wills and her own position on the island. And always back to Rory. Rory, Rory, Rory, like a hum of bees. She wished she could drum him out of her thoughts, yet she longed to feel his arms around her again like that day on the beach. She lay for a moment reliving the pleasurable memory. Her thoughts brought Rory so close that she stretched out her arm and felt the space in the bed beside her. Her hand connected with a warm furry body. Ginger! He'd jumped up onto her bed as she slept. She pushed back the blankets and disturbed Ginger. He stretched and yawned, his tail thumping happily. Then he sprang up and almost knocked her flat on the bed again as he licked her face with boisterous affection.

She was glad of the distraction which blotted out her thoughts of Mick's frightening onslaught and her stupid quarrel with Rory yesterday. Her cheeks grew hot with shame as she remembered how she'd stalked off from him like a spoiled three-year-old after he'd rescued her from Mick's clutches. God knows what would have happened if Rory, guided by Grizelda, hadn't arrived in time. In fact she'd behaved in a very similar way to Great Aunt Grizelda in her fear of letting people get too close to her.

Pushing Ginger down onto the floor, Alyssa went into the bathroom and took a quick shower. She tried to clear her head. As she towelled herself dry, she became aware of an emptiness in the room. Grizelda wasn't there!

The ever-present shadow at the back of her consciousness was missing. How strange! Had Grizelda really left her? Was it a relief or not? Contrarily she now missed Grizelda's misty presence.

After breakfast, Alyssa pulled out her laptop which she hadn't touched since she arrived on the island. She put it on the small table in the sitting room and borrowed the wooden stool from the kitchen. As she perched on the small stool, her mind was sparking with a stream of ideas. What the Island of Mora needed was to be well and truly connected to the Internet if it were to move with the times.

She would work toward that aim. If she set up classes in the village hall she could train some of the islanders in computer skills and how to use the Internet. She'd be able to use her IT skills that she'd spent so many years acquiring. What a great starting point to help her to find her place in the island community. She could write articles too because over the Internet she could send them to suitable magazines or journals. But first of all she'd need to get hooked up to a telephone line.

Her fingers pounded the keyboard as she composed some letters to her friends and connections in London. What a hassle it was to be without an email connection. Now she'd have to find paper, a printer, envelopes and stamps. At least she had a small stock of paper and her portable printer but would it stand up to the sudden extra flurry of activity? She could send her letter over the antiquated fax machine behind the counter of the post office? That was a quicker and less cumbersome way than the ordinary post.

She worked swiftly, fired up with a sense of purpose, and closing her mind to shadows and movements. She shut her ears too. No strains of haunting music were going to slip past her guard. *Grizelda, you're not going to disturb me today*. Soon she had printed out a pile of letters ready to be faxed from the Post Office.

She flexed her fingers and stretched her aching shoulders. She looked at her watch. One o'clock in the afternoon. She'd been working for four hours. But she felt good, as if a burden had been lifted off her shoulders. And she would forget the supernatural.

In one of the island's lightning changes of mood, the rain had slowed to a light drizzle and the sun broke through again, its rays catching the raindrops and scattering slashes of rainbow colours across the grassy banks alongside the road.

Alyssa shrugged on a jacket. She and Ginger set off down the road to the Post Office. As she fingered her letters in her pocket she discovered her ancient Walkman. Pulling it out, she clamped the earpiece to her head and tramped down the road to a rousing rendition of Scottish pipe bands. Ginger followed at her heels, tail aplume.

She still hadn't felt Grizelda's presence. Perhaps the Walkman was an effective way to exclude her, if she should be hovering about. Alyssa continued to stride along, swinging her arms in time to the music, like a kilted highlander warrior. The rousing music lifted her spirits, but as she marched along, a thought struck her. She was behaving like a typical Londoner, using the Walkman to block out other sounds, even the beautiful sounds of living nature. Rory would've laughed scornfully if he'd seen her. She pulled out the earpiece and switched off the cassette. She shoved the Walkman back in her pocket and listened to the peewits calling to each other across the fields.

Two cars swept past her and Ginger. 'Traffic's heavy today!' Alyssa told Ginger flippantly as she pulled him into the side of the road.

They began to climb up the slope. Alyssa strained her eyes managing to make out in the distance the contours of a horse led by a small man. Could it be Davy? Alyssa waved at him as he approached holding the reins of a young colt which was dancing nervously around him.

With a loud roar and amid a swirl of dust, a large white van hurtled past her and Ginger, filling the whole road. She jumped back hastily and scrambled up the grassy bank, dragging the dog by his collar.

The van lurched on swaying from side to side on the road. Alyssa's hand flew to her mouth as the vehicle bore down on Davy and the horse.

She leapt down the bank and rushed down the road. 'Stop, stop!' Her desperate cry rang through the quiet fields. At the last minute the van swerved wildly away from the horse. With a grinding of metal, its two left wheels sank down on the crumbling shoulder of the road and it came to a shuddering halt.

Alyssa ran toward the stricken van, Ginger at her heels. Davy and the young horse lay collapsed in a tangle of legs and branches where a group of birch saplings had broken their fall. As Alyssa watched, the terrified horse made a great effort and lunged to its feet. Davy lay still and white-faced with his eyes closed.

Heedless of the van and its driver, Alyssa rushed down to Davy's side. 'Are you hurt?' Anxiously her hands felt along his limbs.

He opened his eyes and stirred slowly. With Alyssa's help, he pulled himself to his feet and steadied himself on a branch of one of the trees. 'I'm just fine, lass. It's the colt I'm worried about.' He reached out his hand and ran it along the colt's brown coat, which was now stained with rivulets of sweat. The animal stood trembling, its liquid amber eyes showing flashes of white. It was resting a foreleg as if in pain.

'Where's thon divil of a driver?' Davy's eyes sparked fire. 'I'll gie him something to remember.' The small man looked fierce and threatening as Alyssa tried to pull him out of the undergrowth, but he writhed away from her and went back to the colt.

'Thon bastard's damaged the colt, driving like *An Diabhul* himself on these roads.' Davy spoke through his teeth in controlled fury. The birch trees behind him shivered and rustled, heralding the arrival of a large creature. To Alyssa's dismay, Mick emerged from under the branches. He slithered heavily down towards them. His big boots clanged on the stones as he forced his way through the saplings. His jacket caught on a branch, which held him back for a moment until he broke it off the tree.

'You, of course!' Alyssa was resigned. Always he dogged her footsteps, bringing in his wake insurmountable problems and bad luck. Now his face was white and his eyes staring with fright. 'I didnae mean to hit you,' he said hoarsely to Davy. ''Twas thon woman. She was all over the place like a piece of mist. I couldnae see because of her.' He looked fearfully over his shoulder.

'What woman?' Alyssa tried to keep calm to avoid stirring Mick into one of his rages.

'Thon will-o'-the-wisp, did ye no see her?' Mick fumbled in his pocket and brought out a large checked handkerchief to mop the drops of sweat from his brow. He was still panting heavily, an unpleasant reminder to Alyssa of how he'd held her pinioned against the wall of the bedroom in Balvaig House yesterday.

'Did you see a woman, Davy?' Alyssa turned to the old man.

'I did not. Thon eejit's had one too many.' Davy scanned Mick contemptuously and his voice was unforgiving.

'She was there I tell you. Ye must've seen her.' Mick grabbed Alyssa's arm and shook it in his efforts to convince her.

'I only saw your dangerous driving.' Alyssa tried to free herself from Mick's fumbling hold. His whisky-fumed breath made her choke. 'You could have killed Davy and now you've probably injured the colt's leg.'

Mick didn't seem to have heard. 'Did you no see her? She was here! She was like white cobwebs all over the place. I didnae want tae run her down.' He cursed fluently. 'I niver saw Davy and the colt. You've got to believe me, Aleesie!' Shivers were passing through his broad heavy body. I niver meant to steal from you, Aleesie. You've got to believe me.' His tongue seemed to have loosened as Alyssa gazed at his scared and crumpled face, so unlike the bold, blustering Mick of yesterday.

'I didnae mean tae cheat you. I didnae ken aboot ye. Me and Miss Brodie never meant to cheat you.' His words came tumbling out in a stream of excuses.

In a quick-witted reaction, Alyssa felt through her pocket for her Walkman. She tore off the security tab of the cassette and fitting it back into the recorder, she began to pick up Mick's words. He was oblivious to her actions. Fear made him garrulous and the story poured out of him as the cassette spun round and Alyssa recorded his words about how he'd visited Grizelda in hospital and got her to sign the second will. 'I thocht I was the only relative. Ye should've come before. It's all your fault, Aleesie. I niver meant to cheat you. I brought the old lady flowers every week. Big expensive flowers. She owed me for that.'

Alyssa continued to hold the Walkman close to Mick to catch all his words. If she were lucky the recording of his confession would help her to prove her case to the lawyers. Undaunted by the spinning cassette, Mick carried on speaking. 'What does a fine London lady like you want with an old rundown house in Scotland? You dinnae need it. You dinnae belong here. While I've got a wife and bairns to think about.' His fleshy lips formed a rictus of an ingratiating smile. Then he sat down with a thump on a nearby rock, his body slumped over like a shapeless potato sack. The torrent of slimy self-justification ceased.

Alyssa was concentrating so hard on Mick that she scarcely noticed Davy had vanished. Then she saw he had climbed up to the roadside and was waving both his arms.

The familiar Land Rover drew to a halt. Alyssa's heart tried to leap out of her ribcage, and an embarrassed flush rose in her cheeks as Rory jumped down from the vehicle. He strode down to the little group by the birch trees. His first glance was at Alyssa. 'What's happened here? Are you all right?' He took hold of her arm, and searched her face intently.

'It's Mick.' Alyssa was annoyed to find her voice high and tremulous. 'He almost ran over Davy and the colt. He keeps saying he was trying to avoid running down a woman in white. But none of us saw anyone.'

'He's no' sober,' Davy interjected.

Beside Alyssa, the colt plunged nervously, jerking its head up and down like a puppet on a string. The halter rope dangled loose. As if it sensed a way to freedom, the colt tossed its head defiantly. Turning on its haunches, it set off at an uneven gallop through the trees.

Leaving the men standing, Alyssa rushed after the terrified horse. If it ran back up onto the road, it could easily be struck again by a passing car. Alyssa ran faster, puffing a little as she gained on the colt. Then it slowed down and limped painfully. It came to a sudden halt, sides heaving, and liquid eyes full of suffering. It held up its foreleg.

Alyssa crept toward the frightened animal. She whistled softly between her teeth, her eyes holding those of the colt. One false step and it'd be off again. This was her only chance to grab the frightened animal. What would Rory do in such a situation? At the thought of him, she relaxed a little and continued to move slowly toward the colt. She spoke soothingly and slowly she raised her hand, inch by inch.

Her movements were imperceptible and seconds lengthened into minutes. In fact it seemed like hours, but she knew she had to be patient or she'd destroy the confidence she'd had built up with the animal. In a split second it could easily plunge past her, and be lost. Her fingers brushed the trailing halter rope, but the colt jerked up its head and turned away.

There was a rustle of leaves behind her, but she kept her eyes on the colt. 'Come on, sweetie, we'll get you home safely in your stable with some nice fresh hay and plenty of water to drink.' Her voice coaxed and soothed. 'Come on, sweetie. It's time to go home.'

The colt kept looking at her outstretched hand, and then with a sudden movement it came toward her, dropping its head for her to grab the halter. She seized the rope, and let out the breath she was holding. Her heart pounding with relief, she pressed her face against the colt's warm body. As she stroked its neck she heard Rory's voice behind her. 'That was a very brave thing you did, Alyssa. Just like a real country girl!'

Tears of tension streamed down her face, as Davy, followed by Mick, pushed through the densely growing trees.

Rory ran his hand expertly down the legs of the colt. 'I don't think there's much wrong with it that a couple of days' rest won't cure,' he said. 'It's just sprained its foreleg lightly. I can put a light bandage on him.' He handed the halter rope over to Davy.

Then he turned to Alyssa. He bent down to look directly into her eyes. 'What was wrong with you last night? I know you'd had a big fright, but to run off away from me like that when Mick could've still been lurking in the bushes was foolhardy. What were you thinking of?' His face was full of hurt and accusation.

Chapter Twenty-Three

Alyssa flushed in embarrassment at Rory's question. Then she flung herself against him. 'Forgive me, forgive me! I was out of my mind. Perhaps I'm just too like my own great aunt, awkward and suspicious.'

Rory brushed this aside. 'Look, I know you've been through a lot. It's no wonder you overreact. But my father's very worried about you. Why don't you come back to the house with me? You can have supper with us.'

'Thank you, I'd love to see your father again,' said Alyssa. She climbed into the Land Rover and Ginger sprang up beside her on the front seat. She flung her arms round him and hugged his silky coat.

'Ginger's really taken a fancy to you,' said Rory. 'That's okay. You can keep him. He's not a very good sheep dog, but he's very affectionate, and a good watch dog.'

Back at the manse, Mr MacDonald came out of the front door to meet them. He seemed very pleased to see them. 'Have you come to have supper with two lonely men?' he asked and gave Alyssa a welcoming embrace.

'I'd be honoured to have supper with you both,' she said smiling at him.

'Don't flutter away like a frightened bird this time.' Rory's teasing words held an undeniable accusation.

Alyssa writhed inwardly, her guilt at her foolishness stabbing at her heart.

'Don't hang about. I need you to help me,' said Rory. They walked through to the old-fashioned but spotless kitchen. Rory lifted an enormous apron down from a hook on the wall and tied it round her waist.

'Where's Barbara today?' Alyssa asked.

'Oh, she's out with her fiancé. You know - that doctor who treated you at the hospital.'

'But I thought she was your girlfriend!'

'No, of course not. Whatever gave you that idea?'

'Well, she's very pretty, and attractive, so you might have gone out with her.'

Rory raised his eyebrows and looked smug. 'Not my type,' he said, dismissing the subject.

He pointed to the kitchen drawer where the knives and forks were kept. Alyssa collected them and as well as some glasses for setting the table.

'Why did you leave so abruptly last night?' Rory persisted as he set about lifting pots and pans from the cupboard. He produced a large salmon from the refrigerator and laid it on the table.

The direct question was a relief to Alyssa. She took a deep breath. 'Forgive me. I was out of my mind last night after that dreadful encounter with Mick. All I wanted was to get back to the cottage and pull the covers over my head. I didn't want to speak to anyone.'

'But why?' Rory was efficiently cleaning and filleting the large fish. He put the frying pan on the hot plate and turned on the heat, his movements neat and decisive. 'I came and rescued you and then you ran away from me,

238

too.' For the first time Alyssa noticed lines of strain running from his nose to the sides of his mouth.

Alyssa flushed. 'I've made a complete fool of myself,' she admitted.

'Okay, I suppose it was understandable. But it was very dangerous taking off like that.' Rory paused. 'I spent several hours last night patrolling the road outside your cottage to make sure you were all right.'

'Oh, Rory,' Alyssa floundered in a mixture of embarrassment and gratitude. 'Did you really? How can I ever tell you how grateful I am for all you've done for me.'

Rory looked at her quizzically. 'You've had a funny way of showing it.'

'You've no idea how stressful it has been over the past weeks,' Alyssa rushed in with explanations. 'First there was you, then the lawyer, the inheritance, Mick and to crown it all, Grizelda. I didn't dare tell you about what was happening with her. I didn't know myself what was going on.'

'Couldn't you have trusted me?'

'No I couldn't take that chance. I wasn't sure you would understand.' Alyssa's hands were busy shelling the pile of freshly picked green peas. 'It was so hard to distinguish between reality and Grizelda and her incessant demands. Perhaps it was all a dream.' She sighed. 'Maybe you're right. I'll never be one of you.'

'Is that the problem then?' Rory leaned forward as if trying to read her face. 'Of course, you will. You'll fit in easily. Indeed the people here will all welcome you. Your family comes from here, and like it or not you're Grizelda's great niece.'

'But you keep telling me I'm a Londoner, a townie.'

'Not after your prowess with that colt this afternoon.' He washed his hands and dried them on a paper towel. He drew Alyssa close, placing his cheek against hers.

'I can't just stay here doing nothing.' She leaned against him, trying to still her racing heart. 'I'll have to earn some money. Look at the decrepit old house. If it does become mine it'll swallow money for breakfast, dinner and tea.'

Rory stroked her hair. 'Grizelda was much respected and liked. So people will admire you for doing up her house.' He let go of her gently and brought out two baskets of fresh raspberries from the refrigerator.

Alyssa smoothed her hand over the well scrubbed kitchen table. 'Perhaps I can start working over the Internet.' She took one of the baskets from him. She started to clean the fruit. 'I'm going to gather material to write some articles. I have lots of good ideas, and I still have some good connections in London.'

'Well, maybe it isn't possible to run a farm with a hundred head of milk cattle anymore like your great aunt,' Rory conceded. 'But I know you can find your niche.'

'Perhaps I could even help to expand the museum which would bring more tourists to the island. You once suggested that.' Inspiration came to Alyssa. 'There's so much local history. It needs to be sorted out and the stories told.' Ideas of what she could do to contribute to the island community were coming thick and fast again.

Rory put a pot of potatoes and one of freshly scraped baby carrots on the stove and turned up the heat. He brought out a bottle of claret from the cupboard and uncorked it. Pouring it into two crystal wine glasses, he offered one to Alyssa.

He toasted her. 'Here's to your future, Alyssa. Stay with us.'

She took a sip of the ruby liquid, and looked out of the window at the distant sweep of the calm evening sea, her eyes dreaming.

'I think you could get to like it here, Alyssa.' Rory's caressing voice beguiled her.

She caught his challenging gaze and refused to look away. The tension stretched between them and her throat grew dry. The intensity of their feelings hung in the air between them.

'Alyssa.' Rory's deep voice sent a delightful shiver of desire shooting through her. She stepped close to him and he slid his arms round her. They stood tightly locked together, hip to thigh, while her lips opened willingly to him, and his tongue explored her mouth. She revelled in her softness against his hardness. With difficulty she resisted slipping down to the floor of the sparklingly clean kitchen. Desire was making her whole body liquid and melting. Rory's breathing had quickened and she could feel him hardening against her.

Whoosh! A sudden hissing came from the pan of potatoes as they boiled over, spattering water all over the top of the stove. They jumped apart like two guilty children caught with their hands in the sugar bowl. They laughed together at their foolishness. Alyssa's cheeks were hot. Her gaze met Rory's. His eyes were slumberous and dark with desire.

He smiled at her. 'This is unfinished business. Just wait until later. That's a promise!'

He turned back to the cooker and began dishing up the food.

'Raspberries and cream, mm... my favourite,' said Alyssa. 'A real Scottish delicacy.'

*

Alyssa, Rory and Mr MacDonald sat in the sitting room, with the coffee pot on the table in front of them. Rory lay back in his chair stretching out his long legs. His father watched him proudly. The two men were obviously very fond of each other.

Mr MacDonald rose stiffly from his chair and brought out an ancient map of the island and laid it on the table. 'Look, Alyssa, see how far the lands of Balvaig Farm used to stretch before it was sold off many years ago.'

'Goodness that was a lot of land.' Alyssa was impressed. 'How sad that only the house is left. But you can be sure that once the will is sorted out, I shall renovate it all. Once I get a new job that is.'

'It's a marathon task,' said Rory.

'Well I'm up to it,' she said. 'Nothing's going to stop me now.'

'Why don't you take Alyssa up to see the loch where Fordyce abducted Grizelda and her new husband?' Mr MacDonald said to Rory. 'It's a strange, wild, beautiful place. Perhaps if Alyssa sees it at last, it will bring the matter to a close.'

'You'll have to show me where it is, Dad. Remember it all took place long before I was born.' He moved over to sit on the arm of his father's chair and together they pored over the map.

'Of course, the Loch of the Black Horse.' Rory helped his father to fold up the map. 'A very lonely, desolate place. Was that where it happened? That's where a lot of sheep go missing, and probably drown in the depths of the loch.'

*

In the late evening sun, Alyssa and Rory drove in the Land Rover to the other side of the island, and up a winding road.

'This is where I got lost on my first night on the island,' Alyssa said, recognising it immediately. 'Perhaps even then Grizelda had a hand in it.'

'I remember it very well,' said Rory. 'You were pretty distraught that day! Lucky I stopped by to rescue you.'

He parked the Land Rover as far as possible off the narrow road, and they got out. Rory held out his hand to guide her as they climbed down, scrambling over rocks and slipping and sliding on the scree which led down to the glimmering black waters of the loch at the bottom. The touch of his warm hand sent small shivers of desire through her and his intent gaze revealed his expectation of what was to come before the evening was over.

They stopped at the edge of the water. Rory drew her to him, and they exchanged lingering kisses. The air was soft and still. Sweet scents wafted around them.

The trout made silvery arcs as they rose to catch the evening flies, and fell back with a soft plop in the water. The rings made by the fish rippled and spread over the loch until they disappeared.

'Rings in the water from Grizelda to me,' Alyssa said. 'Poor, unhappy bride. Was it here that she was thrown out in her wedding finery? Imagine her feelings of anguish. How cruel of that awful Fordyce. It's miles from anywhere. She must have been furious as well as terrified that no one would ever find them.'

'Yes, they were certainly wild highlanders in those days,' Rory said. 'Weddings and even funerals would carry on for two or three days and the whisky bottles were passed round endlessly between young and old.'

'It must've taken them a least a week to recover from all their carousing,' Alyssa said. 'But I suppose the work was hard and there weren't so many other entertainments.'

Arms entwined, they walked further along the path through a canopy of tall pine trees. Alyssa inhaled the resin scent, which wafted from the trunks of the trees. They passed the ancient ruin of a crofter's cottage and came to a huge boulder, which was gashed in two as if by a giant's axe. A graceful rowan tree had seeded and put down roots in one of the crannies of the rock. Red berries were already forming on the branches of the slender tree. An early sign of autumn.

Rory stopped, and together they gazed across the black waters of the loch.

'What's that?' said Alyssa turning her head, and straining her ears. 'Can you hear it? I think it's the sound of the bagpipes.'

Rory cocked his head. 'Yes, just faintly. They're playing a strathspey or a lament. Who on earth's playing the pipes here?'

Alyssa felt uneasy. Her heart beat faster. 'They're coming closer and now I think they're playing a march.' She staggered back and almost fell. 'Ouch, what was that?' She was finding it hard to breathe, hard to stand up. She was jostled from all sides by unseen forces. She put her hands to her spinning head, and half shut her eyes to block out the shadowy figures flickering past her. She leaned against the split boulder, her breath coming in short gasps.

'What's wrong with you, Alyssa, you look dreadful. Here sit down for a minute.' Rory's voice was anxious. 'I should never have brought you up here.'

'Help me, Rory.' Her voice was a thread of a whisper. She began turning first to the one side, then to the other.

The kilted highlanders filed past her, drawing closer and closer, stifling her, trapping her, hemming her in. Their boots clanged against the stones as they marched and the bagpipes skirled in a wild lament.

Several crows rose, cawing wildly from the pine trees spearing the sky, and fluttered away. Rory stood close to Alyssa and put his arms round her. He tried to calm her. 'Quiet, quiet,' he said as if soothing an animal or child. 'It's all right, there's nothing here. You must be dreaming.'

Alyssa tore herself out of his arms. Shimmering figures buffeted against her. Horses, a bridal veil, a black gown, a faded bouquet, a man with gaunt face and piercing eyes. The figures continued to brush against her. Eyes in dark faces terrified her. Sharp chills coursed through her body.

'Come with us, come with us, Alyssa,' an insidious voice implored her. 'Come, march with us. You belong with us.'

The trees seemed to form a dark, impenetrable ring around the loch, blocking out the dying rays of the sunlight.

'Come, Alyssa, you belong with us,' the soft voice crooned.

Rory seized hold of her hand and tugged her back. His face was chalk white. He was mouthing words she couldn't hear. He seemed so far away. 'Alyssa, stay here! Alyssa, stop! What's the matter with you?' His voice grew louder, then fainter, but he kept dragging on her arm. She struggled to break his hold on her, then fell back whimpering, trying to brush away the frightening shadows with her free hand.

The wail of the bagpipes grew louder until it reached a deafening crescendo. Now several insistent voices whispered in her ear. 'Come, Alyssa, come away with us!'

Rory moved in closer until he stood right behind her, both arms firmly round her waist. The bagpipes droned on and Rory gripped her tightly, his body a protective shield, but she kept struggling to break free of his hold. Then her hands went up once more to her ears to block out the wail of the bagpipes as the discordant sound wrenched at her soul.

'Leave me alone!' she screamed twisting and trying to break Rory's hold. 'Leave me alone!' She wasn't sure if she was shouting at Rory or at the cacophony of sound. Rory clung on to her, anchoring her to him.

'Alyssa, I love you, you must stay here with me,' Rory's words resounded in her ear. 'Stay here with me!'

'I love you too, Rory.' The words seemed forced out of her.

Suddenly all was quiet. The shadows receded and slipped away. The evening sky burned orange. There was no sound except the soft rippling of the loch and the gentle evening breeze murmuring in the trees. The air was cool and calm, and again Alyssa caught the summer scents of pine and flowers.

She sagged against Rory. His strong, warm hands grasped her arms and lifted her up.

'Time to go home,' he whispered.

A vision of Balvaig House, well-tended and repaired, with smoke curling out of the tall chimney, rose before Alyssa. She straightened up and seizing Rory's hand, she said, 'Goodbye, Grizelda. Your mission's accomplished. Now you must leave us in peace.'